Colin
The
Bakelite-Man
(Book 2)

THE
LONG WAY HOME

By

David
Clifford Bell

Colin the Bakelite-Man
Part Two

The Long Way Home

Written by
David Clifford Bell

Woodrow Publishing
www.woodrowpublishing.com/

ISBN: 9798662634626

WITH MANY THANKS TO:-

Gill Ratcliffe

Emma Bloom

The Bells'

My Friends

And Tea Growers Everywhere

Cover Art by Maya Mitten

I would like to dedicate this book to people who know when someone else needs to laugh and obliges. You know who you are.

Introducing the Author

David Bell was born in 1968 in the seaside town of Deal, Kent. By the age of ten he was living in Plymouth, Devon, and had already decided that he wanted to be involved in the creative arts.

Fortunately for David, by the time he left school Plymouth had built one of the biggest theatres in Europe, where he found a job as a stage technician. However, a life behind the scenes was not satisfying enough so he began acting and writing, hoping that a path would show itself.

Here he wrote short films, pop videos and comedy scripts. He also performed as an actor on stage in England, Italy and Poland. He also performed as a comedian in and around Devon and Cornwall, as well as at the Glastonbury Festival.

He now lives in Bath, Somerset, where he suffers with both chronic back pain and endless insomnia, allowing him time to revert to his first love of writing and his second love of laughing, (better than pain killers any day!)

"Colin the Bakelite-Man: Colin and His Plastic Coffin" (available on Amazon) was his first novel and this work is the long awaited follow up.

CHAPTER 1

Morale was exceptionally high, as you would expect after a successful escape. No longer were we prisoners, no longer were we exhibits, and no longer were we the unpaid living museum interns. Albeit nicely fed and always a decent supply of tea on hand. Now we were free and hurtling towards Pic and Don's home world full of vitality and beaming smiles. If at any time there was a lull in joviality someone would break a joke about me being a dark shade of blue, completely stained from being submerged in Squid ink during the escape. No one else suffered this fate. They took the same final journey onto the President's ship as me, in a jar full of ink, but had the good fortune to have all in one overalls provided to them before they got in. I wonder sometimes if they didn't have enough on purpose? Oh well, might as well have a laugh whilst risking your life in an escape attempt, right?

After the two days of scrubbing myself raw Marilyn finally told me that there was no known substance or method of cleaning this stuff off and that I should just accept that I'm going to be blue for a very long time. Until the deepest layer of skin had worked its way to the top and then finally end its journey becoming dust, leaving me a pale milky English white. Ray told me that I could have my own paint range and then started singing Michael Jackson songs...... It could all have been a stag do prank that went horribly wrong.

It was hard to tell where I had cut myself whilst shaving. Blood doesn't show well on dark blue. Which was a problem as it wasn't long before every razor was blunt from constant use and they began to rip the hairs out rather than cut them. So after about a month we all started growing beards.

Blue jokes were soon out and Marilyn took the brunt of joviality for a while, everyone telling her that her beard was coming along nicely. This didn't extend to Mona. She could have eaten anyone of us who dared a 'bit of banter' including her uglier bigger brother, Bernie.

I was very glad of the rabbits that he had brought along, less so of the amount of poo pellets they left everywhere. We went in pairs cleaning them up three times a day. They even had their own unfurnished officer's cabin, the grandest hutch in rabbit history. In which they multiplied like bacteria on a warm day. Of course a regular culling took place every other month or so. Keep the numbers down and filling up the freezer.

We did have a lot of other food in storage. Smokey had indeed been busy loading the ship before we stole it. He told me that he simply told the guards that, "I'm going be loading a load of junk for a while, keep the doors open." They agreed, "Not a problem," they said. So he kept on loading the stores with as much as he could get, which was a lot because nobody knew what he was really doing. It was his job to deliver all the food anyway, after all, and he didn't just get food, he got engine parts, tools, two golf buggies, seeds and soil, tons of salt, tons of electrical boxes containing stuff that needed assembly, and tons of other stuff we never got to know about.

Marilyn was very happy as there was a large stash of coffee. We were all very surprised to hear that she intended to ration herself to one large, which turned out to be enormous mug, of coffee a day. We openly discussed bets in front of her as to how long we thought that she would last before she gave into the inevitable second cup. I thought less than a day, nearly everyone else said a day. The only one who said longer was Marilyn. Just as well none of us had any money as she would have won. The coffee she had was massive and very strong though. I decided that I could aid the stores by not drinking any and only drinking tea, let's go one hundred percent traditional English, for the common good. She was very grateful for this. I think that's why she told me my endless washing was a waste of time. I would remain blue for a while.

The only time we thought or spoke with any severity was during those moments that Don and Pic imparted their concern for their home planet, Crrrrrk. There is a lot of clicks and croaks in their natural tongue. They would often start a conversation in their own language but then change to English out of politeness, or the fact that Ray would be standing nearby giving a live translation. Only he would pick two separate voices in which to relay the non-understandable language. Normally an ill matched voices as well. Something you might find in Sesame Street or similar, or John Wayne and Marlon Brando or someone else as equally improbable and mismatched for the job.

Generally Pic and Don's conversations started badly, in a desperate way, but then they'd pick themselves up quickly by remembering that they would be in time to warn their planet before the Squid had their chance to launch their missile.... If the Squid didn't learn the true potential of the warp speed button that was? The one Nelson told them was only to be used in case of emergencies and for no longer than three seconds at any one time. They actually believed him, as far as we knew? They haven't caught up yet, and we're on a direct course.

Well, the Squid are going to be mad with the whole lot of us for a very long time now, and even longer after that. We'd have been put on some sort of list. One that designates us as undesirable and to be messed with, as soon as we are found and don't do anything unless it involves death....... Our only hope in that case would be some form of mercy from their new President, Doctor Sandra. She may be able to pardon us in some way. I did help her win the election after all.... That is if she actually went onto win the election. The aggravation that the escape must have caused would be huge in the opposition arsenal. We were only on their ship and living due to her and her medical experimentation after all... They needed to have insurance on immortality, death by misadventure or stupidity. The space herb I was poisoned with had immeasurable qualities that helped provide the Squid with an elixir on demand, but it's rendered useless, if you get your head cut off, unless you have in particular a Bakelite coffin, giving at least thousand years of stasis and time to perfect whatever was needed to fix you. Nelson had brought some Herb along with him, enclosed in a case that when opened revealed what looked like a backgammon board made from finely groomed high-grade golf course quality grass. The herb changed directions to form the triangles you needed, from the shade and angle of the blades.... It would then go on to give you a good game and nine times out of ten it would win. It probably let you win the one time you do. It would communicate by text, and write you messages, each blade moving in a precise way to achieve this.

Nelson resumed old practices. He studied the ships computer, reading the charts and all and any information he could get. He already had combed Ray for everything he was worth. The ships computer held extensive and detailed records but still there were holes in its knowledge. There were still uncharted areas, systems and galaxies, planets and moons. Ray also studied the ships computer. He plugged himself in via two tiny wires going into a tiny jack socket, one behind each ear, uploading the data in a matter of moments. He then announced that he had to reboot for the change to take effect and that he needed to shut down. He then became a tiny bit dramatic, nothing new there. Before he shutdown, he got dressed into a makeshift robe made from a spare bed I presumed, then lit some candles and burnt something that stunk. He would have used incense if there was any available I'm sure. He then spoke in a language that nobody understood. Fortunately, nobody understood. He was busy looking up, hands aloft, it looked like he was praying in some way, to the God of the universe and the architect of all his electrical connections, probably, maybe.... For the next two hours the only sign of life or in his case power was a high-pitched whizzing sound. Just like the fan on a hard drive. No changes there then. Apart from in this case Ray's right eye span east to west whilst his left eye north to south. We all left his ceremony feeling dizzy and nauseous. He joined us about two hours later complaining of a headache and migraine.

Later, a prudent order from Nelson arrived at breakfast at the end of the first week. A week that was like the best holiday you could ever get. The orders were we were all to learn all aspects of the ship. How to pilot? How to fire the guns? Who said playing computer games is a waste of life, eh? The only person better than me was Ray and that's because he plugged himself directly into the system. Sam was also good, better than Nelson even. Everyone else was basically quite rubbish. Although, I'm being slightly harsh, I was a two-star general on 'Call of Duty,' after all. I think Jeb was rubbish on purpose. The idea of it being him that could pull the trigger wasn't sitting comfortably. He did however spend a lot of time in the bridge staring at the stars and anything else that that glittered, which was a lot, and it was stunning, he compensated his lack of violence by taking extra driving lessons and it was too long before he could pull off some manoeuvres that nobody else was trying. "Just like riding a buggy," he'd say.

Bernie also felt ill at ease not being able to contribute much in the running of the ship so he took it upon himself to ask Nelson to take a look at the mechanics of the engine. Nelson agreed but, he had to be supervised by Ray who was of course the best person to ask when requiring technical info concerning anything to do with the ship. Nelson then asked, and ever so politely, Mona to accompany her brother and also get stuck into it....... She did and slowly it began to appear that she would be better than her brother...... I think Nelson knew this.

Pic and Don quite naturally crawled through the bowels of the ship without being asked. It seems that they felt quite at home in confined spaces. At times it was as though they were missing. There wasn't anything to fix but they needed to know what they might have to work with if and when it did go wrong. They also found a homing beacon that they felt it prudent to disable. Nelson simply nodded when they told him. It didn't occur to anyone else that we could have been tracked and discovered that easily. They just had to launch a guided missile. Being able to live forever wasn't much of a defence against obliteration. We all new that and it made us all focus just a tiny bit more on staying alive.

Even Smokey who was intent on finding somewhere where he could cultivate tobacco stopped hacking...... Or at least did it in private. He did it once just before dinner which no one appreciated, least of all me. I had memories of earlier hacking sessions and near misses. Whilst I held it down everyone else told him to go to the bathroom....... Not as politely as that though and not many continued eating after....... He must have thought about what he had done as the next time we saw him he didn't have a cigarette butt in the corner of his mouth. Shame really, I was just about to start calling him Popeye. Marilyn kept him company and hopefully taught him some other manners. She would then help Ray in the kitchen, with 'one other', we were all on the Rota, even Nelson. He set the example by taking the first shift and making a damn good job of it. Ray and Marilyn let us know.

Nelson for some reason didn't give me much to do. I learnt how to use the canon quite well. We would practice by trying to hit jettisoned waste. Very rarely did we hit anything but we were close and the targets were small. Vegetable peel mainly. We would be better on the simulator as the targets were much bigger. Often during practice I would stop to take in the view. More than once Nelson noticed and more than twice he let me get on with gazing at the passing stars and gas clouds easy past. There was always something different to look at, always something to be amazed at, always something to stop any conversation mid track and demand to be observed and given attention.

Just like Ray, who would launch into an impression of some character from Star Trek or Star Wars at any time. Which was funny, having Darth Vadar serving tea at breakfast and suggesting no milk with coffee to Marilyn, thereby having it on, 'the dark side' always got the day started with a laugh, and then Spock, explaining that beans with breakfast was illogical and disrespectful, it too was also amusing, for a while. Singing 'Bright Eyes', whilst serving rabbit stew did not last long on Ray's repertoire, not funny.

CHAPTER2

It's never too long before your environment can get boring, staid, or just regular. The sparkle is extinguished, the beauty wanes, the new becomes old. It was just over two weeks before I noticed this happening to me. I had settled into the routine I suppose? Nelson noticed one evening just before dinner when I sat down with a big crease across my head from where I had it squashed up against the port hole in my cabin, as though I had slept with my face on a plate. I then understood what the term 'Cabin Fever' meant. I did need to get out and do something, set my feet on land. Unfortunately there was nowhere and no way I'm getting out just yet. Besides where was there to go? We couldn't just stop so I could go for a spacewalk. We couldn't just pop down to the shops or go to a site of beauty or interest. Even though I was surrounded by everything that was beautiful and wondrous. In short, I just wanted to go for a walk, stretch my legs and feel the wind in my hair. Definitely no sticking my head out of the window.

I took to volunteering myself, upon people and their chores and work, during the day. In the evenings I'd ask Ray to project a film or two. I took extra-long baths to help the process of losing my blue body stain, any way to stretch the day out, but still I got slightly bored. I put in extra time on the canon simulators and potato skins. I would take on the Herb at backgammon and lose of course. I found out a few things about the herb along the way. For instance, it can't remember its' own planet or place of origin. That it doesn't mind being the essential element in my immortality and that it depended on whether it liked the host and fortunately, in my case it did...... It also told me that my ex-Squid captors hadn't ever used the herb for themselves and that they didn't ask whether they needed permission in order for the magic to happen. The Squid simply presumed that it works naturally. Pig headed, big mistake. It told me that it itself didn't know how the magic worked it just did, and, that it existed in order to simply exist. That was it, happy...... I was jealous.

I needed things to happen, at least every now and again. Something to stop the rot of boredom becoming the norm.... Which is what was happening to me when I looked around and only saw the same four walls, again...... Maybe there was some paint on board, I could paint them? No perhaps not, might only mess them up, besides I do like them as they are. You see, boredom making me consider things that I could do, even though they are the wrong decisions....

plus, the room will stink for days....... I wouldn't be able to just open a window.

Marilyn and Mona had the right idea. Stay busy. They took to making themselves clothes and outfits. They found the ships clothing store full of uniforms mainly and complete with a small workshop and tools. They came to my cabin one night and gave me some clothes that they made for me. I was very touched and thanked them profusely. The clothes themselves mainly consisted of military dress uniforms that had all the braiding and sparkly bits removed. Sometimes maybe ripped off, button threads still hanging proud. I kind of looked like a less colourful Adam Ant. de-blinged. I kind of liked it. At breakfast the next day everyone turned up looking like a drab Adam Ant too...... Apart from Mona and Marilyn who wore mainly the braids and buttons. They both seemed to swoosh and jingle everywhere. They soon toned down their swooshiness with more and more new outfits. Something else which soon became the norm.

Sam felt very much at home in his new attire. He gained a swagger in his gait and was spotted in the gym soon after. Which in turn led us all to take to a visit twice a week or so. We didn't take it as seriously as him. When quizzed he replied, "Got to look good for the ladies." He didn't mean Mona or Marilyn, he meant a yet to bump into lady. I admired his hope, his sense of very forward planning. Could be decades before we bump into another human. Would it be bestiality with an alien who could morph into a human shape and look? I was fooled by Doctor Sandra's look and appearance. As you would have been.

It was at breakfast one morning that I realized that this was just like being at work, only it was a live-in position and that I was actually a shareholder. We all did our fair share of everything and a bit more of the things we were good at. The system seemed to work and of course there was good reason for it to work, as it was paramount in our survival. There was no need to say this outright as we all fully understood where we stood...... However, if we stumbled across a planet that could offer most of the things I needed then I would leave and not think too much about it. I've known my companions for several months now and consider them all friends. All would be on a wedding list and my door always open, but, it's a door. Behind which you'd find a simple man who likes hot beverages and the right to be able to do nothing..... Especially when you're good at it….. I didn't share my thoughts and there was no need.

Nelson poured himself a second tea and purposed a question which turned out to be a leading one,

"We need to give the ship a name?" he said smiling. Ray smiled along with him and didn't offer a suggestion. Something was up, they knew something, and a good something.

"What's going on?" I said.

"That's a terrible name for ship," said Ray with a generic pirate accent adding, "Mi lad." With a huge hammy wink. Nelson looked at me and smiled. He knew that I knew he knew something.

"Every ship needs a name when they need to dock Colin," Nelson said frowning, "don't you know anything?"

"Dock. Where?" I said as everyone else was rendered silent by the news apart from Ray who clasped his hands, giggled and bounced on his seat enjoying the moment like a seven year old upon seeing a large box covered in wrapping paper with their name on it.

Nelson replied, "Well we haven't made contact yet, but the computer has detected a slow moving ship and a lot of Life. Its design and lack of fire power suggest it's not a warship of any kind. Which means it probably a science vessel?"

"We should be prepared though," said Sam. He was right too. This was to be our first encounter with another ship and Life. We had no idea what was going to happen.

"If we go on alert they will know," said Don.

"Which might make them go to some sort of battle station alert?" said Nelson.

"Has anyone thought to give them a call and say hello?" said Marilyn.

"We can't do that until we have a name for the ship, and a reason for being here," said Nelson.

"Can't we tell them the truth? That we've just escaped from a bunch of mad Squid intent on blowing up my home planet," added Pic. He had a point.

"I thought about that, however, they may get nervous. Harbouring escapees could make them a target? Or they could detain us and hand us back over. They could be anyone?" said Nelson looking around the gathered faces.

He was right. We had no idea who they were, or how they would receive us. Every ship would have defences. Every commander would have procedures that probably started with a big red button being pressed announcing some sort of alert. When we meet a stranger we naturally judge and assess what they are about. What are their intentions? Do they have any? Friend or foe? Can I trust this person or not? Especially if they have the power to blow you up and return you to dust.

"So any suggestions for a name?" Nelson asked again.

"The official name would translate as Flying Fish," said Don.

"Not very spacey, but does it have to be?" I said.

"It looks like a hammer head shark," said Ray as a suggestion.

"Sounds a bit aggressive. But can hardly call it the 'Swan' or 'Bird of Paradise' can we?" Nelson replied.

"Aren't they going to know that we have guns?" I asked.

"Yes," replied Nelson.

"Then we can't go calling it something soft and fluffy."

"Mmmmmm," replied Nelson knowing I was correct. He tapped the table, drumming his fingers.

"Ooh, ooh, I know." said Ray adding, "What about, what about, the Phoenix, because we've been re-born, in a way. It makes sense?" There was no reaction to Ray's suggestion.

"Maybe just a bit obvious and corny?" Nelson said, phrasing it as a question rather than a statement as that would have had tones of idiot attached. Then we were all saved by the bell. Or at least the single note produced just before the ship's intercom was about to be used, it could only be Smokey who was presently in his chair on the bridge with his hands on the controls.

"Hmmm, hello ship. Mmmm, Nelson you might want to come here? We're being hailed, I think. There's no one else around at least, but they think we're called the Flying Fish. Shouldn't we be called the 'Hammer Head'?"

Nelson stood, "Ok Smokey, I'm on my way." Nelson strode off and everyone followed. He looked behind him as he went, there was nothing he could do about the troupe that followed. He would have only of had to tell us later anyway. We reached the bridge in single file and crammed in awaiting further contact. Ahead of us on through the screen we saw a mass of metal. Struts and stanchions exposed to space, the outside being clad in massive metal sheets by even bigger machines. A self-build Planet under construction. The skin being laid seemed to be an external layer covering a smaller yet still huge metal sphere that lay at the centre. It reminded me of the Death Star, the first one. Only this one wasn't dark, the internal sphere was brash and colourful in every imaginable way, massive bright logos advertised products, bright lights illuminated them. A mixture of the Glastonbury festival and Blade Runner.

The ship hailed again, "Hello Flying Fish. This is Planet Mall. Is there anything you need? We have engines, food, water, casinos, hotels, theatre, museum, waste disposal, and more, more, more. You fancy eating some Garunchee from the seas of Alpeth 7? Some fruits from the forests of Sarnche? Free docking and ten percent off everything if you join as a member."

"There's always something, something free, there's always something free." I repeated to clarify.

"Not normally," replied Nelson adding, "Someone pays."

Nelson approached the console and flicked a switch whilst pressing a finger to his lips indicating that he wanted silence, "Hello Planet Mall, permission to land please?"

"Sending you the coordinates, fly in on auto."

A bleep bleeped and Smokey turned to Nelson and waited for the orders to hit the auto pilot button. Nelson nodded. The engines came to life and we shifted into a banking dive towards the building site planet. As we got closer we could make out bodies floating amongst the jagged edges of the jumble of metal. They seemed to be welding and cutting, drilling and whacking. Activity everywhere.

"It's just one huge shopping centre," I noted.

"I wonder if they sell tobacco?" said Smokey to himself, salivating.

"They may well do, unfortunately we have no money," Nelson reminded him.

"But we do have rabbits," said Bernie.

The ship levelled out and took a sharp turn to the right. We now faced the internal sphere and headed straight towards it. In front of us two massive doors opened up and beckoned us on inside. We glided through a tunnel of jutting metal struts towards them. The dock was a dark grey, the floor discoloured with years of work scuffed into it. Patches of oil and grease stained areas broke up any uniformity. Other ships stood in rank whilst figures dressed in overalls tended to them. The figures were alien. A gentle bump told us that we had landed.

Nelson turned to face us all, he paused for silence and attention, "Now, we're going to have to do this in shifts. Pic, Smokey, Jeb, Bernie, and Mona stay here guard the ship, don't let anyone on board. The rest of us....... here we go..... and, I can't stress this enough, I am not an admiral, I am not Lord Nelson. I'm just a crew member, called Horace."

"Horace. What sort of name is that?" questioned Marilyn.

"One that you won't forget Marilyn. Plus, my real name is Horatio. Can't have anyone taking any interest, locally or beyond."

"Okay Horace," Marilyn replied.

The first contact group made their way to the main door. Nelson hit the button. The door opened with a hiss and a rush of cold air swept passed us all. A set of mobile stairs was already in place to aid our descent and standing at the bottom a party of uniformed guards stood to attention. They looked a bit lizard-like, chunkier legs, no tail, smaller scales around the face than on the head, all green and muggy browns. Too one side stood a smartly dressed reptilian, about one metre tall. He looked happy to see us, nodding to us as we descended. He held a clip board at his side. Another similar looking alien placed a trumpet like instrument to his mouth and began to play a non-melodic tune. Must be the welcome theme, I thought? They should change it. Sounded like a three year old on a recorder for the first time. More like a tuning session than a tuneful session. We still smiled. The guards did have guns.

"Welcome crew of the Flying Fish, to Planet Mall. Sign here." The clip board was thrust Nelson's way. "Just a landing ledger, nothing official." Nelson scribbled something down. The small reptile continued, "Now is there anything we can do for you, anything in particular?"

Not sure how to answer that question Nelson replied with the failsafe line of, "Just looking."

The alien looked stumped by the response. Maybe he had never heard it before. I suppose anyone who came here on purpose had a purpose. We on the other hand didn't know or have anything.

"Is there a trading point of any description?"

"Commerce on level three. But may I just inquire as to what race he is?" The alien was referring to me. Hadn't he ever seen a blue human before?

"I'm human. This isn't my normal skin tone. It's normally more like his," I said whilst pointing at Nelson, "I had an accident with a large jar of ink."

"You have ink. We'll pay a good price for that. Do you have anything else?"

"Rabbits," Ray responded.

"And what are Rabbits?" asked the alien.

"They're small fluffy cute animals that like to hop around and eat carrots," Ray continued.

"Mmmm, I see. Maybe?"

"Which way to level three?" Nelson inquired. The small alien pointed to a lift at the other end of the dock. The trumpet player stopped and looked glad to do so. I think everyone was happy.

Once out of ear shot from our welcome party as we walked towards the lift Nelson spoke, "Did you notice that when Colin told him that he was a human he didn't flinch. Does that mean there's more around, and possibly here?"

No one spoke but the pace quickened, all suddenly eager to see if the theory stood up. We crammed into the lift and hit the button marked with a three. Seconds later the lift arrived at its destination and the doors slid open. I felt a rush of excitement run through my bones. I thought of Christmas for some reason. Why I don't know, I haven't enjoyed Christmas since I was a child. Since I stopped getting wonderous presents and started to get sensible items. Like a calculator or diary, or the inevitable pair of socks or underpants which in fairness I really did need. I was twenty three before I actually needed to buy my first pair of undies, and because I had never bought any before I made the mistake of getting the wrong size, too big. The day I first wore them I was constantly hitching myself up. People at work started to avoid me, probably thinking that I had a sexually transmitted disease. Well, if they saw the pants I was wearing they would have known that there wasn't a chance in hell of getting anywhere near one of those. I looked relatively slim but, in those pants, had a sack of potatoes for a posterior and groin. Piles gargantuous. Unfortunately they're not the sort of item a shop will exchange if only worn once.

Level three looked like a massive indoor market. A botch of stalls, shops and kiosks. The stall holders were just as varied and colourful as the decor. No humans so far. Our group shuffled around like tourists, slow and out of place, gazing up and grinding to a halt most of the time. Creatures and aliens stopped to look at us then they would nudge their colleagues who would then also stop to look. We nodded and smiled as we shuffled along. They would only stare for a few seconds before the power of commerce made them realize that they were losing time and therefore money. Which, was probably the same thought that convinced one stall holder to approach us. A creature like a stick man, human in essence, but taller, thinner, very spindly. A male, a very thin but long jawed face, a drooping chin and high sweeping forehead, with cheek bones higher than the eyes, elongated arms and fingers, very slender bony long feet, three times the size of mine, on the end of some bandy legs. He could easily have a part in a Pink Floyd video. Just put him in a suit and a bowler hat. This guy however wore a long work jacket over some work trousers, factory style.

"Hello gentleman and lady, can I help you with anything? You seem to be lost. Is there anything you're looking for in particular?"

"Yes, we have some ink and rabbits and need to sell them," said Nelson.

"Rabbits, what are rabbits?" the alien said.

"Cute little animals, four legs, fluffy tail, two big front teeth, big ears, like to eat carrots and hop about," I added.

"They're fresh?" he said then inquired, "How many do you have?"

"Now or by the time we get back to the ship?" I answered, only Nelson laughed. The Floyd alien smiled. "Their paws are said to be lucky," I continued. The alien stopped smiling. In fact, it turned into a frown.

"So the saying about them is wrong. What's the point of having a wrong saying? Oh no, that won't do. Not sellable with that bit of spin."

"Lucky charms. That's all," I said almost defending the idea.

"Yes, I understand," he replied, "but it's fundamentally flawed isn't it? I mean, it's not very lucky for the rabbit, as you say, they've got four legs so presumably they have four paws. Four lucky charms, four." He shrugged his very long arms then asked, "What would they be good in?"

Nelson and I answered over each other, "Pie's and Stew."

"With mash," added Ray smiling. The Floyd creature had no idea what we were talking about. He shook his head.

"Maybe I should taste some?"

Ray stepped forward bowing deeply. Nelson looked towards me and rolled his eyes as if to say, "Here we go" and then proceeded to watch an over enthusiastic Ray make a complete idiot out of himself and us by association. He surprised us all. Stepping forward again he bowed even deeper, then said something in a language only he and the Floyd creature understood. He translated afterwards. The conversation went as follows.

"To your House and Heirs and the generations that follow, I pray that health and prosperity reign," Ray said, sweeping the floor with another over enthusiastic bow. Instantly the Floyd creature reacted in a similar manner and proceeded to outdo Ray in his gesticulations and greeting. His stretched body seemed to drag along the floor, he was that long and spindly. Then they both then squared up to each other, facing one other as though they were about to start round one of a boxing match. In fact, it was just a part of the business deal. Honour your customers' custom before getting his cash. Ray spoke first.

"If there's one thing these creatures are good at it's reproducing. I could give you a handful of rabbits now and within a year there would be more of them than leaves on your family tree. A self-producing commodity that only requires minimal feeding."

The Floyd creature nodded to himself, pondering something, he then screwed up his nose, "I'm not very good with poo."

"Who is?" Ray said quickly, "There must be such a thing as a 'Poo Bot?'"

"I'm still going to have to taste it, or cuddle it, or snap a paw off and go to the casino."

"You could do all three? Just make sure you cuddle it first. Provisionally I suggest that we supply you and you act as our agent and take an agreeable percentage?"

The Floyd bowed deeply knowing this was indeed a fantastic offer, possibly easy money. He bowed deeply once more replying, "I would indeed be stupid not to accept your most gracious offer."

"I shall be back in a few hours with some samples. What about ink?"

"Next level up, look for 'Stationary Planet.'"

"To sell, not to buy."

"Oh...... Maybe I could take care of that too?" the Floyd said looking eager, "and I will take small reduction in my percentage?"

"Very noble of you. I shall relay your terms."

Ray chuckled as did the Floyd. They then nearly crashed heads as they indulged in bigger and grander sweeping bows. The Floyd then nodded to the larger party and left.

Ray explained that the Floyd's culture demanded all the pomp of ceremony and that the provisional business plan seemed to be more than acceptable. It was now a simple matter of agreeing a percentage.

A thought ran through my mind, one that made me feel a little sad. One that made me realize that my newly acquired sense of freedom was about to be squeezed, the boundaries lessened and

20

constricted. We were going to have to open some form of bank account..... Details required, forms to fill in....... I bet somehow we'll still end up getting a load of junk mail. Insurance offers and deals on double glazing. Millions of miles away from anywhere yet someone will be trying to tempt us with a two for one offer on a pizza.

Ray turned to the Floyd and opened with, "Twenty percent."

"Twenty two and a half."

"Seventeen and a half."

"Twenty then," the Floyd responded. Then bowed slightly keeping his eyes on Ray. Who responded by bowing to the same half completed extent. Only then and after a moment more did they continue with another flurry of sweeping bows and salutations.

"Be here in four hours. With as much of everything as you can, and something prepared."

Ray clapped to himself and turned to all of us but mainly Nelson and nodded, saying, "I need to go and prepare a few things. I'd better go. We need to be back here in four hours. And maybe Marilyn should come with me?"

"That does sound like the best idea. Would that be all right Marilyn?" Nelson said asking in a tone of a person asking for a favour, a pre-emptive apologetic call for a little help. That of releasing a few bodily fluids, one for the cause, ok? Marilyn smiled as she nodded back. Nelson continued, "We'll be back within a short time, but before you go could you ask the gentleman if there are any humans here," said Nelson adding a small nod.

Ray relayed Nelson's question to which the answer was clear.

"No.... but there are a few on one of the sister malls. I think it maybe Meteor Mall..... I think?"

My heart broke a step. I think everyone's did, maybe not Marilyn? She'd probably had her fill of humans for a while and was more than used to us, but we, the three humans here now, had the potential to meet up with more of our own. I don't think Ray has a heart as such, not that he's nasty, far from it, but it's probably a battery of some sort. So I'm not sure if he would have missed a beat, I'll have to ask him. Not right now though he's got to get busy with some preparation, and Marilyn needs to get busy doing whatever it is that she needs to do. From my experience I think it works a bit like the remedy of scaring someone when they have hic-cups, the sneak attack culminating in a loud shout of some description, normally a 'boo' and normally useless.

We bade or farewells to the Floyd and went into the unknown. The first thing I noticed was how soon we were looked upon as just a bunch of potential customers, leading me to think that humans weren't so rare after all. I myself, took in everything I could, the textures and colours of skin on so many differently constructed heads and faces and bodies. Dressed every which way you could consider. Most creatures came with two of each, legs, arms and eyes. Some had variations, the one that had no holes for eyes scarred me the most. It could still see us. No eyes at all, something moved under the skin but you couldn't see what. Heat sensitive or something? It tried to encourage us into his stall for food and drinks, we all declined and made out that we had a prior engagement somewhere, which he knew we didn't, somehow? We were all freaked out, it wasn't just me. The creature's body really didn't help, it was like a six-foot fat cobra with a very lazy head, that flopped around, on top of its body.... no neck.... no eyes.... scaly. There were more and even scarier looking aliens though, but this one managed to do it for all of us. There were also creatures that wouldn't be out of place in the 'Toys are Us's girlie doll, cute as fluffy can be section...... All creatures were friendly though, they all seemed decent. Obviously they followed some sort of law, they upheld the one that says you can't just punch someone without cause..... I like that one.

I remember someone at work once punching a box because they were angry about something, he didn't realize that in contained tins of tuna, he couldn't avoid hitting a rim, what an idiot, he broke a finger, so he kicked the framework holding the box of tuna, broke his little toe. I drove him to the hospital resisting the urge to call him a complete idiot. He really didn't like it when I told him that he was only going to be paid sickness payments whilst he was off work, I did warn him not to hit anything prior to telling him this, he was that stupid...... To prove it, he went onto threaten suing for an accident at work, even though he knew there were cameras watching everything in every corner. He couldn't comprehend the fact that he was responsible for his own numptiness. He didn't understand that the injury had to be a work-related injury, not just any old injury, especially self-infliction. If that was the case we'd all stay at home and continuously trip over things surely or have repetitive sitting injuries? He never showed up again. He didn't sue though....... I hope he had rich parents, he was going to need some.

It wasn't too long before we made our way back to the Flying Fish. Window shopping is not the preserve of males throughout the ages it appears. In fact it only serves to wind me up, looking at things that I couldn't afford, even when there's a discount. Once inside we were overcome with most beautiful aromas coming from the galley. Ray had surpassed himself, and Nelson was very happy with the knowledge that Greg, the intelligent herb, was prepared to shed some itself in order for all dishes to taste amazing no matter who or what was eating it. It only took a pinch and he did volunteer. As suspected the taste was divine. Nelson opened the box that Greg lived in and thanked him heavily. Greg responded with dignity saying, by twisting and laying flat his individual blades thereby creating the shapes required, "My pleasure, my honour, plus it like one of your haircuts, well not yours Nelson, you've got terrible hair, but the point is it'll grow back, plus you know me, love to help, and I can have a small adventure, love it..... Fancy a game of backgammon?" Nelson declined, not because he knew he would lose but he had things to organize and get on with. Greg didn't mind, it was only on the off chance, he decided to have a snooze instead.

Nelson then left with everyone who stayed earlier. He was off to find a bank or some form of credit system. We were going to need cash. Hopefully Squid ink was expensive and the rabbits would go down as a treat and luxury. Smokey didn't go even though he had a chance. Both he and Marilyn were far too exhausted after their efforts. I think they over did it, they were not their usual tone of colour, they both had a grey tinge about them. Marilyn was slowly sipping a huge coffee. "Medicinal," she told me when she saw me looking, "and I'm going to have another one when this one has gone." I didn't argue. Smokey just stared off into the distance, drained of energy. If you didn't know better you may have thought he was no longer living, his sinewy skin pulled down by gravity made him look like a gone off lump of melted tofu. It seemed best to leave them both alone to recover. I left to see if Ray needed a hand in the kitchen with anything. He didn't, but I ended up doing the washing up and other porter duties out of near boredom. Not the sort of thing you would normally enjoy, but Ray was talking in the voice and style of Gordon Ramsey and called me a so and so every other minute. I never knew cleaning could be so much fun. Once everything was complete the only job remaining was loading a golf buggy with some live rabbits and ink. We wanted to transport the food hot, so we waited until the last minute before we dished everything up, allowing enough time for the second landing party to return and further plans to be made.

Nelson inhaled deeply as he entered the galley, "That smells good. Well done Ray. I've called a meeting for five minutes, you both need to think what we might need, what you might want, nothing stupid though. It would be welcome break to stay for a while but we have to get on with returning Don and Pic home, there's the small matter of trying to save a planet." There was a slight pause whilst Nelson drifted off somewhere, his chest inflated with a slow intake of air and the corners of his mouth curled slightly, not because he was thinking of a joke he had heard earlier, he wasn't smiling, he was enjoying something though, and I think it might be the thought of the grander importance that his life now had, as in the old days, his old days.......... Momentarily I realize that I must be underestimating the job in hand myself. I could die, again. We could all die, in one moment. Sneak attack, and now that I'm thinking about it, a sneak attack from anyone, not just the Squid.

"You alright Colin, you seem to wearing quite a big frown?" Nelson asked.

"Yeah, yeah.... No, well yeah, I was just thinking, that, we now have to be wary of a lot more and that even though we're going to live for a very very long time, we're in the same boat as the Squid, nothing is going to save you from blowing up in the middle of space."

Nelson and Ray stared at me momentarily, then at each other.

"What's new?" Nelson said.

"Nothing has changed there then," added Ray, a moment of silence followed.

"Apart from someone is actively gunning for us. It's a bit like not being able to go out on a Friday night because you might bump into someone who has a bit of a beef with you and something might kick off."

"No it's nothing like that, we could die in an instant and not even see what hit us, probably the best way to go in some ways?" added Nelson, who nodded in agreement with himself, "You've got to get a sense of proportion Colin."

"Yes Colin, he's right. Get a grip. This isn't a little brawl, this is an undertaking of massive consequences for millions of lives, either way."

"Yeah, thanks for that I needed cheering up." Another moment of silence, there was nothing at that moment anyone could say. Nelson broke the air.

"Well there's one thing I think you need, a sense of humour transplant. Only joking, only joking. We should be able to get there in time, make further plans, but I would argue we have a good chance of saving the planet, as the device delivering the virus they intend using needs to be delivered safely, slowly. From what both Don and Pic tell me I think they have enough capability to take care of it. They did after all rebuild the Flying Fish, and the ship we escaped from. You alright now, you feel a bit better, huh, huh, you want to take a little nap or something?" The smile across Nelson's face grew more and more as the insults came. I eventually joined in.

"What was it you were enjoying a moment ago?" I asked Nelson.

"Eh?"

"You smiled at some thought or other?"

"Ah that, yes...... Life has purpose, I was remembering the horizon going up and down, up and down, the wind, the spray, but always the sense that I was doing something fundamentally important, something not for the sake of oneself. The adventure....."

"The adrenalin," Ray added.

"Yes that too," Nelson confirmed.

"I miss that, so much, I'd be no fun at a fun fair at all,"

"Oh I don't know, you have your moments Ray," I said, "but you're right, you'd make for a better accountant."

"Thanks, I needed cheering up." Ray said mimicking my voice.

CHAPTER 3

Everyone assembled and wished they were there for dinner, the smell was amazing. Nelson tried calling us to order.

"Well that was a mistake, can everyone put their tongues in please, thinking caps on." Ray smiled over the worktop that separated the pushed together dining tables from the kitchen and took a moment from packing containers full of food into thermos boxes to appreciate the sideways compliment.

"Now, Marilyn and Smokey are taking a moment to rest, we must all take the time to thank them for their efforts, hmmm, maybe don't use that term though, 'Efforts', just thank them, anyway, anyone with any requirements speak now."

"Well, we could do with some large rubber gloves, wire brushes and bleach," said Don. Pic nodded furiously alongside him.

"Alright," answered Nelson in a drawn out manner, sounding like he was expecting something slightly more important.

"We could use some static free gloves," Bernie added.

"I'd quite like some oven gloves," Ray said seriously not realizing that now someone was bound to make a glove related witticism. Or maybe that was only me thinking that?

"I'd like some fingerless, just to add to this piratesque little outfit I'm adorning at this moment in time," I said, batting my eyebrows.

"You dick," Nelson responded half smiling. I in return responded with a single bat.

Nelson continued, "Apart from pumping out, charging up, getting supplies, is there anything else we might need?" everyone seemed happy with Nelson's shopping list, "Well may I suggest we get some guns, the ones in the armoury are a bit too big. Not something you can easily hide or even just casually hang around your neck and we're not invading anywhere. By the same token more medical supplies might be in order. We have lots, but it doesn't take a lot for them to disappear."

I'm so glad, I thought, that one of us at the very least, was thinking ahead. One of us knew what was needed without thinking. It was only natural that that role was fulfilled by the most qualified person. I had done an audit of most things on board, hey that's what I'm good at, but the end figures actually still meant nothing to me. I could work somethings out of course, especially what we might be low in, but we weren't, Smokey had done a great job, stocking everything, Nelson would gain more information from the stock sheets than me, for sure, I was just good at correlating them.

Jeb huh hummed, he didn't speak that often, probably busy having an internal chat with God, one in which God was trying to tell him to chill out and that not everyone was a heathen. He frowned deeply before he began, "Thank you. Now in light of our revered colleagues I'll keep this light." He smiled, or at least curled his upper lip upwards whilst looking between myself and Nelson. He went on, "A lot of the first generation of settlers were so stupid, so incredibly stupid. Somehow you English thought that the world would just lay down before you and provide everything. Including the wax for the wigs you thought more important that nails you might need to construct the homes you wanted to live in. And of course the saws you would need to use to make the house and it would all be growing on the famous 'Soaring Saw Tree' that sprawled across the plains. Everything was going to be so easy."

I lent in slightly towards Nelson, "I don't think he likes the English?"

Nelson lent back, "Who does?"

"All I'm saying is that at some point this journey of ours needs to end and at that moment we might need a few things that makes it easier for us to settle down, that makes it easier for us to build. We need tools."

Nelson nodded and scribbled something down, "Some rock, metal, wood laser saw thing. Heavy duty plant gear....... Nice." There followed a small moment of silence and then Mona laughed.

"You've got to be kidding, you all in your own little heads were actually using it just then, all cutting through something big and heavy imaginary huge thing. Yeah, really big and heavy. Yeah even you Jeb, blokes and their toys. Probably wouldn't even know how to turn it on."

She was right, I'd seen myself, with a massive laser gun, oil stained arms, biceps rippling as they pushed back against the force created by the firing laser. The laser itself was busy cutting a clean archway through a massive block of metal that somehow was in my way. I could have easily stepped around, but I had a massive laser tool and the mind of a child.

"Some of you are doing it again." Mona said incredulously shaking her head. Dare I mention shoes, no, better not, a slap from Mona even in jest would be enough to break whatever bones were in the region of contact. No one else offered a retort for the same

27

reason, not even her brother. He was too busy agreeing that she was right.

I then did have a bright thought, "Umm, how about we also find out who takes care of monitoring and ask them to inform us if a massive fish tank floats by on a path that takes them to planet Crrrrk." The was a moments silence, one in which they struggled to understand what I meant by fish tank. Sam got it first.

"Oh yeah, good idea." He looked around the confused faces, "Come on. Even you Horace? The fish tank. A container containing fish, or in this case Squid. Huh?"

Everyone else got it as a collective, lots of 'Arrs'.

"That's cunning Colin, I wonder how much that would cost? I shall find out. Ok we have an appointment. Colin, Ray, Sam, Bernie with me, everyone else stay here. Mona, unlock the armoury, load everything, lock the loading bay ramp, once we've left. Open for nobody...... Weird things happen when there's money involved."

Somehow we all squeezed into the golf buggy with the Rabbits. With Bernie in the back you could say it was tight, my left buttock didn't have any contact with the seat, I'm sure it was the same with Sam on the other side of Bernie. A second later and the glare confirmed my suspicion. I was actually surprised the thing moved considering the total weight it was having to deal with. The tone in the engine was definitely lower than I'd ever heard. It must have been struggling, but once we hit the deck and got going it was fine.

We had to use a different lift to go to the third floor where we were due to meet the Floyd and hopefully come to some beneficial arrangement, and we had to travel at crawling pace.

Something was different this time though. We passed the same faces, the same stalls and traders. Last time we were a slightly rare sight but still essentially customers, but we obviously had no credit, we did look like tourists, walking at half pace and getting in the way of locals. However, because of our motorized transport and the delicious smell wafting after us we now appeared to be at least traders but just maybe a bunch of idiots with wealth going off on a little jolly. A picnic amongst a jumble of steel and shouts of amazing offers.......... A bit like those people in the 1950's who thought it most wonderful to have a roadside picnic. Pulling into a lay-by and getting out some deck chairs and a flask, eat your dinner as other drivers whizzed past at 40 miles an hour, plastering your cucumber sandwich in a thin layer of exhaust fumes...... Yeah 50's sophistication, the freedom of the open road. The freedom to not have a picnic at a site of beauty a park or beach.

I began to notice a trail of stall holders salivating, taking in the air, stepping forwards to smell the air again as we crawled by. This was good, we were drawing a crowd already or at least interest. They wanted to follow but never left the near vicinity of the property. The phrase 'leave at owner's risk' came to mind. The remaining 50 meters to the meeting point seemed to take an age and the engine growled like it had a hangover all the way. The Floyd bowed heavily as he did before. We all for some strange reason imitated as best we could the same greeting. Although Sam looked embarrassed by the whole thing and gave a much-restricted version, and twice as quick, which he followed with a half apologetic shrug. Ray opened the conversation and invited the Floyd to taste the goodies. We all knew that there was no way he would be disappointed. I'm sure Ray would have done an equally good job without Greg, but his sacrifice guaranteed delight. The Floyd's eyes widened with the first bite, and he then did what you could call a slow dance, a sway left to right whilst humming a, "Mmm, mmm, mmm." He then went on try everything else, each in turn receiving the same response, he seemed to be in gourmet heaven. It was a good thirty seconds before he was able to speak.

"You should be a chef?" he said to Ray and bowed.

"I know," Ray responded with no hint of modesty.

"May I introduce my brother's wife's cousin's friend who owns a food franchise here and on other Malls." Another Floyd stepped forward from under a nearby canvas. Nobody noticed him at first but after the obligatory ceremonial bowing session everyone was more than aware of his presence. We all went down the Sam route and offered a quickened but similar enough response. Apart from Ray who went to the other extreme and went off with a long speech in the creatures' mother tongue, probably containing phrases to do with, "Your House" or "Forefather's blood", "your mother's ears and your uncle's wit." Some such platitudes.

Turned out I was wrong. He suggested that they watch the following commotion and see fit to offer a price worthy enough considering the passion it will raise. They frowned, I didn't, I also knew what was coming next, we were used to this in the supermarket I worked in. Simply go around with a tray or a small stand offering very small samples...... Never on a Thursday though, they were never good days, pension day, the blue rinse brigade would turn up by 10 a.m. and devour everything, well for some of them it was all they needed and I'm sure for some of them they actually needed it.

Ray asked myself and Sam to offer the remaining food to nearby stall holders. None refused, all loved it and wanted more. Then they came to us and within minutes we were surrounded and the food disappeared before I even had the chance to say, "Wo," fingers were licked. I could see the two Floyds slowly nodding to themselves. By the time I pushed my way through the ever growing crowd both Nelson and Ray were shaking hands with the Floyds and each other.

I did find out the Floyds' names but as with Pic and Don their actual names were too hard for me to pronounce, the original Floyds' name sounded like, "Derrrf" if coming through one of those microphone on the neck machines, for people with no larynx, and the new Floyd had a name for which you'd have to use the same machine to pronounce it properly, it sounded like, "Wwarga" but to me, because I had already applied a term, and probably in a racist sort of way, that of Floyd, I decided it only fitting that I called them Dave and Roger, because they were in the Floyd you see, and well I'm quite stupid at doing things like that. If you knew me you would gradually just accept this.

Nelson then called for a little huddle and explained that not only had they struck an excellent deal on the Rabbits, they were to be paid for every new born, a self-perpetuating pyramid scheme, the ink was a standard price for weight, but the price was a good one, apparently, and we now had to walk back to the ship as we no longer had a buggy to take us there, we had sold that too. We did however have enough money to get some heavy duty laser cutters, and Roger Floyd, employed a chef who spoke English who had a brother who worked for the chief of security, and it was his job to know what was going on in the space around the Mall. Nelson, Roger Floyd and I were to go there right away whilst Ray, Sam and Dave Floyd were going to open a credit account, deposit a lump of cash, and then get whatever they could from the shopping list. Nelson implored Ray not to spend a single credit on fingerless gloves, even though the cash we now had was the equivalent of three years wages to me at the time of my removal from Earth, Ray informed me after tutting. We went our separate ways.

CHAPTER 4

We met the third Floyd who pronounced his name as, "Keeef" so obviously I called him Keith. Ideal for me as he was still dressed in his kitchen gear minus the hat and as he was already built for basketball he didn't need one of those. We then went straight to the top level, where we then met Keith's brother. I was glad that I didn't get his name. Both myself and Nelson thought it wise to provide a more gracious attempt at a Floyd welcome than previous attempts. This seemed to help as he wasn't expecting it at all. In fact it was the first time it had ever happened to him on this Mall. We then realized that there actually was no need to flourish the meeting with such a greeting but for some reason like dumb sheep we followed Ray's original example believing it was the done thing. We should have come to this conclusion earlier really. How would they ever get anything done if they had to spend all that time greeting everyone with a five minute routine? Social events must take an eon.

Nelson did all the talking, which suited me as it gave me the chance to catch a look at the universe through the clear domed ceiling directly above. Still as beautiful as ever. Fortunately the area I was in was so dimly lit there was no light pollution. It also made sense to avoid advertising yourself to anyone wishing ill harm, lighting yourself up like a beacon, especially as you are the security department. Although they did have a lot of gear. A lot of gear that back in my Grandad's day was enough to do one or two amazing things, back in my day a lot of gear was enough to do a lot of amazing things, so a lot of gear now surely could do some mind-blowing things. Why so much for so little? Unless it wasn't so little? Or the universe holds peoples that are just like any other civilization and have its' fair share of thieves and vagabonds. I was beginning to scare myself again. The news that we weren't going to have to pay for any help and would be notified if the Squid flew passed for free cheered me up though, at least for a bit. It seems our over the top ceremonial gesticulations and Ray's salutations earlier had earned us some respect that meant favours and cash were not required.

This did two things firstly reassure me and fill me with hope seeing that there was a still a sense of respect and honour left somewhere in the vastness of space, and secondly, confirm my utter dread and horror because that sense of hope was rare, and all around me there was a need for this much security, personnel and monitoring equipment, only because there were 'Baddies' around in the same vastness of space. I was beginning to look forward to the moment we were out of here. It should have been more refreshing to see other creatures, different life, to be free from captivity, to be free to walk for as long as you want without restriction, until you meet an obstacle, like the sea, or a border customs control centre and some bloke with a gun, a border control gun of course. Another moment in which infinity somehow gets smaller, and the space around you is no longer fully yours. Other people don't necessarily play by the same rules. I wouldn't breach your personal space, but some people don't care about that, and if they don't care about that, you can often find that your space is breached by one of their fists.

I had always hoped in the future that we would be at peace. That we would have finally just stopped, everyone took a step backwards for a moment and said we won't if you don't and since then nobody started anything else, it just never kicked off again..... but I guess I was wrong. Everything was still the same, only now the weapons were far superior and more powerful. No longer would brass bullets be ricocheting around the internals of the body, those days were long gone, now a laser pulse singes a way through everything, kind of hard not to hit anything of major importance. I read somewhere that there's a Convention whereby bullets were banned from being messed around with so that could spin around the body once it hit a target. It was considered inhumane. I imagine the soldiers really appreciated that, shooting me is fine just don't make it more painful than the hell it must already be. Gee thanks for that...... Maybe you could spend more time stopping wars than arranging the rules and courtesies of them. Arrrghh I need a cuppa' and I'm pretty sure my friend Nelson could also do with one.

"I think we should celebrate Horace, cup of tea?"

"Ouw, that sounds like a good idea. Would you gentleman be interested?" Nelson said. They declined, both needed to be elsewhere, but wished us well with our celebrations.

Keith escorted us to the fourth floor, the most likely place to find Ray and Sam. Here on this level the harder industrial outlets purveyed their wears and workshops. It was much harder to hear anyone talk as the noise was quite loud. You had to face them and raise your voice.

"If we walk around the circumference, you that way, me this way, we should bump into them, right?" he asked, unsure of his own question.

"Should do, if we keep a check on the aisles, they're the only humans here, shouldn't be that difficult."

We arranged to meet diametrically opposite. The floor was basically a huge round shape cut into 6 segments, albeit massive large huge sections. These were surrounded by a wall of more workshops and shops for those workshops it seemed. We were nearly at the widest point of the Mall. The best place for the bigger units within I suppose. The segments were intersected by 3 corridors, more like avenues, as wide as a 2 lane road and from where we were the centre seemed to house a throng of activity and smaller stalls.

"They're going to be in there aren't they?" I shouted nodding towards the crowd. Nelson grimaced at the idea and wished me good luck.

I didn't have any and neither did Nelson. I wish I could say I had a pleasant walk but I couldn't the shrill noise of metals being tortured by some unforgiving tool sang like a Banshee having a really bad time of the month, right through my head. It wasn't long before I resorted to putting a finger in each ear. Which is how I found Nelson. We were glad to make our way to the centre junction. Although we still had to speak loudly we didn't need the finger mufflers as there were no workshops directly near, sounds still caterwauled through me, everything from a stampede of angry cats to a rampage of angry dentists.

It wasn't long before we found Ray. He was it appeared acting as an arbiter in a dispute. He didn't seem to be enjoying the moment. I caught Sam's eye and he didn't look to happy either, he rolled his eyes. I had already realized Ray had maybe said something he shouldn't have, I also assumed he would have done it innocently too, whatever it was. The problem was some voices were raised, and that had resulted in the what was already a dense crowd to bunch in even closer to the cause, Ray. It took a gentle nudge and few side steps and apologies to get close enough to Sam before he could tell us more.

"So, we go into an engineering shop and Ray here notices the colour on a particular laser wasn't, according to him the correct shade, 'and that it maybe costing them on energy consumption, only a small amount but well add it over the year and I'm guessing it adds up, I mean I don't know what the fuel consumption is but I imagine it's not free? Eh? Ha?' .... he says, so this Guy here, the one with the wrench, storms over here and promises to smash someone's head in, this Guy here, the one with his tongue out and those horny spikes all lining up in the other guy's direction every time they moved alignment, well, apparently they are really poisonous, deadly, so watch out for those. Well anyway, as you can see they're being held back, but I'm sure that's not going to last, and Ray is insisting that the laser is burning at the wrong colour, and spikey poison boy is saying he can't be responsible because he's just buying it and selling it on. He's kind of right, but it doesn't matter the Mall police are on their way.

He was correct. Just wailing high enough above the already ultra-high pitch frequencies squealing and the commotion of the crowd, a siren or alarm of a nature anyone would recognize could be heard. More Dutch sounding than anything else. I visited Holland once with the Ex, their sirens seemed to sound more drunk than we got, 'Weee orr' followed by a quick, 'Err, ooo' which oscillated briefly, and repeat till fade, or you reach the hospital..... I wonder if the 'Health and Safety' people ever required anyone in transport to wear headphones as the sound so close to a siren, within that proximity was, bloody annoying?

Ray was shaking his head, "No, no, no no no. It's the wrong colour I tell you. Oh, hello Horace, Hello Colin."

"Hello Ray, what seems to be the problem?" Nelson inquired.

Ray didn't get a chance to answer, spikey Alien spoke up, "The problem is your friend is calling me a liar and now security are here." He then looked towards Nelson and his spikes followed.

"Now now, violence rarely sorts out a problem."

"It sorts out getting ripped off, after eight years of custom," said wrench Alien.

"Yes but it's hardly worth the grief, especially with all these witnesses and security within eye shot." I said, kind of pointing out the stupidity of the present situation. The wrench disappeared, the spikes on spikey receded until he just looked like a teenager with a massive zit problem. The crowd then parted allowing the security team to approach. Two heavy set creatures with a bright yet greyish skin covering a large face who's features it seemed turned down at the edges giving the appearance of sadness, for all I knew it could be their birthdays and they're having a ball but I still feel like I want to hug them and tell them that everything is going to be alright. Being dressed in black really didn't help, it only aided their graveyard pallor look. Which in its own way only added to the feeling that these guys really did not like time wasters. Which was only reinforced by their massive eight foot frame and huge bulk.

"What's going on?" one of them said. It was hard to tell which one as everything was grey, tongue, gums and teeth.

"I was sold a laser cutter that is defective."

"It's not defective."

"How do you know it's defective?"

"This human told me."

"Oh, and what do you know about laser cutters, you qualified in some way?"

"Nothing validated by a university but I'm sure even a Doctor of Colour would agree with me that the laser was the wrong colour to be doing to what it needed to be doing to fill its' maximum potential," answered Ray.

"All I did was buy it, and then I sold it to him."

"And all I did was buy it, but it's off."

Silence. Apart from the din of metals and materials crying from the workshops. Someone really should be selling earplugs.

"So you sold a low quality laser and you bought a low quality laser."

Silence. Whichever one of those security guards spoke he was basically right, although a thought did run through my head.

"Ray, could you just check the schematics against similar better quality items and work out the difference?"

"Yes I suppose I could, why?"

"It could be a really easy fix, something somebody could do in a massive workshop, for instance."

Ray went off somewhere into cyber land, he closed his eyes this time so the now slightly less substantial crowd couldn't see his eyes spin wildly in their sockets, it was a bit disconcerting, especially if you were eating.

Something inside told me that it was probably best if the crowd didn't know Ray wasn't totally human. Only in appearance. Which was enough to attract attention by itself, Ray being an ex-Egyptian Royal who liked to look like one. He's probably already spotted where he needs to go to find eye-liner. He would have liked the 1980's. I didn't know if androids were a normal thing or not, or how they may react, but as Ray had the sense to close his eyes it may not be welcoming. He's never bothered to do that in front of any of us. I spoke up.

"My good friend Ray here has a photographic memory and anything he has ever read he can recall." Ray stopped what he was doing and open his left eye, looked at me and as I did I noticed an ever so small mischievous grin. He caught my little white lie, he then closed his eye and continued. As did I, "Just one of his many party tricks is recalling whatever happen upon your birthday." I hoped nobody asked.

"But you can't read a colour," some bright spark noted from somewhere. He was right, and having a photographic memory meant nothing.

"He also sold paint for a living," I lied my back teeth off, sometimes if you're going for the bluff you may as well go for it. I could feel Nelson's back stiffen as he began to realize I was digging myself a big hole. He then he jumped in with me.

"And as he lived next to a desert he's quite good with all shades orange, I suggest you just give him a second and......"

A moment later Ray open his eyes.

"Ah, I have it. It appears this laser is made by the same company that make the top models, but they use a different housing silicate that has less tensile strength thus you simply need to move the whole plate away from the contact point....... I believe by 13 microns only. You have a torque driver?" Ray asked the disgruntled purchaser.

"Yes."

"Go on then," urged Ray. Even the security ghosts gesticulated that he should do so. The remaining crowd grew silent, everybody waited for him to complete the task. The creature next to him held forth his hands and made a makeshift rather small and soft work top. Ideal for the first four screws, he then offered the small screwdriver with torque settings to the security guard to double check. Everything was good, he then fiddles around within the laser unit, quickly finished and calmly replaced the housing.

"Right, done, need to go to my workshop to have a look, cut something, check the power consumption and errr, make sure all's in order. It's just over there." He pointed the way and it seemed that because everyone in the crowd had invested so much time already they had to see the result and the conclusion if any resulting from the tests. The crowd parted so he could lead the way, the two security guards followed on behind, followed by everybody else who had a direct connection to the drama and then finally everybody else. Not a lot can be happening around here if this is enough to promote this level of interest....... Or maybe they all hoped that it would end in failure, there's a massive break down in order and a big fight ensues?

Maybe it so appealing because at the same time it was also very boring around here?

On the way to the workshop I noticed Nelson look me over whilst deep in thought. I instantly had the feeling I was in trouble, a telling off was at some point in order, just not best here amongst a crowd, and if it related to my improvisation over Ray then he'd give the game away...... I think I'd be angry, it was out of the blue, and a big fat lie, and we don't really know what the law is concerning whoppers.

The workshop was full of machines and tools and boxes of stock, and piles of cut sheet metals. The smell of carbon filled the air and shouts of 'Eyes' as flashes of blinding bright lights exploded from metal joints being welded were just audible over the scream of whizzing blades and whirring drills. The only thing missing as far as I could see from an engineering works on earth and this place was a heavily stained tea mug somewhere..... I checked, there were none, yes, I wanted a tea that much and yes I was beginning to salivate and yes, that's sad. Whilst I yearned for a hot beverage, wrench alien croaked some orders to one of his workshop colleagues. He in turn opened the nearby junction box and peered in. He then raised a hand whilst continuing his gaze. Wrench alien then placed a sheet of some metal on a bench, placed the laser into its place on the end of a sleek robotic arm. He checked that his friend was watching inside the junction box, he then nodded to the security guards, who nodded back and then finally to Ray. Ray didn't nod back as he noticed that the nod wasn't so much a sign of, 'ready' but more if this doesn't work I'm going to be really really angry, and the only thing Ray should get 'ready' for is running away...... He pushed a small green button. The metal sheet was instantly sucked down securely onto the bench and the arm sprang to life dancing around in its' own choreographed routine. It then just as swiftly returned to its' home start point and sank down with an exhausted pneumatic hiss. The alien watching the box shouted over to the wrench alien, who in turn paused and ran something through his head. A slow turn towards Ray prompted a silence.....

"........ I owe you an apology, does your culture allow contact?"

"Well, human's do..." said Ray and before he could finish what he was saying the alien was hugging him, firmly, he then let go and Ray finished what he was saying, "... but I might not. Bit late now, but that's alright." I laughed and Nelson joined in, personally speaking, more out of a sense of relief than anything else. Spikey alien broke the mood.

"Accuse me, embarrass me in front of everyone!"

"I'll take ten more."

"Would you like them delivered?"

"No I'll collect. Give me ten minutes."

With that everyone was happy, apart from nearly everyone who really wanted a fight. The crowd dispersed quickly, the guards stayed momentarily just to give Ray a word of advice.

"It's best not to stir things up, you've only just got here and you're telling us what's what. Best not to do that. Especially from a human."

"Yes Ray, watch your tongue," said Nelson.

"Yes, yes, I will, sorry everyone." Either Ray was a very good actor or the fact that he was mainly a computer allowed a neutral tone that just happened to sound sincere, very sincere. The guards left.

"Right, I think we should get back to the ship before we get in any more trouble, don't you? Or tell any more porkies, what do you say Colin?"

"Yes, umm, I should have just kept quiet."

"No, speak up, speak away, just back it up and don't endanger the people around you. Mistrust from the off will doom any relationship."

I got the idea. I suppose he was much more responsible with other peoples' lives as a matter of course, it being his trade and all.

"Before you go is there anything I can do for you? You're going to save me and a lot of us around here an awful lot, and the colour was different," asked wrench alien.

"Well, if there's one small design problem I've noticed with our ship it's that, there's no splash-back in the kitchen, you know, where the sinks are." I nodded, he wasn't wrong. Nelson looked slightly more incredulous, probably hoping that just because Ray had asked for the first favour it didn't necessarily mean that others might not be considered and that that was all we needed. I now knew how Nelson felt about me just blurting something out, surely there was something slightly more important than a splash-back to be had, or at least asked for? The alien did offer after all.

"Could we get back to you on that, Ray was just thinking personally as he spends most of his time in the kitchen."

"If he wants a splash-back, whatever one of those is, he's going to get one."

"I only need a strip of metal, that's all, nothing much, a metre long and less than half as wide. Look there's a piece." Ray pointed to a small strip of shiny metal. The alien handed him a small tube of adhesive.

"Take what you need and come back if you want more or something else. If you go out this evening, find the 'Uumergorn' restaurant, on the third floor, my wife's brother is having a new food evening, something called Rabbit, you come, you come, it's on me. All the Rabbit you can eat."

Strangely enough we all smiled and chuckled our apologies at the same time. No one needed to speak for the group we all declined in unison.

"Although, do they have whiskey?" inquired Sam.

"Lovely thought Sam, I must admit, however I think we may have gone by then. We can't hang around too long. We could meander back via a shop though, there might be a few things we wouldn't have thought about unless you see them."

Oh dear, I thought, I'm going to have to wait for my cup of tea. Ray must have noticed as he asked me if I wanted to go back and help put up his new kitchen design feature.

"Only an idiot would ask for a hand in doing that, all you need do is stick it to the wall, but it would give me a chance to get a pot ready, keep the kettle hot."

Nelson saw the sense, "Yes, good idea, keep that kettle hot. Anything you want, and don't say fingerless gloves."

"What about some, normal gloves and some scissors?"

I think the Admiral in him stopped him giving me the finger.

CHAPTER 5

To my amazement Ray actually did want me to hold the sheet metal splash-back in place whilst he stepped back and pretended to make sure it was level. He eventually made sure he was correct by projecting a thin beam from his eye right eye. He double checked his own correctness with his left eye, scanning the line across its length for a small moment my stomach urged. He looked up at me with his left eye, making me urge again.

"You alright?"

"Yeah. Everything fine here, may I slap it into position?"

"Yes, sure, all levels are correct," he said and blinked his eyes to their normal position.

"I know, it's resting on the worktop and I'm not actually touching it." I pushed it into place and held it for a couple a seconds waiting for the glue to adhere, "I'll put the kettle on."

"Shouldn't we go and help someone?"

"Yes," I answered taking a seat.

"Anything wrong Colin?" Ray asked in an Austrian accent.

The answer was, yes, but I wasn't sure why. I wasn't sure if it merited being something worthy of even having a bad side. I sighed deeply and made it last, deciding if I should mention anything.

"Take your time," Ray offered in a softer version of the same accent.

"I need a day off, a Saturday, a lay in. A locked front door, even unplugging the phone. Slippers, pyjamas, dressing gown, coffee, toast. Radio, shower, more coffee, 'Football Focus'."

"Yeah, everyone feels like that, that's quite normal."

"That makes it worse. If we're all burying our heads at the end of the week then surely the system needs to be tweaked? It would be good to be satisfied at the end of the day. At work it often felt like I was the agent of someone else's deceit and they'd underpay me for the privilege of working for them. I didn't like that."

"Who would?" Ray coughed, "yes the generals hated it when I told them they were taking a pay cut as I needed to up the bread allowance for the slaves."

"What happened?"

"Not sure…….. Next thing I knew I awoke on a starship. You would have thought I would have a chip on my shoulder, wouldn't you? No, turns out it was in my head. Eh? Eh?" Ray laughed loudly,

I chuckled, "come on, that was funny," he continued. He was right, it was, I just feared encouraging him.

"You seem to be more than just a computer though Ray? You've almost got a sense of humour, you know, you can nearly crack a joke."

"Yeah, yeah, you're very funny yourself. When the Squid took me, they also got the remnants of my brain and all the bits. The bits they chucked away, and replaced with mechanics, a small amount of the brains worked in some sense, I had fragments of memories, some of the involuntary switching systems still worked, and I still felt something of a life force energy surging through my being."

"Mmmm, you sure they didn't simply over charge the battery?"

Ray stared at me for a moment, and then shook his head, "Idiot. The point is that with the aid of a supercomputer I suddenly knew more than I ever did as a human. And now more than most."

"But you were entombed right? So how did they get you out in time?"

"Quite simple really, they used the old alien trick of painting the underside of a space shuttle or smallish ship in the design of a local animal, say a bird. Swoop down, tell the locals that you've been sent by the Gods and that we are to convey the body of whomever to the heavens. Can you get on it and put the body into the loading bay, I mean belly of the bird. Easy."

Wow, I thought, that really does sound easy. Were we that stupid? Is it wrong of me to think that we were? We are more intelligent now though, aren't we?

"That's another thing Ray? Why is it that a thousand years after I died the first bit of life and civilization I encounter feels like a town centre on a Saturday afternoon?"

"Commerce, it's everywhere, what were you expecting?"

It appeared that was a much more difficult question than it first appeared. I pulled a few faces, grunted once and Umm'd a few times and then realize I'd wasted my time doing any of that.

"I just wish there was less of it. Or, less desire to make too much of it. It still looked like it was all about the cash, you know what I mean?"

"Yeah, yeah, I think I know what that means? I think it means you're a hippy. A big scruffy hairy blue hippy. A big beardy blue hippy, hey, I know, 'Hippy Smurf' right?

Ah, the sweet medicine of laughter. I howled a bellyful. Just what I needed. The remark also made me peer into the new splashback and try and gleam how I looked in the misty reflection. It wasn't good. The skin was a lighter shade of blue of course than the first day we escaped, but Ray was right, I still fitted into the 'Smurf' range on the colour chart. As already seen, he was good with colours, the beard needed to come off. I never liked them, but at the same time I hated being told that I had to shave for the sake of work. I have to rip out my facial fluff, yet my boss covered her face, and not very well, with bucket loads of war paint. Doesn't seem right. If I saw her now, I'd have to tell her that I'd taken up acting and was presently an extra in a Tim Burton film. Wouldn't matter which one.

"Ahhh, you've got so much to learn Colin," said Ray. I obviously didn't understand. I tilted my head and Ray pondered something. He then continued, "Do you want the long story or the short story? No, no, the long one will take too long, you'll ask too many questions, and, you'll probably then ask even more questions, no no, that won't do?"

"Short story please Ray?" I offered as an excuse to get to the point. Ray paused once more.

"Well, if you say so. Ok, this isn't easy you know?" Ray said, and then shuffled his shoulders and coughed several times, "Ok. For thousands of years the earth was visited by Aliens, it was easy, turn up with a dazzling display of colours and sounds, put on a bit of a show, wait until the locals bow down, get what you need and off you go. Man was quite stupid for quite a while. Then came telescopes, easy at first to avoid, but then in the twentieth century especially, it started to get a bit more tricky. A bright young thing called, Jocelyn Bell, saw something in the data and hit upon Pulsars. That also meant that ships or anything of movement can be detected if you know what you're looking for. That was a big problem for anything at long range. Much closer to Earth however, there were just too many cameras. A few made the mistake of thinking they could avoid being caught on film, but failed, and then, well you remember the mobile phone? Everyone had one, and they all had cameras…….. This had a twofold conclusion, firstly; everyone agreed on no more earthly intrusions, secondly, there was no need, all those cameras needed a home, the Internet, everything was uploaded and broadcast, we simply couldn't go back, but there was no need, you beamed your lives to us. Just as well, several times the planet was about to be taken over or simply annihilated, but along came massive events like the football 'World Cup', the 'Super Bowl' or the 'Olympics' or the 'Eurovision Song Contest' and everyone would park up, by which I mean assemble in a safe zone, slightly obscured by the moon but enough to capture the signal. Everyone agreed that these events were wonderful, amazing, and beautifully eccentrically human....... Plus who can resist a bunch of cats enjoying the cardboard box as much as they do?"

"I don't think any of that really helps explain? Although in itself, that's quite amazing...... Am I being told that a ball, a box, and a jolly love song saved the planet and everything on it."

"Yes that's a good way to put it..... But more than that, the systems, the mechanics, the guts of how humans used trade, money, markets, it all filtered out. The human view was far more technical than any advanced alien system had, they learnt a lot. The best bits, some the worst bits..... How about this, maybe you should think of the Earth, as a shared dwelling, a house of multiple occupancy. Your room is one of many, on just one floor, of many, in a house, on street in a borough, in a city, just one city in many cities in a county....."

"Let me guess, alright, I get it. The point, being, it's pretty much like Earth everywhere, because of the Earth."

"Yeah..... But not completely, but that's the longer story..... so we'll leave that for another time."

"That sounds great. I think I need another cuppa anyway..... and maybe a long bath, and an even longer shave, and, this may sound stupid or, or, irrelevant, but a good chat about football, for instance how did Arsenal do? What are the chances of England winning the world cup? Is Dennis Bergkamp the most underestimated greatest player ever? I miss 'Football Focus', I think it's as simple as that? Something in that order of things, not the Galactic history for dummies thing, no offence Ray.'

I noticed an audible high pitched tone emanating from Ray, his eyes spinning in different directions. I tapped the side of my tea mug with the spoon. Ray looked at me with one eye and smiled, "Mmm Arsenal. Yes they won the league that season, the one you died in, in some style it appears. They didn't lose a single game and went on into the annals of history, known as the 'Invincibles'. Well done that team. Something wrong Colin?"

There were indeed many things wrong at that moment. Most worryingly the image of my murder and kidnapper and I thought latterly my friend, wearing a Tottenham shirt laughing manically. I clenched my jaw and grimaced, this was my Team having what sounds like their best season ever and Doctor Sandra denied me what I'd waited all my life to see!!! What was I supposed to think! Now,

I'm not normally the sort of guy who runs around when something goes wrong proclaiming, 'Poor me' or anything of that order, but this time and for at least half a minute I toured the canteen looking at the floor, shaking my head and tutting all the way.......... Must remember to breathe, and not waste hot tea, but whilst I'm in this mood already who cares about air and beverages.

"Anything else happen that would have really annoyed me. Did Jim Morrison apologize for his hoax death and reform the Doors, along with guest guitarist, and neighbour Jimi Hendrix, and they were announcing a small venue tour starting at my local? Anything like that?"

"Alright, alright, don't shoot the messenger," Ray said, pointing out that he wasn't to blame.

"I'm sorry Ray. I didn't mean to......."

"That's fine, don't apologize. Do you want to know how the national team got on?"

"Noooo."

"They lost to Wales in the final in the, joking, joking...."

There was no need to reply as the door of the Canteen crashed open but I didn't see anyone come in. A small shiver ran up my spine. What was going on? Either the shiver was caused by the small breeze caused as the door swung open or, and more worrying, it was a ghost. Then something appeared at my side.

"Ahhh!! Smokey, don't do that. I thought you were a ghost. Although you do look more ill than normal. Won't be long."

"Gee thanks, that maybe down to the extreme over exertion obtaining my ink, and the fact that during my sleep I remembered that there were Squid who volunteered to stay at places like this and act as the eyes and ears and restocking officers."

"How do you know this?" I asked.

"I volunteered...... I thought I might be able to get my hands on some tobacco. I was refused, and told to stock up the volunteers with everything they needed and make sure everyone had a 'Space Messaging Service' communication unit."

"A Space Messaging Service?"

"Yes, that's what I said," said Smokey.

"Mmmm, an S.M.S. Tell me, would that be a text message? Like a mobile phone application? They can send a text. Wow, a thousand years later and the only development with phones seems to be the size of its' range. Must need a big battery?"

"Yes," said Smokey," but you're missing the point, we need to get away as quickly as we can, our position is probably known. Where's Horatio?"

"Shopping. With Sam, I think everyone else is onboard."

My spine shivered again. No ghost, no breeze, simple adrenalin, my guts telling me to act.

"We need to get hold of everyone and send out a search party…… Although, if there are Squid here they'd recognize everyone but me. Damn, so, I'll go out and search. Ray, can you get hold of our man upstairs and see if he can locate them."

"I would if I knew what you meant, 'Our man upstairs'."

"You know, 'Our' man. Nudge nudge….. No? The brother of the chef that works for the Floyd we sold the rabbits to?"

"Oh, couldn't you just say that?"

"Yes, I could have, but it doesn't sound as good. Right, got to go. If I'm not back in half an hour send out the search party." Nobody laughed, not even after I did. "Anyone got a mobile phone?" I didn't hang around to wait for an answer.

I went straight to the lifts. Thinking it best to start on the floor I left them on. Just as well Ray wasn't with me, he'd probably be asked about calibration of lasers and asked how to tweak them. It wasn't too long before I realized I wasn't going to find them. It would be sheer luck if I did. There must be a system, a way. Dave the Floyd would know, and just might have a phone, or something equivalent.

He was easy to find. Spottable in a crowd due to his height, his very slender frame, and the fact that he was at his stall. He bowed, less flamboyant than before and then said something that sounded gracious but could have been a complete insult. I wouldn't know, I didn't speak the language. Go slow, I thought, I need to be understood. Don't over explain. Stick to the message.

"Hello." Oops, foreigner mode, over loud. Decrease volume start again, "Hello, I've lost my friends, and need to contact them…." Followed by little finger to mouth and thumb to ear. The planet Earths' international hand signal for a phone. He looked puzzled, so I shook my phone-hand, "Phone, telephone." Dave squinted and then smiled broadly.

"Ahhhhh, yesss." He made his way to the back of his stall and picked up a small clear thin piece of plastic, the size of a credit card. He tapped it a few times and Nelson's face appeared on the plastic. Dave handed the screen to me.

45

"Err, Horace, hello, you good?"

"Hello Colin, you're my first caller, these are great aren't they? I've brought one for everyone, and few more bits besides. What can I do for you?"

"Nothing but get back to the ship as quick as possible." I refrained to add any immediacy to stress why. The neutrality of my tone in itself suggested something was wrong. I knew Nelson would understand that I had something to say but I wasn't able to simply blurt it out. I was correct, he nodded ever-so-slightly.

"I will do as you suggest. Now, how do you turn this thing off?" The image rocked about. Nelson turning his device over to look for an off switch. Hasn't he got small feet, nice shoes though? "Seriously, where's the button, how can there be a button on something that is flat anyway?"

Dave giggled and pointed to the bottom right hand corner of the screen. I instinctually tapped it. A few symbols appeared, one of which was a red 'X'. My turn to giggle.

"Tap the bottom right of the screen and then the big red 'x'. See you back at the ship." I pressed the 'X' and handed it back to Dave, "Thank you," I said, and feeling the urge bowed and rolled my hand in a very regal sort of way. Which in truth made me feel embarrassed so I turned quickly on my heels and left.

CHAPTER 6

Everyone was waiting in the canteen and for a quick getaway Ray had prepared a superb lunch, basically everything left over from earlier. Amazingly no one started until everyone was gathered.

Nelson spoke, but huffed before he started, "Firstly, thank you Ray for this amazing spread, however, given the circumstances I fear we won't be able to appreciate it as you would like...... We need to initiate our first 'Alert'. But, I guess we're all starving, so I'm going to say everyone has five minutes to get ready and in position. You can eat this now and rush or save it until the alert is over. I don't know when that will be."

Nobody ate, for a few seconds, then some one's stomach growled like a thunderstorm trapped in a barrel tumbling over a waterfall, so, we all dived in. Nobody had time to speak. You wouldn't have been able to hear anything anyway as the sound of cutlery smashed and clattered on the plates, I think they may have been ceramic. Bernie didn't look out of place, as he always used his hands to feed himself and he always ate like he was never going to see food again. It was actually quite disgusting to watch. Simple solution, don't watch or, join in.

Bernie was first to leave, but in quick succession we followed. Nobody thanked Ray, which was a shame because he always made whatever he was making fantastic, and he always took the time to do it. The sound of echoing burps from different areas of the ship, did however reassure him that we did like it, very much, and it wasn't wasted.

"In some cultures you know," he said from his position on the bridge and then started to laugh.

Nelson laughed proudly too, "That's my boy. You hear that Colin. Ray here, able to laugh in the face of the danger just around the corner. Good on you, Ray." Another burp resonated through the belly of the ship followed by a high pitched chuckle. Then from somewhere else someone joined in with the laughing, and then someone else.

Nelson, Ray, Smokey and I, all that were on the bridge, joined in with our own howl and then from everywhere the ship echoed with cackled and hoots of laughter.

From my position in the gunners chair I noticed the staff within the dock stop whatever they were doing and look around for something, some noise that they'd never heard before, not normal to their working environment. I wasn't the only one to notice, both Nelson and Smokey blew up into hysterics as they noticed the same thing. They buckled for a moment, but as ever Nelson drew himself back and switched on his sensible mode and the communication unit.

"Flying Fish requesting a speedy exit."

"Flying Fish, Flying Fish, leaving us so early. Did you remember to get your loyalty card and get it stamped, it wouldn't have been worth much as you weren't here that long but every credit helps right? We hope you had a nice stay and hello it's me…. That's ten percent when you…. A transmission went out….. and inclusive of breakfast and first wife stays for nothing……. With your name attached, we noticed it as it was a very strong signal, it had to travel some distance so whoever they were……. That's right sir if you want your breakfast in the spa that's possible, could be arranged you'd have to speak with the management on that one…. They were very far away, but you wanted notification if that happened, have a good trip….. And yes we have a new food available that's making a stir in all the restaurants, it's called a 'Wobbit'. Is everything alright with your engine, there are some very strange noise emanating from your ship and some very perplexed dock crew asking for maintenance.

"No, nothing to worry about. That will be the Wobbit we had earlier."

"Oh, I see, I'll let the dock know, have a good safe journey. I'll send you the exit route, ok, you can hit auto."

"Fare thee well," Nelson said and flipped the switch as quickly as he could as he was just about to howl louder than I had ever heard him do so thus far. Again pockets of laughter erupted from around the ship. Resonating through and around it. The workers in the dock began to join in.

We left the Mall as gracefully as a lazy dolphin using minimal movement, banking and rolling perfectly to avoid all the new construction works, and away we went, laughing in the face of adversity and adventure. Someone did let one last ripper loose before we got going.

"Anything nearby Ray?"

Ray scanned his scanners, "There's a few small ships heading for the Mall, nothing going towards the planet Crrrrk."

Nelson nodded to himself, happy enough with the situation, "Smokey, stick it on auto. Ray stay here and…. And join us when I send relief." Nelson flicked a switch and lent in towards his console, "would everyone please make their way to the Officers' mess."

"Glad you didn't choose the canteen because that really is a mess," Ray said and then tutted slowly.

Nelson lent forward once more, "Scrub that, would everyone make their way to the kitchen. The place needs a good wipe down." Nelson smiled towards Ray, "Alright?"

"The place needs to be wiped out, you lot need bibs or something. For a minute I thought I was in the adult version of Bugsy Malone."

"We're all very sorry Ray, we'll clean up our mess, and then once everything is clean, to your satisfaction, you can relax, with the present I bought you. Would that make you happy?"

Of course it would. Ray's eyes sparkled with excitement and he jittered about in his seat, "Can I have it now, can I, can I, please, please?"

"I'm afraid not, Ray, I haven't got it on me." Nelson flicked the intercom button once more, "Sam, would you please grab a volunteer and take the goodies to the canteen, please." Nelson smiled again, a sneaky one, the sort of smile that says, 'I know what's going on, you don't, you don't, Naa naa, don't worry it's something you'll like but in the meantime I reserve the right to wind you up a bit and have a bit of fun at your expense." This thought is generally followed by a moment of hesitation where you wonder if the thing you have is actually worth it and have you just blown it all out of proportion. You hope you haven't, otherwise you'll end up looking like a complete numpty and no one will ever trust your opinion again when you tell them they should do something because you believe it's excellent.

"Smokey, Colin, I'll wash, you dry, you put away."

By the time we got to the kitchen most of the work was done. Marilyn had woken from her slumber but still looked very exhausted, she was sat in a chair, lent over with her head firmly pressed into the table. Even the coffee that lay in front of her wasn't enough to make her in any way seem alive. Smokey was almost asleep whilst sweeping the floor, his eyes closed, only his momentum keeping him moving. Everyone else were busy wiping something or other or putting the freshly wiped item away somewhere also freshly wiped.

"Good timing Colin eh?"

"Yes, I' might as well get the kettle on. Show of hands for a cuppa?" Everyone raised a hand, except Marilyn. She appeared not to be even raising a pulse.

Nelson strolled over to Sam who pointed at a pile of boxes and bags laying on the floor. They smiled to each other. I smiled and had a quick internal giggle too, I love seeing other people's happiness, never fails to make me smile. If you are ever feeling down, just go to a maternity ward after feeding and hopefully during a play session. I defy you not to smile. Like a contagion of innocent happiness. That would be something worth catching, why not, you'd already be in a hospital. Seem to catch everything else in those places.

I was the last to get seated, I made two visits making sure everyone had access to hot beverages and then finally sat myself. There followed a moment of silence, everyone smiled, broadly speaking. Nelson just smiled, broadly. Again I laughed which he noticed and understood, he did the only thing he could do, he gave me a wink.

"You enjoying yourself Santa?" I asked.

"Certainly am Colin, aren't you? If there's one thing I learnt at sea it was that small distractions to your reality can save an awful lot of respect and trust, but what is more important than all of that is? You have to laugh, enjoy the moments that can provide a wellbeing that money can't buy. And this Colin, is one of those moments."

Something then hit me in the face. Soft, very soft, wool like soft. That would make sense as a pair of fingerless gloves slipped down my face and into my lap.

"See what I mean Colin?" Nelson said. Once more I had no choice but to agree and join in. I was last at joining in everyone was already pointing and laughing at me. I tried the gloves on.

"Perfect, thank you, and the moral of that story is, wish for bigger things?"

"Like Smokey here. What would be your wish Smokey?"

Any of us could have answered that question for him, instead we simply watched him wonder off whilst he considered this notion. Wherever he went he was there for quite a while, and his facial expressions changed more than once.

"A view, involving the sea, a sea full of easily catchable food, near a beach, on which is a lounger and low table with umbrella, mmmm, a sweet yet non fruit based cocktail and a bowl of the finest tobacco with thousands of cigarette papers." Most people seemed to be at that beach with him. Eyes drifting off hazily into the distance.

"Well I can help with the first sequence of requests but I do have a little something for you. Nelson shoved a wrapped box in Smokey's direction it stopped dead in front of him. Smokey paused and swallowed deeply before slowly savouring the moment of unwrapping. Building up his own sense of anticipation. Nelsons' smile became grander and wider the closer Smokey got to finishing his slow undress of his present. He must have known what it was already. Even before he unwrapped it he inhaled deeply and after exhaling stopped at the final moment and graciously nodded towards Nelson.

"You deserve it, the only thing is you're going to have to go outside to smoke it." Nelson face didn't move a muscle, "only joking, just make sure you're near an extractor when you do light up. So you can have one now, here under the cooker hood, and then relieve Ray on the bridge, alright?"

"More than, thank you."

"Don't thank me, that stuff is going to kill you, don't thank me for that." Too late, on the way over to the cooker Smokey passed Nelson and gave him a complete one hundred percent unescapable fully embracing hug and squeeze.

"Get a room," shouted Sam.

Nelson just grinned, or maybe that was just the look of a man who hated everything tactile...... Especially from a bear hugging loving Squid. I don't think anyone saw Smokey make his cigarette, dexterous or gasping, either way the thing just appeared in his mouth and off he chugged. Where did he keep his lighter? Smokey slowly sank to the floor, sliding down the side of the cooker as he went and exhaling as he went. We all seemed to be having a phantom or sympathy smoke with him. We all exhaled at the same time.

"Get your own," said Smokey noticing the amassed crowd looking on enviously at his moment of joy. Nobody else smoked, but we all recognized that moment of, 'Ahhhhhhhhh, mmmmm, rrr.' Mine would be the single malt whiskey I save for very special occasions or particularly difficult days. My last bottle was hardly used, and what little had gone was mainly followed by a barrel load of tears when the missus left and the world went sideways for a while. Then I realized life was actually better without her and had a double to celebrate. No more overtime wasted on shoes, endless shoes. So much overtime I never had the chance to see her wear them...... Somebody else had that pleasure, poor man.

Nelson dipped his hands into his goody bag, "Ah, some excellent coffee for Marilyn, and others."

"Get your own," Marilyn just about managed to say and then raised her head from the table, smiled towards Nelson, said, "Thank you" and returned to her original position.

"You're with us....and no you're not...... don't waste your coffee Marilyn."

Marilyn bolted upright, opened her eyes as wide as possible, which was a lot considering how flexible her Squidgy skin is and pretended to be awake as possible. She then delicately raised her mug to her mouth and drank, everything, in one, "Ahhhhh, yessss, that's the one. Where are we? I need another one, anybody, anyone want another drink, I'm making, say now. Smokey what the hell are you doing slumped on the floor like that?"

"I think he's just getting up and fetching Ray?"

Smokey stood up slowly, which wasn't very long for him as he was quite small. Big volume, but not very tall. He slapped nelson on the back as he passed, causing Nelson to spill a small splash of tea.

"Just as well I got more, Eh Colin? I got more tea."

"Hey, there's never enough tea?" I answered. Naturally.

"So nobody for a refill?" Marilyn double checked, "Good..... Get your own." Yet again I chuckled. Everyone seemed to be on form today, in as much as the 'Banter' was flowing. In its' own way a beautiful moment, willfully opening up your being ready for insult or ridicule all in the cause of cementing and bonding a relationship. Easily misunderstood as bullying, and unfortunately used as an excuse when bullying is spotted and confronted. "No, no, I was only joking, you know, havin' a laugh."

All the insults flying around were definitely in the friendly zone, as they all ended with a smirk or some other facial giveaway. Unlike the clenching of teeth that leads to a snarl at the end of an insult, that's not 'Banter' at all and it's definitely not funny, unless you know that the 'Insulter' has completely underestimated the 'insultee' and is going to get what he may well deserve. I still wouldn't want anyone to get seriously hurt though.

"Ok and yes, this stuff." Nelson placed large pot on the table, the size of a sweet shop sweet jar, "this is great, check this out." He opened the pot and rolled up a sleeve and dipped his hand into a white gel. He then retrieved his hand and the gel covering the hand pulled itself taught and made a perfect glove, he then slowly peeled it off and replaced it back into pot where it returned to a gel.

"Amazing, brilliant for any messy job, and, excellent as bandage, self-cleaning when you return it to the pot. I know I can't really call this a present, but whoever needs it, it'll be here in the canteen. There's also a crate of tools ready to be unpacked in the loading bay."

At that moment Ray entered, "I think Smokey maybe ill, has anybody smelt his breath? Seriously, there's something wrong, I could smell the path he walked all the way to back here."

"That was just an unhealthy reunification of tobacco and addict, nothing to worry about, he is old enough to make his own decisions. It was a little present, as is this." Nelson once again withdrew something from his Santa bag and placed a small metal case on the table, polished and silver looking, in itself a nice object, "There you go Ray, I just happened to pass a particular place."

If Ray could blush he would have. He did look shy and embarrassed for a moment and then he sat down in front of his present. He gave Nelson a very regal nod, one which the Floyd would indeed be honoured to receive. Nelson simply and quickly nodded back.

The first thing Ray did was slowly caress the edges of the box, as though he was a pilot feeling the skin of the plane before take-off, or the way a man might check the skin on his face after the shave that is reserved for the night he goes out thinking he 'May get Lucky', the one that goes against the grain, dangerous, but worth it if successful. Ray then brought his fingers to the centre clasp and flipped the catch. He still took his time opening the lid, why I couldn't understand because he also had his eyes closed and he was looking away.

"Just open it already," shouted Sam. Ray broke out of his childish spell and looked down.

"What the hell are these? Sunglasses. Am I near home? Wait a minute?" Ray opened the glasses and put them on. Yes, to anyone looking at Ray they would have thought, why is that idiot wearing sunglasses inside. You know I hate that, right? However, Nelson and Sam who acquired the present knew different and then half a moment later Ray knew different, "Ahhh, I get it," he said, and then a good ten seconds later everybody else got it. Ray took off the glasses to reveal his freshly placed eye liner and make up, "that's perfect." He then immediately ran to the sink and wiped everything off and started again. Five seconds later and a new look.

"It's behind you," I shouted. Ray frowned, fair enough I forgot that might need an explanation, "Pantomime baddie, it's a line the audie.... never mind." Again ray had a quick wipe and started over.

"Ok, let's go trad. Where are you, where are you." From the side I could see that Ray was blinking rapidly, he must have been scrolling through a menu of some designs and by the sounds of it looking for something. He tutted lifting the glasses up slightly with one hand, "Typical, does this sound offensive to you, he replaced the glasses to read from the inside, 'Egyptian Pharaoh Style; Ancient human culture, very very simple basic, not really worth calling it a design. No imagination, creativity, or panache. Why!' Why indeed? Idiot, to make me look more important that you, just do you job." He blinked then revealed his Pharaoh pout, pose, and perambulation. The pop star swank as he strolled back to his seat. Either that or he was doing a very camp version of John Travolta's walk from 'Saturday Night Fever'.

"One thing Ray, I only got three cartridges to refill it, so don't go nuts."

"Shouldn't be a problem, no colour, simple design, not much waste, you know? And thank you so much, I'm impressed. Better hide them from Marilyn and Mona."

"I could punch myself in the face and end up looking better than that," said Mona and grinned smugly.

"I could help you with that," answered Ray. Bernie roared with laughter and patted his sister on her back. Mona looks surprised but nodded the acceptance of a good come back.

Maybe, just maybe it was a sign that in fact we all worried. An underlying resonance of fear. Not only were we wanted, but we could now assume that the Squid had a fix on us, or at the very least a good idea of where we were. It was just as well Nelson was using this get together as a stress relieving exercise.

Nelson then produce the credit card size plastic phone I had seen earlier. He bought one for everyone. He asked Ray to give demonstrations as and when he could and if people weren't otherwise busy. Most of us were going to be quite busy straight away, Nelson asked us all to attend to our areas and double check them and their systems, and then slid a jumbo pack of razors across the table. Pic and Don grimaced, they foresaw a clog coming along. There was going to be a lot of de-bearding and trimmings to contend with. Before we left our seats Nelson asked for silence.

"……… Men, Ladies, I need to say something, to you all, and to myself too. Now, I know you all feel that I 'm probably the best person for the job, that of final decision maker, captain as it were, and, you'd be right, but here in lies the problem, none of you are professional military men, no one is getting paid and, what's maybe worse is, you're all very much my friends. Which kind of makes it difficult for me to shout at anyone, or bark an order. So, bearing this in mind, I just going to say, If I do, it's only probably so because it needs to be done straight away. So I'll apologize in advance of this event occurring. I would also like, in this sense, to say that, it should come down to me to try and bluff our way out of a situation, and nobody else, Colin. If it goes wrong, I will raise my hand, 'Mia culpa', but, I think I might just play it cooler, I'd panic less."

"Yes, Sorry about that. You're right I did panic. It's just as well Ray knew his colours, sorry."

"No, no, don't get me wrong Colin, I like invention, spontaneity, thinking on the hoof. I should have said something before we left, I take responsibility. I should have said something. It worked out, everything is good, there's no problem. Just, next time, be slightly more patient, relax, you didn't need to justify anything to anyone."

Nelson of course was right, and I'd have to say that was the best telling off I'd ever received. It wasn't even a telling off, it was more of an educational tip, the art of 'Bull'. I don't want to be the man that says Lord Horatio Nelson knows a lot about the subject, but we are dealing with a man who would ask his men not to fire the canon until well within range. When most would simply want to fire and run away, you're going to need procrastination levels normally reserved for sloths to achieve this.

"Don, Pic, we're all with you. We're still ahead in the race. The fact that the Squid now know this doesn't change a thing. Everybody be alert, concentrate, we've got a job to do. Everyone to their stations…… please."

CHAPTER 7

To tell you the truth I wasn't too sure what my station required. My position was the gunners' chair. That was my station. All I had to do was aim and fire. Tracker ball and button. I didn't even have to load any artillery first, there was nothing to load. I was firing something produced by a massive energy producing battery on constant trickle charge from an engine I had no grasp of. How do I check that......? Maybe I should employ the first rule of the shop floor manual; if you're not busy, get a brush and sweep, get a cloth and wipe. I suppose a good wipe down of the console wouldn't be out of the question. Good maintenance of equipment and all that. The second rule would be don't rush what you're going to do if you're only doing it to make yourself look busy. What are you going to do if you finish that early too?

So a slow walk to the stores and poke around amongst the cleaning equipment was in order. As soon as I closed the door it instantly felt as though I was back, in my time. If I were wearing a watch I'd be looking at it wondering how many hours remained before I could saunter home and collapse in my armchair...... I did have a watch somewhere? Is it still in the replica house on the Squid ship? The morning Smokey politely offered to stash my things on the Flying Fish I was rather rude to him. Well, I told him where to go and how to get there. He rightly took offence and got on with something that would be worthwhile. He kindly took a few things, but no clothes, as a form of punishment? Or politeness, as they were stored in the wardrobe in the bedroom, where I was trying very hard to get some sleep and not be so grumpy about it. Anyhow, my escape was mainly done in my birthday suit and I had nothing to change into once we were away. I had been wearing the altered uniforms ever since. I had no idea what the material was. It felt very comfortable, I just didn't necessarily like the look. Was I off to a themed fancy dress party somewhere, mainly based on the Nineteen Eighties? A quick blast with Rays' new glasses and I would be complete. The Adam and the Ants look from the eighties...... No thanks. 'Kings of the last Frontier,' eh? Sorry that's only relevant if you know anything about Adam and the Ants. Please excuse me if you don't.

My musings were interrupted by Don and Pic bursting in.

"Hello Colin, what are you doing here?" asked Pic.

"Looking for something to clean my console with, give it a wipe or something."

"Busy then?" said Don.

"Yeah, rushed off my feet."

"There's the spray." Pic pointed to a can.

"There's a cloth." Don pointed to a cloth.

"Thanks."

"You know what you're doing?" they both said together and in the very same tone.

"I'm pretty sure I've got this."

That too, was exactly like being back in my own time. Every time you met someone coming into the storeroom you occupied you'd automatically consider the chances that they too were just wasting a bit of time. Like the smoker who nips off for a sneaky cigarette.

Back on the bridge I got to work wiping down, quite slowly, my console and chair. Still it didn't take long.

"Smokey, anything need a wipe down?" His console was directly in front of mine, his half of it at least. Smokey was on the left, Nelson's chair was to his right. From there they steered the ship and monitored everything else.

"No thanks."

Sam had his console directly to my left. More buttons and sliders and small screens displaying dancing data in various graph forms.

"Sam?"

"No, that's alright, I need to use these buttons. I'll tell you what, why don't you get a suit on a do the screen?"

"Spacewalk to do a bit of window cleaning? Are you quite mad?"

"Hey," interrupted Smokey, "I'll come with you, I could do with another cigarette."

I had to pause for a second as I wasn't sure if Smokey was aware that Sam was joking or not, because if he wasn't that could quite possibly mean that he is also serious about coming along for the smoke. That's dedication. So for a second a few things ran through my mind, and then for verification I looked at him for any more clues...... Head down rolling away, ok, he was serious. I know it's been a while for him but really?

He then looked up, "You dumb Bass. You thought I was serious.... I'm done here for the moment. Colin would you take my seat please, don't press anything, you got me? If you do need to call me, and really I wouldn't know why you should, then that switch there, flick and speak." He pointed to a flick switch on Nelson's side of the console.

"Where are you going?" I asked, stupid question, he held up his cigarette and shook his head all the way as he strolled passed me, looking up at me all the way.

"Better look after this one Sam," he said as he opened the door, still shaking his head. I took his seat and admired his console. Then quickly suppressed the urge to spray the whole thing a make it shine. The row upon row of buttons and switches looked too delicate to scrub and I'm sure the spray would get down the side and interfere with the electronics hidden beneath. I might be wrong, but I'm not going to be the idiot who fuses the ship leaving us stranded, wallowing around in space, hoping and waiting for some passing ship to save us….. No, I'd better not do anything just sit here and do nothing…… I could clean Smokey's chair, in fact I'll do that, I should have done that before I sat down. I'm not saying he's dirty or filthy or anything, he's got his own salt water hot tub, that must take care of a lot of things, but, he's a Squid….. Well, that didn't take too long…. And neither did Nelson's. Phfffff, and once more phfffff. That didn't bode well did it? Super boredom?

"You ok?" inquired Sam.

"Debateable."

"Why don't you just sit there and look at the supremely amazing view whizzing by? Or if that's no good, sit down and wonder how that's even possible? If you're still stuck, grab Ray's new glasses, turn an image of your own eyes into a design and print them back onto your now closed eyes thus making it look like you're completely awake and paying attention rather than bored numbless and mostly asleep, as you are now."

Wow, I thought, have I annoyed him in some way? I don't think so? Maybe he just hates bored people? Maybe it's more than that maybe I'm boring! No, that can't be right? I like to moan a lot, but there's so much to moan about. I like to drink tea whilst I'm doing that, so I drink a lot of tea. Maybe he hates tea? No, probably just the English? Better check though.

"Everything alright with you Sam?"

Sam looked at me with the grumpiest face I'd ever seen him wear. Oops, it that was anything to do with me, then it must be quite serious? Sam looked away for a moment and then looked back directly at me.

"Is it something I've done?" I asked and then clenched my teeth.

"No, why would it be anything to do with you. Oh no, sorry, I forgot, you are English, always apologizing for nothing in particular. Have I offended anyone? Just in case, I'd better offer a jolly sorry, 'Sorry Everyone' that was probably me.... Hmm? Did I just bark and snap at you a few times? I'm sorry Colin."

"That's alright Sam, it happens."

"Sorry, what happens?"

"You know, It, it happens, we lose our rag, we say that in England, sorry did... did say that."

There followed a pause in time for both of us at that moment. We were both swept away into a daydream, or memory, or absorbed into an image that conjured a feeling of home, it was glorious, unique, made you forget all else. Obviously, we weren't sharing the same vision, I presume Sam was off somewhere crossing some plain on a horse, camping out at night under a blanket of stars, warmed by a roaring fire, looking out over the Death Valley horizon or some such place. I however, was just finishing a pasty in any Cornish town, just about to start a clotted cream ice-cream, mmm, better put a flake in that, and then punch a few dive-bombing seagulls who must have learnt how to deal with 'Brain Freeze'. In the foreground camper vans and sand, squeals of excited kids, squawks of freshly Black-eyed seagulls, and maybe some mid-nineties funk fusion kicking out of an even older ghetto blaster...... Eventually I sighed heavily, Sam whistled as he exhaled, making his exasperation tuneful. For a few moments I truly believed Sam had to be one of the best whistlers that I'd ever heard. It seemed that during his melodic sigh, at the end of his trip down Nostalgia Avenue he was also able to add a metronome on a very regular beep. Reminded me of the music you might hear at the beginning of a news programme on the television..... I then had the good sense to realize that this was a highly unlikely musical talent and that it was probably worth shushing Sam. I hate doing that to people but somewhere something in my brain shouted 'Alert' and I acted upon instinct. I would never shush someone simply because I couldn't be bothered to listen to them. I'm not a jerk..... My suspicions were correct.

Sam instantly span around in his chair and scanned his domain for information. I ran over to the only switch I was allowed to use.

"Stations everyone! This is not an exercise. I'm not having a laugh, everyone, stations, now!" I looked for a button that might produce an alarm sound, I couldn't see one. "Shift!" I then jumped into my chair. It instantly hoisted me up a metre to meet my console.

"Damn, who's driving?" I said. Sam instantly left his seat and took over control. We could all do everyone else's jobs but primarily it was Smokey's role, simply because he was the best. I had played a lot of 'Call of Duty', hence I was the main gunner. Nelson then strode in directly towards his seat.

"Calm down Colin, you don't have time to panic. Sam, spin her one eighty on her axis. Colin, are you ready? Where's Smokey?"

"I'm ready, all systems on, primed, scanning now….. Smokey's have a smoke." I cringed as I dobbed on Smokey, again not my normal style, I'm really not a jerk, but, it's best we're all honest, and right now other things were far more important. Like the answer to my question.

"Why is that beep getting faster?"

"Whatever it is it's going faster than us," Nelson said as he followed a sequence of lights that told him something or other. The door to the bridge then crashed open. Without turning nelson greeted Smokey.

"Hello Smokey, take your seat. Sam's done a lovely job turning us about.

Sam returned to his own seat and humphed, and then added, "Whatever it is will hit us in forty seconds. It's on course to hit."

Smokey looked up and shrugged, "Oh well, at least I got my last cigarette in."

I then saw a moment of magic….. Or madness? Nelson slowly turned his head and looked at Smokey, paused momentarily and then shook his head, disappointed, or, still playing it ultra-cool?

"Oh ye of little faith. Eh Colin? You can take care of it can't you?" Nelson was still facing Smokey. I knew he wanted to hear a positive tone from me, but I also needed to be straight with him, and everyone. Myself included.

"Yes, should be alright… Once I can see it." Not totally laced with self-belief, enough for Nelson though.

"You see Smokey. Colin's got it." I noticed a quick glance over towards me as he tried to convince Smokey…… Unfortunately it wasn't necessarily Smokey that Nelson should have been trying to convince….. My heart rate seemed to be going as quick as the quickening beeps and my finger trembled in time too, causing a moment of doubt and the thought of a fumbled button crossed my mind.

"How big is this thing? What am I firing at?" I asked trying to invoke action mode. As with my game play, before every mission start, load all weapons and use the correct gun for the right scenario setting. Not just your favourite one all the time. Sam leant in and studied the data, pressed some buttons and nodded to himself.

"Mm, small, very small. Twenty five seconds. The size of your head Colin, a football…. It couldn't be the virus payload, could it?"

Well that news cheered us all up. I don't know about anybody else but my mouth went dry instantly. I needed a drink and anything would do. I couldn't even swallow.

"I'm on maximum magnification here and I can't see a thing," I said.

"My scan is very long range, you should have it in a moment."

"Everybody strap in!" Nelson announced over the ship's tannoy. Generally that meant the warp button was about to be pressed. He had indeed flicked the switch that opened the housing exposing the bright red ignition button. His finger hovered over it. I was very glad it wasn't one of my digits, small but noticeable tremors would have accidentally triggered it I'm sure, and my panic would zoom us off a billion miles away….. It could just be a simple delivery drone or something, carrying messages and tokens of love…… Better safe than sorry though.

"Too small for a fragment burst, a missile might get it, and us." I said to myself, but everyone heard.

"Breathe Colin, relax, take the single shot canon, you done this before, practically endless supply of fire, you'll be fine."

I felt myself sink into an alpha zone, it may sound like an oxymoron but my vision tunneled as my awareness grew. My fingers stopped trembling and suddenly found a familiarity mapped within them. That moment when playing a game and you no longer have to look down to the buttons in order to know exactly what you're doing, a moment of Zen. Thus allowing me to concentrate on the sights and not the menus. I couldn't hear the beeping anymore, at the very same time I knew it was there.

"Fifteen seconds," Sam announced his tone and volume both raised.

"I'm putting a lock on it." I said, and it sounded like I'd said that a thousand times before.

"Slow down a smidge Smokey. Sam, can you check if it alters its' course to suit ours?"

"Ten, nine, eight. It's altered its course. Seven, sorry, yes it's on us. Five, four."

I swallowed heavily, my hands had become instantly sweaty.

"Three," continued Sam.

"Ready Colin," demanded Nelson, "and f."

"It's stopped," shouted Sam.

"Stand down Colin...... What's it doing? Get it up on my screen Sam."

Nelson and Sam started punching buttons, a small screen flipped out from Nelson console and the image appeared.

"That's tiny, what is it?"

Ray walked over to have a look and bent down to study the whatever it was.

"I think that maybe a police probe? Hang on." Ray must have nipped off into his circuitry. "it's an Auto Stop Bot."

No one knew what he was talking about, not he did?

"Hang on, wait a second, it will contact us any sec....." Ray didn't have time to finish.

"It's hailing us, in fact it's, it's, opened up a channel all by itself," announced Smokey. Everyone looked towards Nelson hoping he'd know what to do.

"Get ready Colin," he said.

"Ready," I answered.

"Oh, don't fire on it?"

"Why?" I asked.

"It has a built in disrupter, we fire on it, it explodes and suddenly the crystals in our engine shatter and we can't get anywhere, or, or, do anything. No power."

"Smokey get ready to hit the warp button. Colin, you still ready?" He didn't wait for an answer, "If I shout warp, hit the button Smokey, and at the same time Colin fire. It's risky but we need a contingency..... What do they want with us anyway?"

"I'm sure they'll let us know," Ray responded. He wasn't wrong.

"Flying Fish, Flying Fish, please come to a halt, if you do not do this immediately we will stop you."

"All stop Smokey," ordered Nelson.

"Thank you," said the bot.

"Stand down Colin, I think we're stuck?"

"Our records indicate that you may have been involved in an incident. Please answer in a clear voice with a 'Yes' or 'No' after the beep. Please be advised that your response may affect your mortality….." Beep.

"Who hasn't ever been involved in an incident?" Nelson said turning away from the microphone on his console. "Yes," exclaimed Nelson.

"Thank you. You answered, 'Yes'." Nelson's voice echoed around the ship. "Thank you. Our records show that you have stolen the vessel you are in and must return it to the rightful owners. Is this correct? Please answer in a clear voice 'Yes' or 'No'."

Nelson tilted his head and considered something, "No," he answered and then hit the intercom button, "Pic, Don to the bridge as quickly as possible please."

The Bot butted in, "This is not in accordance to the complaint."

"How could that be? We nicked it off the Squid that nicked it to begin with," I said, exasperated.

Smokey tutted, "Well, nearly, but not quite, we claimed it as salvage, the original owners wiped themselves out on board, what were we supposed to do? I think we filled out all the correct forms and did everything we had to?"

The bot spoke once more, "Can you explain why you said 'No'? You have ten seconds to record your answer, please be precise, and start after the beep."

"Ten seconds, how can I explain everything in ten seconds?" Nelson said to himself.

Beep.

"We have two off the original owners here, well, not in the bridge but on the ship they'll be here any second, you can ask them."

Good answer I thought, that'll confuse them.

"One moment……. Answer requires interaction I shall put you through to an advisor." There followed a couple of scratchy clicks and hisses.

"Hello Flying Fish, our records show that the original owners no longer own the mothership and therefore the vessel you are in. It was taken as salvage and therefore the original owners have no authority."

"Well we also have two of the present owners here," responded Nelson.

"Hello," shouted Smokey.

"Excuse me?"

"We have two original and present owners onboard, how did we steal the Flying Fish, I think that someone maybe pulling the wool over your eyes."

"Is that some sort of insult? Are you calling me a long haired sheep or something?"

"No sorry it's just a saying from my home planet. It means I think someone has lied to you."

"Oh, someone lying to the police hey? You better stay where you are. I'm sending one of our shuttles out to you. Should be there in two days, do not move anywhere. Clear."

"Yes sir," replied Nelson and then proclaimed his annoyance with a massive, "Hummppphhh."

At a moment like this the world and everything in it could so easily break down. People could panic, risk something they need not have bothered with, all because we, at that moment, could lose sight of our own rationality, and at a moment such as this there is only one thing you can do?

"Tea anyone?"

At that moment Pic and Don entered and looked towards Nelson. It was easy to spot his concern.

"Everything alright?" asked Pic.

"What's happened?"

"We've been accused of stealing this ship," responded Nelson whilst shaking his head. Pic and Don didn't reply.

"We've got to stay here and not make a run for it. If we do then apparently our engines will be disrupted and will be stuck with no power, and it wouldn't take too long before we freeze to death."

"Mmm, I see."

"Mmm, so do I?"

"Mmm I don't think you do. We're now stationary, we have to wait for the police to turn up, and who knows, maybe we all get arrested because we have the most amazing story that they don't believe because no human lives for more than a thousand years." Nelson's voice was becoming angry, not with Don or Pic, but the whole situation. There he was, with us all, and we're trying to save a planet and all the life on it. Yet someone else is stopping us all because they don't know what's going on, what's it got to do with them anyway?"

Don grimaced before answering, hoping not to frustrate Nelson any further.

"Well, technically we did ste….."

A single look from Nelson was enough to stop Don in his tracks. He responded by looking down, sheepishly, embarrassed. It was slightly harsh of Nelson, Don was only trying to point out that we had stolen the Flying Fish, technically.

There we go, another perfect opportunity for me to speak. What do you need in a moment where there is an awkward silence?

"Tea, anyone?"

"Very sorry Don, that was completely out of order for me, will you please accept an apology? And everyone, if I turn into an arse will you please let me know?" Nelson first looked towards Don who simply waved away the need for Nelson regret. He then in turn caught all our eyes just to make sure we heard. When at last he looked towards me I couldn't resist.

"Ah, ok, well I've asked you twice now already. Do you want a cup of tea? You arse."

Nelson could do nothing. Apart from smile broadly, laugh, and finally accept the offer.

"That would be lovely Colin, thank you. Tools down everyone, take a rest, sorry Smokey, can you stay here for a while and keep an eye on that Bot?" I'll be back soon, give you the night off." Nelson then hit the intercom button, "Can everyone make their way to the kitchen please, finish what you're doing and get there as soon as you can."

CHAPTER 8

It didn't take Nelson too long to inform everyone of the situation. About as much time as it took me to make a cuppa and place it in front of him. He cupped it and sighed heavily at the same time, 'Ahhh'. His shoulders dropped as he reached the point of tea induced serenity.

"Ideas, solutions, strategies, go!" Finger tapping drum roll. What was that? I've never seen him do that before. And by the collective amount of raised eyebrows it appeared that nobody else had either. Was that one of those awful management ideas? Rapid high energy snowballing nonsense? It could have been that but by the same token, he could have known that he needed to change his own mood to get into the right mood? Yeah, I'm going to go with that one. I'd better start.

"Can someone tell me how this 'Disrupter' works? Please." I instantly looked towards Ray for an answer, as did most. He pondered, looked up, a quick side to side shimmy, look down, raised each forefinger, weighed something imaginary with them, he's got an idea, and indeed he did. He briskly waltzed over to the sink grabbing a tall glass on the way, which he placed directly between the taps. Good idea, I thought as I believed I knew what was coming next. I leant back, quite far and alerted my hands that I may need a rapid response from them any second. Colin got himself ready, as only he could. He placed himself about eight feet away and bent over to the exact level of the glass. For a moment he looked like a surveyor checking a level, or, a snooker player lining up a shot and giggling about a bit in order to relax. Then he settled.

"Iiiieeeeeeccccchhhhhh," he sang, awfully, and with such an awful sound. Imagine a soprano reaching the highest note he could and then without warning someone else grabbing tightly his testicles. Everyone followed my example and leant back. I myself leant back a tiny bit further. I shouldn't have. The glass exploded and within fractions of a second Ray had to spin around as quickly as he could, which wasn't quite fast enough. A large shard of glass had retaliated and launched itself at its' attacker with a perfect bulls-eye, hit in the middle of the for head.

"Owww," he said without really being bothered.

"Owww ha ha ha haaa, the splashback works then," I bawled as I crashed backwards hitting the floor in crash laughing like a hyena on nitrous oxide, setting even more of us off into a similar state.

"Excuse me I just need to go and, glue this up," said Ray, plucking the offending object from himself and flicking it into the sink. Of course Ray's answer set us of again. It took me a while to gather myself and the chair. Nobody seems to mind as they were busy brining themselves down to a sensible state too.

"Well, that's how that works Colin, it certainly disrupted everything here," Nelson said in a calm tone.

"Can we dampen the ship, or the engine, or the crystals?" I asked.

"If you could I don't see why they wouldn't be," said Sam. Bernie nodded.

"And having spares wouldn't matter. Disrupters are only good on smaller vessels, useless on a battleship or destroyer, cruisers, larger ferry's ships of that size," said Mona. Bernie almost did a double take. Mona just smiled.

"What about getting into a suit, going out to the bot, and, doing something there? Punch it, or something, I don't know?" I was on a roll.

"I imagine the thing will have a proximity detector and will either kill you or just move away," Nelson suggested.

"What about turning the ship around, getting the bot in line with the thrusters and letting rip with the engine?" Another wild guess.

Ray returned to the room, patched up, "That too wouldn't work, somebody must have tried that before, nice idea though."

For a few moments there was silence, everyone holding the expression of deep thought and concentration.

"Never leave anything to chance, but always remember that chance will rear its' head when it wants to, not when we ask it to...... It's always good to minimize failures to a minimum, you'll never hit zero, and sometimes you might want something unexpected to happen if you're quick enough to react to the change that chance brought," said Nelson.

"Are you suggesting we should manufacture a 'Chance'?" asked Bernie.

"Nope," responded Nelson, "Just saying there's always hope that something unexpected might happen to change the course of events, you never know what's around the corner, a change in the tide, an unexpected storm, getting stranded on a shifting sand bank."

More silence, no change there then.

"Could we remove our identity chip?" asked Nelson.

"We could do but that would render us unlicensed and therefore uninsurable and make us look like a hostile vessel, far worse than our supposed offence at the minute, I do believe we would be blown to kingdom come," Ray answered.

"In that case I suggest we do the next best thing and obey the bot, and take the time now to make ourselves presentable instead of looking like a bunch of pirates. No offence Marilyn, Mona. Everyone back here in four hours. That should be enough time for all of us to have a shave.... No offence Marilyn, Mona."

Mona raised an eyebrow, which actually could do with a trim.

"I could grow a better one than any of you guys," said Marilyn, and I figured she wasn't joking.

It didn't take long for everyone with a beard to disappear, and it probably took even less time for the beards to vanish too. The best thing was that the razors we now had would self-sharpen, apparently the more they were used the sharper they would get. The warning on the packet recommended they be thrown away after twenty shaves as they may become extremely dangerous. The exact opposite of the ones I had used all my life prior to this. A disposable item that improves? Not a normal business ethic. After my shave I noticed that my shade of blue was fractionally lighter. At this rate I shouldn't be the milky white I was before my ink emersion during the escape. I wasn't happy with it but there was nothing I could do. Not even Greg, the life giving herb could do anything about it. Although my skin had never been so blemish free. He did a good job on that score. He liked the idea that I looked different, it would make me stand out in a crowd. That would be the last thing I would enjoy. Not for me, I'm more the melt into the background, don't do anything to get yourself noticed, don't volunteer for anything even if it sounds like fun, sort of guy, most of us I think are like that.....
Unless there's a girl involved, then I'm completely prepared to make myself look like anything in order to get noticed. Aren't we all fellas', and right now a clean shaven blue human I think would work in most situations of attention seeking? It's just a shame there's no human females around..... Sorry Mona, I don't mean her any disrespect, but even if she was the last human female she's still not my type. Bigger than me, stronger than me, but mainly hairier than me...... maybe she has gone for a shave?

Suddenly the lights turned red, this was accompanied by a squawky alarm that sounded like a parrot in distress having a fight with a hectic cat. Fortunately I wasn't shaving at the time, it could have been fatal. As it was my heart missed more than beat.

"Red alert, red alert, positions everyone, this is not a drill," shouted Smokey, nearly breaking the speakers on the tannoy. Why do people shout into microphones, because they are panicked? I grabbed a clean shirt as I ran towards the bridge, putting it on as I ran. I only managed to do up half the buttons, somehow running barefoot made dressing at speed more difficult. I then suddenly realized why the Squid loved everything so clean? Because half of them went around barefoot or pad or whatever you would call it?

I then had another thought? Isn't it odd how we think of something strange at moments when we should be thinking about something far more important? For instance, I, at that very moment was considering what it would be like to be wearing slippers made from giant slugs. Why? Probably because that was the easiest way for me to imagine what it must feel like for a Squid to be walking, using the ends of its' tentacles as feet. I nearly went on to the 'Yes, but why' never ending scenario but the sight of the bridge door refocused my attention. Which as immediately broken by Ray.

"Action Smurf."

"What?"

"Action Smurf. You know, you've had a shave, but you still look bit disheveled, unkempt just been running hair. And you're still blue, remember?"

The bridge had a full complement. Everyone in position, my chair and console already descended and ready for me. Someone was a boy scout, preparation. I took my seat and took the system off standby. Sounds impressive to but wasn't. It tapped the fire button once, that's all. It also acts the as the on off switch.

"Don't select a weapon Colin," said Nelson, "You'll only annoy the police bot."

"What do I do then?"

"Just get ready to select a weapon, something small for the bot, and then something very big for something much bigger that's heading our way.....That's as much as you can do."

"Ok.... So what's the problem?" I said as I scrolled through the weapon menu. Nelson span his chair around to face me. His face at first was quite serious. Enough to make me become slightly anxious, I leant forward ever so slightly. The screen in front of me now becoming all the more important and the whole of my vision. I went slightly dry in the mouth, and my fingers started an exercise routine, all of their own accord. Fortunately they weren't anywhere nearby anything important, as Nelson suddenly appeared at my side and my hands, all of their own accord, sprang up defensively nearly slapping Nelson in the face. We both shouted "Wow" at the same time and then "Easy."

"It's alright Colin you can lower your hands, this isn't a stick up."

I lowered my arms and put my hands back to where they were most useful, next to the buttons I might need any second..... Damn, there you go, dry mouth again?

"Is there any chance you can lower your heart beat as well. There's a large ship coming in, hopefully it's the police, but Smokey and Ray both tell me it might be a bit big to be them, so big in fact it matches the size of our previous landlords and they probably don't appreciate us not paying in some way for the shelter that is the ship we're in now."

"Aanch," I said quickly, coughed after going dry for a third time and quickly continued hoping nobody noticed, "and is it?"

"We think so. We'll know soon enough. Gives us a chance to catch up with things, see what's going on in the world of Squid."

I slowly inhaled for as long as I could and then exhaled in the same manner.

"Just as well the bot is here, I guess?"

"You guess correctly." Nelson smiled and span on his heels and returned to his seat.

"I can confirm it is the 'Squid Tank', oops sorry Smokey," shouted Sam.

"And it's heading straight for us. Mmmm very fast too. Ohh here it is."

Another alarm started to scream. Only Nelson resisted bracing himself to the nearest sturdy object. The view of the stars I had from my seat through the ships bridge window was suddenly replaced by the hull of the ship that until recently had housed us all, I say housed, I mean imprisoned. Nelson casually hit a button on Smokey's side of the console. The screaming stopped a small double bleep accompanied with an even smaller flashing red started up in its place next to the button Nelson had just hit.

"Nice parking," announced Nelson.

"Someone wants to talk on screen," said Smokey.

"Do we know who that someone is?" asked Nelson.

"No, we don't."

"If that's a happy surprise Someone, it's probably Doctor Sandra wanting to invite us over for a banquet and celebratory public apology for the cruel behaviour towards other species, mainly humans. You know, it could be good if it's her?" I said.

"Yeah right," said Smokey sarcastically.

"Yeah right," said Ray but followed it with a guffaw.

"Why wouldn't it be her?" I said defending myself.

Nobody answered as we followed the Police bot that had slowly begun to drift from the left, in between our screen and the Squids' hull. The top half swiveled manically, its' last rotation going anti-clockwise, giving the impression that it was concerned with them and not us.

"Without concern for sounding stupid, is that police bot in communication with them at the moment? Can we just scarper?"

"I suppose we could reverse a bit, feeling threatened as we do by the ship in front of us?" reasoned Nelson, "Very slow reverse there Smokey please."

"We won't be able to scarper, as you put it Colin, but yes, the law here would allow us be to taking evasive or defensive action if anything happens..... However in the event of anything, happening, then in most scenarios, no, all scenarios we come off worse. In every event the police bot actually gets most destroyed, but there's no life on that tiny thing, just damage percentage wise, it comes off worse. At the very least our engine gets trashed by the disrupter and then just go up in any scale... Whatever blows the bot up takes us out too but to what level."

Everybody had their own look at that moment. We all wanted to say thank you by punching Ray for pointing out the great happy news he was obliviously giving us. Fortunately for Ray, not some much for us, was the fact that he sometimes didn't comprehend what he was saying before it was too late. We've all done it, but some continue to do it throughout their lives, mostly oblivious, we refrained from violence, for this reason and also because he was mainly computer, and prone to being sensitive. He would disagree with this of course.

The communication bleep went mad for a second and then the police bot opened our speakers and warned us to stop immediately. We did. Nelson even drifted back towards the bot and the hull of the obstacle in front of us. We rested at about one hundred meters away.

"I suggest we take the call and speak to the Someone," I said, whilst the bot is still here, just in case, can someone set the record button on the scene and audio and the time and everything, from in here, and surely the police bot is taking notes, in some, hopefully many wondrous ways. Surely their technology has moved on the last thousand years..... Do I sound like I'm glad to see the police?" Only Sam agreed with me.

"Ok, I'm going to speak. Ray, Smokey behind me, obscure Colin. Sam, pay attention to any systems coming online? Colin forget about the bot, go through what you need to do to unload everything as fast as you can." Nelson pushed Smokey's chair behind him and just to the left and waited until Ray was settled. Which took a few moments.

"Ohh, ooh, hang on," He said very excitedly. He then retrieved his new toy, the make-up glasses.

"Oh plop, I knew I shouldn't have," murmured Nelson.

Ray giggled to himself and then removed his glasses. A broad black band as wide as his eyes and across them traversed his face. Had he had a blond long wig to hand I'm sure he would have put it on and gone with the Nexus 6 Blade Runner look. Nelson shook his head.

"Happy now?" he asked.

"Yes, yes, thank you, go for it." Nelson turned to face the screen that would appear as soon as he hit the communication switch. Everyone settled...... Nelson hit the switch. A few things happened. Firstly the centre panel of the bridge's window, there were only three, but they were curved around and arched back a bit, they were probably about three metres or so in length, maybe just under, but big enough, well, the centre one turned a milky white just for a second and then snapped into the image being broadcast. Now, I had my screen obscuring most of that image, but because of the extra height gained by being in a raised seat, not much more than standing, I could see the top third. It didn't help much, just a forehead of a Squid glistening under a film of slime. I'm going to count that all as one thing. Then another thing happened, my new mobile telephone device rang. Not good timing, especially as I'd not long had it and didn't know how to cut someone off or down. The only thing Ray had taught me was how to call someone and how to change the Ring tones. He had done me a favour by installing the tune to 'Match of the Day', which was presently blaring out at great Volume. I then panicked slightly and the wafer thin, but very loud mobile, spilt from my hands. I watched it rotate and spin and then crash to the floor. It bounced a couple of times before settling.

"Back in a moment," I heard Nelson say, the screen returned to a milky white opaque state, "Ray would you answer that?" he continued, probably aware I was too embarrassed to say anything and it was a procedure in itself just to get out of the chair I was in. Ray obliged.

"Marilyn, how are you? Yes, Colin couldn't answer it. Why? Well he's slightly busy at the moment. Yes, yes, I'd do that. Well how about this? I call you when something has changed? You'll be the first. Ok, bye, bye." Ray tapped the screen and handed it back to me.

"I've turned it off."

"Thank you. Sorry everyone."

"Well you didn't ring yourself Colin, no need to worry. Can everyone just turn off their own. Just in case."

Everyone did as they were asked. Nelson waited for quiet.

"Ok, everyone in position, ready? And go." The milky screen disappeared and the very colourful forehead replaced it. It was frowning, I think?

"Everything alright there, looks like you might be having a party or something?" said a voice.

"Everything is fine here, enjoying the freedoms of freedom. And you, can I help?" said Nelson with beautiful delivery, that of the child that has smeared everything they can get their hands on, on everything they can get their hands on. Well that pattern was boring, and why not, but as you're there, really, can I help? Otherwise as you can see I'm a bit tied up with this smearing, so if you don't mind? Unless you want to join in?

"You could make this very easy and dock, here, where you found our ship."

"Why would we do that?"

There was a small pause before he responded. Is he being fed what to say? It certainly took a while for him to answer. I couldn't tell for sure, his frown did look like that of someone scratching for an answer, he could just be thinking? Finally he spoke.

"Because that's our ship." Eh, was that it?

"Well, the thing is Colin, you remember him, kind of non-descript but would stand out in a line of neat well-dressed people, remember him? Well he was invited out on a jaunt, and I think he asked Pic and Don if he could use one of their ships, I think they said yes, well they must have, we're here, they're here, even Ray is here."

"Yes, I see, hello Raymoon, how are you?" said the voice in a very monotone hollow way. He's either said that very thing a thousand times before and then heard the same answer time and time again or was very upset with him. They definitely knew each other.

"Hello Fred, how are you? What are you doing on the intercom, I would have thought it would be someone else?" said Ray and asked very politely immediately throwing off Fred and my train of thought. Good question Ray, who was Fred and why was he speaking on behalf of the Squid? He doesn't sound like a Military Squid, as I would have expected. I presume Nelson was glad it wasn't the case and not just me, even though I didn't know who Fred was. At least at that moment. Did I know Fred? I questioned myself several times on this matter because at the same time I had realized that I could set the guns with 'Personal settings' and I could then design my own pre-set scenario. I was pondering if I knew Fred at that same time as I had just selected everything on board to simply launch straight ahead, I couldn't miss, it was point blank, and Nelson asked for something big for the big thing. I didn't know Fred. I wouldn't have to feel guilty about putting a big hole in the side of his home, and, or, but probably worse. I hope I don't know Fred, I'm sure I didn't.

"Possession is everything I think you'll find. We had no choice but to take control as everyone bar Don and Pic were dead. If we didn't we all would have just died, run out of food or just crashed into some moon or planet…. I think salvage rights alone would give us the right to claim that ship as ours, let alone it being compensation for everything they did, and before you say, 'well look at what you've done to us, what about our compensation, just remember, we suffered at your hands and nets forever, and we always lost."

Silence being broadcast in space, what a waste of energy I thought as nobody spoke. Nelson's turn to be 'Sctummed' along with everyone else….. Didn't anyone else notice the obvious? It's a shame my phone was switched off I could have sent a message. Yes, the Simple Messaging Service had survived longer than some civilizations, and probably because it was so simple. Don't mess with something that doesn't need fixing I guess you could say was that lesson of that thought.

I know Nelson wanted Ray and Smokey to act as set dressing and block the view but the silence was driving me nuts, unfortunately however after being made aware that spontaneity isn't necessarily the best way forward I wasn't sure if I butted in it would be appreciated. Maybe Ray would hear me if I whispered it, loudly.

"If possession is everything then what's his problem?" I saw Ray's head twitch ever so slightly. I repeated what I said. Ray who already had his hands behind his back gave me the thumbs up.

"If Possession is everything then what's your problem?" he said.

"Ah Hello Colin, how are you? The re-runs of you on my show are stacking the audience figures."

Oh it's that Fred..... Hasn't he got good ears.....? Why is the host of a television show talking on behalf of the..... Oh no, Doctor Sandra didn't win the election. We're not going to get any sort of pardon, apology, ceremony of friendship.

"Hellllllooooooo Fred," I said mimicking the way the announcer would annunciate the opening of the show Fred was referring to," Doctor Sandra didn't win the election then? No?"

"No, she certainly didn't. She's presently in the Tank. The Tank is a prison. President Crab is now Mr. Crab, he's studying hard for his Naval entrance exam, he'll probably pass."

"So who won your election?"

There was no answer. It didn't take long to figure out what had happened though. Nelson, Ray and Smokey all said 'No' at the same time. All suggesting massive disbelief.

"Yep, that's right. You're looking at him."

"No," said Ray one more time.

"Yes," said Fred

"Hang on, hang on, why is she in the Tank?" I asked before anyone else changed the subject.

"Because without the lemons she gave to you, the ones you used in those dispenser sprays, you wouldn't have been able to escape. What else could it be?"

I took my eyes from my screen and noticed everyone had turned to look at me, questioning me. There was something I should be asking myself, something I had missed..... Oh yes, right, I should have expected Doctor Sandra to be at least questioned as to how we came to be in possession of dangerous fruits. Maybe I hoped she would win the election and everything would be alright, brushed under the carpet, or it would be simply overlooked..... Maybe I overlooked it because I knew it might happen and I couldn't tell her because it may have upset my plans on escape... My need was greater but, well, I don't want to say she was a friend, but she nearly was, I wanted to like her at least.... I did feel sorry to hear that she was imprisoned. That didn't last long. As soon as Fred continued I listened but I also looked back towards my console, then stretched my forefinger.

"So are you still doing your awful show?"

"Oh yes of course, I'd be stupid not to, audience figures doubled after your appearance Colin." That's a shame I thought, I could cancel it though, just tap my finger on the button it was hovering over.

"Fortunately for you, we have a Bot between us, otherwise we would blow you all to smithereens after asking you politely if you would all like to re-join us and continue from where we left off, which I image you would refuse as Colin was on trial for being a dick. I won the election on a promise of continuing with all policies until I had a chance to settle in and get my own executive..... I'm sure you can remember what I'm talking about? And then we'll come back for you. Who knows you might still be here. Any way got to dash. Are you all sitting comfortably, wearing your safety straps? See you next time."

In an instant my target vanished off screen. In a second instant I was thrown viciously to the right. I wasn't strapped in but my hips just about held a secure enough position to half anchor me to the seat, my hands quickly followed to give support, grabbing hold of the arm rests. I was lucky. From where I now held position I had a perfect view of Nelson, Ray and Smokey flying, uncontrollably through the air, a mass of flaying limbs landing in a crumpled mass after hitting the wall. Sam who was normally directly to my right in his own chair now occupied the left hand portion of my chair, not actually sitting in it, more slung in and over it.

"Hello," he said, "you get a nice view from here don't you?"

The actual view wasn't at that moment quite so pretty as normal. We were spinning, caught in the rush of turbulence caused by a starship hitting warp speed. There were many names we could offer to someone who would do that sort of thing, none of them complementary, but at that moment it wasn't quite top of the list of things to do, we were all too busy screaming in fright or because of the pain caused by a wall stopping you mid-flight, and or both. I wouldn't know at what rate we were rotating but it was enough for me not to be able to sit upright and all I could see through the main screen was a swirl of bright traces so long they became continuous. Oh dear, I was beginning to see other stars, the kind you get just before you faint, just before you vomit.

I closed my eyes, and calmed everything that could be calmed within my body. Not my heart or plumbing, I didn't want to die in a smelly mess, but everything else that would stop me from hurling my insides out..... only because I knew that if I did it would probably hit the heap of bodies to my right, no matter from which direction it originated. Think of anything not connected to this moment and motion, and quickly.

I considered the design of spring leaf suspension and how such a simple design works so well. Could it be improved? Why bother? Why bother tinkle with something that works so well already. Hang on, do they even exist anymore, does anyone drive a car anywhere in the universe? Or a carriage? The wheel must exist somewhere in technology, so surely the comfortability of movement would be considered, oh well, if that civilization has only just discovered the wheel, then it won't be too long before someone else invents the seat cushion and then someone else yet again invents suspension, hmm, maybe we should find that planet and invent them..... There's a thought, if you can find a planet with a civilization who had some but little and maybe only industrial technology cornering all the markets would be easy. Then you could sit back and watch that planet die amongst its own foul pollution stench..... Unless you also provide a fuel free generation source. Hmmmm, could work? As long as I have enough power to boil the kettle and refrigerate enough milk for a cuppa I'll be fine. Where the hell am I going to find a fridge?

I thought that would be enough thinking to take my mind off the situation. It wasn't quite. We were still spinning quickly. The mass heap of bodies to my right had separated into its' constituent parts and Sam had managed to slide down the framework of my chair and crawl his way towards his station against the centrifugal force wanting to smash him into the wall opposite. The one Nelson and Sam were crouching against, the one Smokey appeared compressed into, it wasn't pretty, he looked like a gone off trifle someone had thrown at a wall. Ooops, time to close my eyes and think again of a healthy distraction, mmm, surely most suspension systems would be pneumatic?

Sam screamed as he reached his console, somehow got to his knees and planted his fingers along the edge of his desk. Afraid to let go he slowly bowed his head over a button, it didn't look too easy, he was having to force his neck muscles to perform like they'd never done before. Again he screamed, not a painful one, but more one that a weightlifter might yelp as he yanked a load I'd get a forklift for.

"Yes," Sam shouted in celebration and moments later the 'Flying Fish' came to a rest. Unlike everybody inside Her. Wallowing moans, heaving breathing exercises and not much movement. Only Ray seemed to be happy with the situation.

"Well, that was fun."

Nelson steadied himself and offered Smokey a hand off the floor, too which he had now slid. Smokey refused, he needed a moment, and then he grew a few inches and seemed to inflate a bit. He then, with a squelch as he purchased himself upwards walked back to his seat. Nelson still steadied himself, his arms outstretched firmly against the wall taking most of his weight.

"Is everyone alright?" he asked.

It took a few moments but eventually we all answered that we were indeed fine. Shaken but fine. Ray was already in Smokey's seat repositioning the ship, smoothly, like a chauffeur, we ended up going around a few times trying to find the police Bot. It took a while and it was Sam who told us to hold a course, his scan giving us the direction, the problem for the Bot being the same turbulence that had turned our ship into a fairground ride had buffeted the Bot miles away.

"It's making its' way back to us," Sam announced.

"We could just go and pretend we never saw it, thought it must have been destroyed, your honour, honestly guv?" I said.

Nelson stood upright and looked at me, he then clenched his teeth. The factors in the risk being assessed. The Bot was getting closer.

CHAPTER 9

"Damn!" Nelson bawled, "Now would be the best time to take a risk. But do we need to take a risk?" He returned to his seat and sighed heavily, "Let's hope it's broken," he consoled himself with.

The Bot drew close enough to see that it was dented in a few places, and there was a wobble. It must have bounced off us.

"Ooh," said Ray and flicked a switch. The speakers came to life but only picked up mid station interference, then a voice flickered in and out and broken. Completely non-understandable, which Nelson made clear in reply. He hit another switch.

"Naa, you going to have to do better than that, can't understand a word you're saying. Nothing, nada."

The signal stopped but seconds later we heard a 'Beep beep' and a small message appeared on the video screen that Fred had just recently appeared on. Nelson read it out.

"Protective mode….. You are requested to follow this unit, '2461-87'."

"Hey, we didn't do that. Why aren't you going after the other ship?"

The message simply flashed and the Bot moved off, wobbling as it did. It wasn't well.

"I don't think anyone can hear you?" said Ray.

The message flashed. Nelson slumped in resignation and sighed tapping a button as he did. The video screen retreated back into the console.

"Is there any way we could find out whether the disrupters still work on that Bot?"

"Some circuits are definitely out. It's lost all stability, and quite frankly we could go faster on a horse," said Sam. He wasn't wrong. It seemed the Bot was on auto, it felt it had to return for repairs but needed to take us with it just because there was some paperwork to do and somebody else had to hear the real story. That gave me an idea?

"Could we find out where we are going and go ahead, report to whomever, and then even get some help?"

"That would in most cases be the best and obvious way forward Colin," said Ray, "but we can't let anyone know that that is the intention and that there's no need to disrupt as we're coming to you, wherever you are and wherever you are? We could even collect their Bot and bring it back for them, cos' we're so nice. No, this may cause problems." He then got out of Smokey's chair and walked over to Sam and started pressing buttons. I'm sure some of those buttons may have been Sam's. He didn't look too enamoured with Ray doing his job. Ray then stood back and stroked his chin.

"Mmm?"

"What are you thinking Ray?" asked Nelson.

"Mmm, as I feared."

"What is it Ray." Nelson said again only with more urgency.

"The Bot isn't on a true course, it's not going in a straight line. It's going left right left right left right left right really really quickly, like a little over wound tin soldier, there are many destinations it could be going to….. Mmm, I don't think any of that matters though as at this rate it's going to take sixty-seven thousand years to reach anything."

"Should have taken the shot Horace," said Sam.

Nelson checked back, "Easily said in retrospect Sam…. It's not just us I was protecting. We're on our way to save Crrrrk and its' inhabitants. It wasn't worth the bigger outcome. Don't lose the war because of a skirmish."

If tension was a musical key it had just gone up in notch in scale and it wasn't a happy 'Major' scale is was a 'Minor' slightly discordant scale, something Jimi Hendrix would get into…. Nelson took a deep breath and stepped into the middle of the bridge, he faced the screen and looked at the Bot bumbling along.

"It's going to annoy me vastly if that thing can't disrupt…. Ray can you tell me how many days we can afford to lose before Fred gets a chance to fire his missile. One bomb, where's the honour in battle?" Nelson shook his head in disgust.

"Can I stand down the blasters, phasers and torpedoes?" I said as sarcastically as I could.

Nelson turned his head slowly. At first it appeared he wasn't too happy and maybe there was about to be another key change. I'd better put a stop to that, I thought, so I winked at him. He had no choice but to surrender. He bowed his head and laughed.

"You arse Colin, yes you can stand down and meet me with Sam in my quarters for a tipple. Sam, you coming? Smokey, go have a smoke. Ray can you stay here work on my question and keep an eye on that Bot? Try and work out if it's still armed and capable?"

Ray nodded and took Sam's seat as he vacated it. Nelson flicked the comm switch on his console.

"Anyone needing medical assistance?" There was silence whilst we waited for a response. There was none. Nelson chuckled to himself," "Oh well, they're either all fine or all dead." He then chuckled again knowing that of course no one had died. He then flicked the switch once more and invited all survivors to his quarters for a drink. Marilyn should make herself a coffee, Jeb should bring his own holy water, Bernie and Mona where to bring whatever they fancied, no-one was quite sure what that could mean? Pic and Don were to find the bottle of meteor water Nelson had acquired and was keeping for a happier occasion just for them as they generally drank water. To put anything in it to them was a sin. Apparently most Crrrkians were plumbers because they craved the purest water they could get their three fingered giant middle finger hands on. There was a lot of algae on their planet and because there were so many plumbers it was said that there were more pipes per capita on Crrrk than any other planet so far known.

I'd poked my head into Nelson's pad a few times over the weeks, I'd been in and hung around in his, what we could call a rest room, like everyone's, a small lounge, two slightly arched plastic moulded chairs, screen on the wall, flip out table. Everything was elegant but not overdone in design as it still needed to be practical, it was still a Navy vessel after all. Nelson's quarters though had an extra chamber that I'd never seen. I wasn't too sure what I'd find inside? In truth, I didn't know what to expect and I was quite glad about that. It was probably a place of sanctuary, I thought, Nelson's sanctuary. For a second I thought that I shouldn't actually go inside. I didn't want to know what was in there..... In the same way I would refuse to get anything out of a lady's handbag no matter what the situation or how many times she pleads. I am not going in there.

This was different though. Nelson held the door open so there was no option, it would have been difficult to decline the invitation. The room itself was a bit of a let-down. It was half the size of the lounge, you could just about get a double bed in there but absolutely no furniture. This room however on the immediate left wall simply had a small round table, oak I think, two chairs either side, again oak, and in the corners next to the table and chairs a standard lamp and on the other side an old globe of planet earth. He tapped somewhere on the Equator and there was a click, he then flipped open the lid to reveal a several bottles and different sized glasses.

"Drink gentlemen? Take one, take a seat too. You don't always need a celebration to break out the good stuff." Nelson proceeded to pour himself a drink, not as large as normal. Not even what I'd call a double. Just in case he needs to get back to the bridge, I thought, good thinking, responsibility. He's not getting drunk.

"Don't take too much mind, there's not so much of this laying around."

Opposite the casual drinking set up and fixed to the wall spanning its entire length a massive screen. The television hasn't developed much over the last millennium then? From personal experience I can say that the shows haven't changed..... Why and how I'll never understand they ever caught on in the first place?

"Hey, you haven't got one of those corporate managerial teamwork videos lined up have you? How to improve productivity and be happier at the same time. Yeah right, I could do the same by not buying the video and not turning up to a meeting when I've already got a stack load of work to do. You haven't got one of those have you?"

"Why would it help? Actually Colin I needed to get climb down out of that chair and take stock. To become rational, calm and steady of thought. The problem with the 'Chase', is it's exciting. Excitement creates adrenalin, which in turn stimulates the brain, the brain likes this, it's having its' own little party, to a point it doesn't care about the body it's in, It, is happy, It is getting its' thing. It can end up steering you sometimes, quite subtly too, you can for instance, end up rewarding yourself with your favourite alcoholic beverage, cheers, for an ever decreasing amount of tendered deeds..... It can make you chase the chase, I suppose, and put quite simply I nearly lost my rag on the bridge simply because I forgot that I'm the only military conditioned being here and I wasn't happy because I couldn't do what I knew I could do. Does that make sense? I was in the moment, considering options that could only really work with a compliment of trained men, this annoyed me, and I got angry, it was no one else's fault. What right did I have....? So I stopped my brain getting carried away, in order to say I'm truly sorry and here's to your health. Cheers." Nelson knocked back his drink. He didn't refill, which in turn made both Sam and I conform to the same limit, probably wise.

CHAPTER 10

By the time the rest of the crew arrived Nelson's mood had lifted even after I offered the line, "Hey on the plus side things can only get better." I couldn't tell whether his blank expressionless response was an indication of agreement or him giving me a moment to consider how much of an idiot I must have sounded at that moment..... I didn't actually need that long, if that was indeed what he was doing. Sam I think must have noticed the moment. He quickly changed the subject to something he could talk about.

"Lovely drop of hooch Admiral. You've been saving this one haven't you?"

"Only from you Sam. Actually, I was going to open it when we first escaped, but it didn't seem appropriate toasting our achievement any more than we did with the possibility of Don and Pic becoming an endangered species."

"So why are we drinking it now? I don't understand."

"Because now we have a moment to pause. An unforeseen has occurred, and at this rate, well it actually feels like I'm on a ship at sea. Never thought that would happen. And, because of that, inconvenience, I thought I might as well take that opportunity to celebrate our escape now, because if I didn't and we fail to help Don and Pic have a home, if we fail in that, then I'll never be able to open it. I hope you all understand?" Nelson looked around the room making sure everyone knew exactly what he was saying.... "We planned and executed a mass escape, well done everyone. Pic, Don, I pray that good weather comes to our aid, and good fortune finds Her way to our door. Cheers."

There followed a solemn soft moment of salutation gracefully directed towards Don and Pic. Bowed heads, a raised glass and down the hatch. Then the room seemed to grow quiet and empty. There was no particular order in which we left but everyone I believe had a sense of raised awareness and readiness, our own personal alert systems raised a level.... Nelson's work complete, saying something without saying something.

I was the last to leave and before going stopped and said, "It's a shame there's no weather in space." I was hoping for a bemused look in response followed with the question, "Why?" I got the first part, which soon changed into a surprised look. One that suggested that it was in itself a strange point, 'No weather in space.' His look then changed once more, this time he quizzed himself as to why I might say something like that?

"Are you going to mention a storm, and then at some point the break in the storm and the amazing clear view that would be gained...... or some such nonsense? You were weren't you?"

I, as it happens was. However in a vain attempt to disguise this I of course said no.

"Your voice and face don't seem to be in agreement...... No need to be concerned Colin. Now if you don't mind I'm going to watch an episode of Starsky and Hutch, the best theme tune ever I'm sure you'll agree and you still need finish your, whatever it is you do in the bathroom stuff. Go away, nothing can be done, at the moment."

I left without saying a word and the door closed quietly behind me. Within a few steps I was in agreement with him about the theme tune, it was probably the best.

On the way to my quarters I met Ray. When I told him that Nelson was watching Starsky and Hutch he paused and said, "Oh, in that case I'll see him in twenty minutes, wouldn't want to disturb him...." I was baffled for a moment, a moment too long, one in which Ray had enough time to turn and walk off. I didn't bother calling after him...... I did have half a beard scrawled across my face that needed seeing to. I decided to hmmm the Starsky and Hutch theme tune to myself. Once inside and with a closed door that soon turned into loud humming, then eventually fully vocalized, Baa's and 'Daa's. Louder still once I decided a hot shower was in order before I started with the fuzz on my face.

I managed several theme tunes during my sustained soaking. Starting with a lung busting rendition of Starsky and Hutch I moved on without thinking to Dr Who, it seemed to fit, and then straight onto the A-Team. Not one of my favourites, it just happened. I didn't get a chance to finish though. Towards the end of my joviality my ear heard at first what I thought was a repetitive squeak, it was slowly getting louder and was beginning to sound more like the notorious violin accompanied shower scene from the film Psycho. I turned the shower off to see if it was causing the problem, it wasn't. The sound continued and from the corner of my eye I saw the shadow of an arm with a hand holding something pointy. It seemed to be raised and slashing down. My instinct to protect myself from sharp thing gave way to another reaction that of putting my arms out as the floor rapidly headed towards me after losing my balance. As I ripped the shower curtain off in the process I managed to spot a now laughing Ray and Smokey and when I say laughing I actually mean clutching the sides to stop them buckling over any further. Why I had any reaction at all was beyond me? I really should have known it was Ray all along. I crashed onto the floor of the shower and a gentle but audible crack stopped all merriment. I would have the last laugh.... Only I couldn't, the pain around my nose and mouth forced me to not proceed with anything other than a light prod. Which produced a reasonable amount of achy pain. Something like a bruise I thought. Only my fingers were red and I could taste blood. I raised my head and sat upright. A massive wave of pain surged its way around my skull and centred on the bridge of my nose. Both Ray and Smokey screamed...... Oh it must be worse than I first hoped..... Mmmm, maybe it's a lot worse than I now imagining, Ray and Smokey are still screaming. They stopped, but only to take a breath, they started again. A massive throb punched my face every second. I put my head down, isn't that the thing we're supposed to do? I seemed to work the throb was fading at least. However I soon joined in with the screaming as I watched a torrent of blood spew forth and splash my blue skin.....

"Dowel" I demanded, unable to fully pronounce my 'T''s. No towel came my way.

"Sdop scweemin nd path me a dowel." No towel came my way. I reached out and shook my hand, "Dowel, dowel, towel." At last a towel.

I slowly stood, taking my time to avoid the trombone player who had found his way into my head from waking up. Then I turned on the shower once more rinsing myself but mainly getting the towel wet. I folded it several times a placed it over my nose and mouth. That hurt. A quick look from me towards Ray and they both stopped screaming.

"Sorry," Ray offered. He was sincere..... then with his aid I got into a robe, again slowly, whilst Smokey opened the door. We were on our way to the infirmary and nobody need mention it.

"Waa ith tha en your hund?" I asked Ray...... He just looked puzzled. He might know every language in the universe but he doesn't know' Smashed up Face'.

"Tha, tha, tha," I said and pointed to the thing in his hand.

"Oh, just a piece of paper, and some maths. I've just been explaining things to Horace. Got in there before he started with another episode. Explained things.... I was coming in to say we're requested in the galley in half an hour, well twenty five minutes now. I promised to make some biscuits. So I'll leave you here in Smokey's many hands." By here Ray meant the infirmary door. Smokey opened it. Ray took my arm, "I am Sorry. Got to go." He left, reasonably sharpish.

The Infirmary was a small office in which the ships doctor would usually work from and a larger room with a long box with a shallow soft looking cushioned work top. The box itself comprised mainly of drawers and small doors of all shapes and sizes. Above the box a robotic arm hung gently, cables for ligaments and a small round lens at the end of its articulated body for an eye. As soon as I sat down on it the robot arm hissed into life and swung down and around directly opposite my forehead.

A soothing gentle female voice told me not to move. Then the snake like robotic arm danced around my head, it bleeped a few times and then moved on nothing else bleeped and the arm returned to it's starting position and hissed out of existence. The voice of the Lady Doctor kindly asked me to lay on my back in my own time and when ready say 'Ready'. A male voice then told me to be perfectly still and not to move. He wasn't so friendly. I wouldn't want to be at their Christmas office party…….. Mind you I didn't like going to my Christmas staff parties….. Does anybody like going to those parties? Somehow I managed to giggle before I rested my weary head. I then tried to control my breathing and relax as much as possible. I closed my eyes and began. In for four, hold for four, out for four, hold, in for four, repeat. I could feel my heart slow and no sign of the trombone player…. In….. Out….. In. Screech. What the hell. That certainly didn't help the moment. I opened one eye to see a stool moving towards me, the seat part, it then stopped and I must admit, with a sigh of relief, Smokey climbed up the frame and got himself comfortable. I then opened my other eye to make it easier to look sternly at him. I had to wait a while whilst he sorted himself out. To which I shook my head….. Which hurt…. It gave credence to my look at least. Smokey quickly settled.

"Everything alright? I, thought I'd, watch, never seen this before."

If you don't calm down, I thought, you'll soon be trying it, and breathe….. In…. Out….. In….. Repeat, repeat, that's better, heart beat down again. Relax my frown and stern eyes. Is that even possible? Seems to help, that's better, heartbeat getting slower, and sweet point. I recognized the place in which I was happy to sleep but active enough to be aware. I hit that moment for a second or two.

"Ready," I said to the unknown expert.

The voices were much more pleasant than the rest of the machine. Even grumpy male voice instantly had qualities. Without much warning four spider like legs sprang out from the innards of the bed I rested upon, although as soon as I heard their approach I became less restful and half the breathing exercises I went through turned out to be a waste of time. The first limb that approached me laid a small towelly thing upon my mouth and then retreated a matter of inches. The next limb with several small clamp heads gently laid what felt like very malleable rubber fingertips over my nose. My heart skipped a beat. Something was going to happen soon. The next arm came alongside and opened a small aperture. Slowly a cold white goo oozed out, and the limb plastered my nose delicately. Then another arm curled over and secure my forehead to the bed, which then in itself raised a few degrees until my mouth met the first limb that provided the small towel. Which I suddenly realized was there for only one reason. The fresh amount of blood about to pop out. My thoughts were confirmed when another arm place a large towel in my hands and not for the sweat that they were exuding.

"Whatever you do Colin...? Don't sneeze."

From where I lay I raised my middle finger.

"Yeah, fair enough," Smokey said.

I felt the soft rubber tips pull as the arm they were attached to retreat ever so slightly, then individually for a moment the same thing, the tips pulled slightly, small tweaks, and then one or two came back in a fraction.

"Awwgggg," I exclaimed and then again. I wanted to scream,'Aaahhhh' but was unable to, too much discomfort and throbbing and sound proofing from a now much bloodstained small towel across my mouth.

"How can so much come out of such little holes?" Smokey asked. I held up a clenched fist and tried my best to say, "You want me to show you." It came out though as just a long stream of vowels.

All the robotic limbs relocated themselves back in their respective homes. Small doors shut tight with a hiss. One final limb then secured a big fluffy cotton pad across my vacuumed sealed nose, sprayed something up each nostril and then handed me a strong looking tissue in a clear plastic packet. It was now all over. This was confirmed by the gentle female voice.

"Procedure over. Procedure successful. Three days in a reclined position, no lifting or running for a week. No contact sports for six weeks. Absolutely no picking of the nose...... Return daily for clean dressing." Then, as I thought grumpy male voice may do, he got the last word in and maintaining his image he said, "Goodbye," but I know he really didn't mean it.... He was probably busy getting jealous thinking his work colleague had a crush on me.

I checked my new look in a mirror back in the Doctor's office. It wasn't pretty. It was more ridiculous. I was still a light shade of blue, all over, apart from the white bandage over my nose surrounded by a straggly beard. I looked like a crazed, just got out of a hospital, accident or insane, Manchester City fan on his way to a cup final.... Or the Hulks' never seen twin, when he gets angry he turns blue, losses some stature and just becomes passive and maybe sombre....

Even though the ships auto Doc had told me to rest I thought it best to still turn up to the Meeting in the galley called by Nelson. If I didn't get a move on though I would be late. I had to get dressed but maintain an upright position, not only did a throb occur every time my head dipped above or below the horizon, but I was also aware that it wouldn't take much to start a fresh torrent to purge itself from my face. I did have a massive urge to scratch away the already slightly congealed blood beginning to encrust itself around my nasal passage. Must resist that, I've just had the whole thing reset.

CHAPTER 11

It's a lovely thought believing that you can depend on your friends and comrades in those moments you think you may need them. The reality is never that giving. I was the last to make it to the meeting in the galley, still on time I'd like to point out. I paused in the doorway to take the applause and whoops and laughter that were flung in my direction. The only person not laughing was Nelson, he just raised his eye-brows as if to say, "What did you expect? Suck it up." I tried to smile, it hurt slightly so I gave up. Nelson soon cheered me up though.

"Ray has explained what happened Colin, and Smokey has informed me of the auto Docs' diagnosis. So you'll be happy to know that I'm ordering you to bed where you will stay until further notice, alright? To ease the boredom both Ray and Smokey have kindly volunteered to be on call for anything you need.... I hope you abuse the privilege," he said smiling, "Before you go though I think that you should know that at the rate of travel we are currently on by the time we get anywhere we will all be dead unless we can get a delivery of everything. We've still got to eat."

"I don't," said Ray. This was of course met with an eyeballing silence.

"Shut up Ray. This also means both Don and Pic won't have to worry about returning home because there probably won't be one..... So if you have any ideas let me know, or pass on a message. Off you go, and remember, no picking of the nose."

Nelson simply looked at me until I left, which wasn't too long as I noticed Nelson's manner had become more abrupt. Ray left with me. Nelson must have given him the nod to do so.

"I don't think I've ever seen him like that?" offered Ray.

"I think the problem maybe that he has our best intentions at heart and it may appear that we don't, or at least we're not seeing it the way he would like us to see it..... Don't you think?"

"Yes, I suppose....... But add that to the fact that if something out of the blue doesn't happen soon everything that can go wrong will go wrong. What we need is a Crystal engine set outside the sphere of any disruptive blast the Police Bot may have, and may I stress the May! I mean, do we risk it? Do we chance it and fire up the engines and try and run? Running the risk of getting our engine shattered in the process or do we hope that the Police are on their way because of the damage to the Police Bot, and then hope even more that they believe our story that it wasn't us that damaged the Bot, and then hope beyond belief that they are all happy to let us go on our merry way….. especially when we explain the reason for our hasty departure, that of course is saving billions of lives on a planet far far away that we've never been to but happen to have two locals on board. Who I'm sure will vouch for us... Yes let's hope that someone will openly believe and trust everything we say. After all I'm sure you know what it's like to get caught up in someone else's paperwork when they need to start at the very beginning to be able to understand what is happening in the present. Because they're always very very understanding people, aren't they?"

"You ok Ray? Getting something off your chest?"

"Yeah, I'm sorry, I was just remembering this one official who wanted details of everything, paperwork for this that and everything else. He drove me nuts, I could have had him removed at any time, but he was just too good at his job. Everyone complained, probably because it meant that they couldn't pilfer from the stores."

"What happened to him?"

"He discovered a mistake, one that only he himself could have made, simple arithmetic, he forgot to carry over some Reeds in a Waterbed. Ended up with way too many cats at the festival of Birds….. It was carnage. He sacked himself."

"…… Right…. Ok, thanks for that."

"But more importantly let's get you sorted out. We've all got orders and yours are to stay in bed. Is there anything I can get for you immediately?"

I pondered this question as we made our way to my room. I had about thirty seconds to come up with something better than a cup of tea….. What on earth was I thinking, what is there that is possibly better than a cup of tea? In fairness, yes, there's a lot of things better than that, but not in my present situation, not a lot. So whilst Ray went back to the galley to make me my hot beverage I, with great caution, no quick sudden movements and trying to keep my head from lowering itself, got into bed and made myself both comfortable and ready to receive my steamy medicine. Which soon arrived along with a plate of biscuits.

Now everybody knows that when you are off work with sickness the best thing to do is recline, relax, read a book, or watch as much daytime television as possible. This can have a few effects; you laugh wildly at the amazing unbelievable lives that some people lead and you feel a lot better about your own, you get slightly depressed at the state of progression within society and realize that we haven't moved on at all. You can't actually believe what you're watching so you turn the television off and read a book instead. I think I tend to do a bit of the first two, and sometimes I'm not quite sure exactly whom I'm laughing about or why and it could be myself that I'm actually laughing at because in reality I'm instantly taken to a point of depression and have no other choice but to laugh..... Since there was no longer anymore daytime television maybe I could, could do, oh damn, I'm bored of being sick already.

A series of heavy sighs and half grunts was enough of a hint for Ray to offer further assistance. He showed me how I could use my new phone like a computer and then 'Throw' whatever was on my phone over to my cabins main screen, which was positioned kindly by Ray to face me directly. All I had to do was put my finger on the small screen and wipe it in the direction of the big screen and it would appear instantly on the bigger one. I then could use my phone as a remote, on which I could call up anything that was ever broadcast from anyone, anywhere, as long as it was recorded. Near enough everything from earth was recorded and near enough from its' first broadcast.

"This is amazing. Wow, I wish I was around when this came out. The future seemed bright for a moment at least?" I said my eyes expressing amazement at the technology. Ray grimaced.

"You only missed this by a few years. This is basic stuff. Great idea, the person who invented this was onto a winner I bet."

I momentarily thought once more about watching the season Arsenal F.C. went unbeaten, but I got slightly angry I wasn't there the first time around so decided to just search what was around from anytime later. Scroll through loads of stuff and wait for something to grab my attention. Something, at first from Earth, then maybe spread out to see what other planets had to offer. Which I knew wasn't great as most other civilizations had simply based their shows on the ones they saw broadcast from Earth, as indeed the Squid had done with us..... In which case maybe I shouldn't bother at all? I could try and find a modern station broadcasting something. I bet it wouldn't take too long to find a station still repeating Top Gear. Yet again Ray witnessed my face contort itself through a range of ponderances.

"May I suggest a film?" Ray asked.

"Well....."

"You could do the complete Star Wars saga?"

"I've seen all those."

"Oh no you haven't. All forty two?"

"What!"

"You see you haven't seen anything. Do you want to? I can set it up if you wish?"

"I'm not sure I can be bothered. Forty two! That seems like a massive investment of time."

"You're in bed. What else are you doing?" Ray pointed out.

"Well maybe I could be thinking about how to get out of this situation with the Police Bot?"

"Go on then, seems like a good use of your time. I'll leave you alone."

"Hang on."

Ray smiled, awaiting my thoughts.

"I can't just be put on the spot like that..... Maybe I should do a tiny bit of relaxing first, eh?"

"Whatever you wish Colin. You want to sleep? I could get you something to help from the Auto Doc if you wish?"

"No I'm fine, I think I just want to channel hop."

"You could do but everything will be old. We are nowhere near any civilization that bothers to broadcast...... You might get some bad reception on a radio station that keeps going in and out of reception, maybe."

"Oh I was kind of used to that, sounds like anything on medium wave."

"Why not watch some comedy? Combine it with some history and watch those 'End of the Decade" shows. The ones that look back over the past year or decade. You could go straight in and with the ones that did the centuries. May I suggest you check out Charlie Brooker and his work. He went onto sign a contract that allowed the BBC to andriodize him after his death. The first of a few stars to do the same in England and many around the world. Pretty similar to myself in many ways but I'm guessing I'm a better cook. Speaking of which I might have to make you soup considering the state of your face. Spoon or Straw?"

"What! Oh, yes, yes why not, spoon please," I replied trying to smile which hurt slightly. Maybe I should use a straw? No, a spoon will be fine. That and some funny looking back over the centuries with an android Charlie Brooker.

Ray left asking a final time if I needed anything apart from the soup he was about to knock up.

"Tea, biscuits, bed, duvet, television and soup on the way, I think I'm alright Ray."

Ray left with a smile on his face humming the Starsky and Hutch theme. Only for a moment. I could just about make out an expletive as he realized he was signing the last tune he had heard. The ear worm strikes.

The beginning of the Charlie Brooker show started with something like this.

"Regular viewers will know that I like to start these shows with something lighthearted and funny. However," uh ooh, here it comes, "the start of this century began as badly as the previous century ended." Without looking my finger pressed the pause button on my phone.

I didn't even know what century he was talking about and I already wanted to turn remain blissfully unaware.

I wondered for a moment if there ever was a moment in human history when absolutely nobody was annoying, threatening, waring with anyone else. If there was ever a moment in which a United Nations meeting had every nation represented and everyone had a lovely time. In fact the world was so peaceful that they went on to disband themselves because man had agreed finally just to get on with things in a much more open and friendly manner. Their final act being the introduction of a law that forces everyone to attend a mass rave held once a year for the sheer hell of it. Lovely thought but only ever just that I'd imagine. A less lovely thought was that of do I depress myself senselessly by watching the downfall of mankind. If I'm going to do that surely I might as well go the whole hog and find something more profound and detailed......? The Squid were right, I wanted, yearned for something other than the absolute truth. I needed to water down the reality I had lived in.....

Ray knocked gently before he entered holding a tray with soup and bread.

"Didn't you like your tea?" he asked. I held it between my two hands, cupping it, it was cold and untouched. A good indication, at least to an Englishman, that something terrible must have happened.

"I think I spent too much time thinking about what to watch, or what to avoid..... Was it as terrible as I think it was? Human history after I left the planet.

Ray paused for a moment.

"Here sorry let me take that." I took the tray from Ray and handed him my cold mug of tea.

"Let me put it like this. There were always problems which caused other problems which only amplified the original problem, so yes in short, it was as bad as you imagine, and then double it. Now I still have some duties on the bridge and Horace as asked for a new menu. One that includes half the food but all the taste and goodness. I think he's gone mad."

"He's just being a good boy scout," I said defending Nelson.

"What?"

"Prepared."

Ray looked mystified.

"He's just making sure that if we need to go onto rations, he's ready, we're ready, and you're ready. It's one less thing you're going to have to do at a more critical time too. Any way it's not going to come to that, touch wood, damn there isn't any, but something will come up, something will have to come up."

"Preparation, I see, and a little faith it appears. Contact me when you need to, but if you can, call Smokey first. I've already made you soup and a cuppa you didn't even bother with." Rays bottom lip quivered frantically and he dipped his finger into the cold tea and placed a drip under his eye, letting it roll down as though he was crying.

"You numpty," I said and laughed and then stop laughing immediately as it sparked a throb around my nose. Ray smiled too and then bowed like an actor at the end of a two hour performance and exited stage left.

His soup was of course delicious. I didn't actually know what it was but that didn't matter and instead of watching anything I decided to play some classical music, just in the background, not too loud, my intention was to finish my meal, close my eyes and sleep. It worked.

CHAPTER 12

I wasn't sure how restful the sleep was as the awakening was anything but. I had rolled over during my slumber and my head wanted to travel further than the vacuum packed nose protection I had would allow.

I didn't need to use my phone to message anyone to grab their attention my scream and after throb squeal was enough. Marilyn and Mona rushed in with a look of concern upon their faces.

"We heard someone scream!" Marilyn said looking into my now slightly watery eyes.

"Yes sounded like twin girls having a fight," Mona added. I think she was being serious. Marilyn gave her a look too. Mona shrugged her shoulders. "I broke Bernie's nose once. He just laughed. It was such a good punch." Her eyes drifted off somewhere and then she smiled. I believe she was remembering the moment she whacked her brother. She abruptly returned her gaze back to me.

"So there's nothing wrong right, you don't need any help or anything? Right?"

".... Right," I answered correctly, "I'll get back to what I was doing, and don't worry I won't disturb you again."

"If you mean you're going to back to sleep you might be disappointed. We're starting a major service any minute. We were on our way when we heard you."

"It might get a bit bangy," Marilyn added in laymen's terms.

"Sounds like a very good excuse to play some loud rock music. You may want to leave."

I picked up my phone and put it into computer mode and called up Led Zeppelin, random, volume up, bass up, volume up a bit more….. Play. "Aaah," volume down volume down volume down. A Whole Lotta Love blared out, and probably still too loudly. It wasn't long before there was a knock on the door, and then a harder knock because I wasn't sure about the first.

"It's open."

Bernie smiled at me from the doorway bouncing his head in time to the beat. He raised his hand and mimed it turning a small invisible dial. I smiled back and raised the volume. He didn't stop rotating that non-existent dial though so, I naturally followed. It ended up louder than my first setting. Bernie then showed me the palm of his hand, enough, he disappeared without closing the door.

Again I knew it wouldn't be too long before someone else came along and asked me to do the opposite. I gave it no more than thirty seconds. I was so confident I set up the stopwatch on my phone....... After three minutes I turned it off. That also allowed me to concentrate on a distant thud coming somewhere from the ship. It wasn't in anyway part of the song, but it fitted, and then from somewhere else a 'Ting Ting' joined in on the off-beat. I began to giggle, it appeared that more than one person was indulging in a 'Moment'. Then the Moment spread a bit more and a whirl of an electric motor added to the chorus by adding two quick stabs on the trigger at the end of every fourth bar. This was slowly turning into a famous scene from 'Delicatessen' and if you've seen that film you'll know the one I'm on about unfortunately from my point of view I would be the character in bed, only in this case on my tod, unlike the guy in the film, who definitely wasn't, enough said.

The joviality continued for the next track, but soon wavered as the reality of the work involved servicing the ship took over..... Part of me was secretly glad to have avoided the work, although that part definitely wasn't my nose.

I was quite surprised to be able to play so many tracks without further visitors. I got through six Led Zeppelin tracks before I decided that I needed to listen to the Stone Roses. The music that was guaranteed to take me back to the best years of my life. I seemed to have so many memories of travel to and fro from the beach in my best mates' car, Jamie and his knackered Morris Minor. Glorious sunshine all day long, and that beautiful rare shade, in England, of Summer Blue, proper blue, blue skies, and a knackered ghetto blaster that only played cassette tapes. On which we only ever played the Stone Roses, we couldn't actually get the cassette draw open so it was completely stuck in there. We didn't mind, they were great. Unfortunately after only three months of 'Play, rewind, play, rewind,' the tape snapped and autumn instantly set in. I don't generally like nostalgia, going back in my memories, I was so happy back then I'd be tempted to stay there, to try and find that state again, which of course is impossible. I might then have the problem of getting angry with the present because I've measured the past, and I find I don't like the difference.

This time however things were slightly different. I was in bed listening to music with excessive volume attached and in that situation anything with a grungy guitar is best, we all know that, even if you don't like music at all, you know that. I had to resist the urge to bounce my head along in time and resorted to finger drumming on my thighs with eyes closed. I let myself drift. I smiled as I remembered that this was exactly what I'd do on the first morning of any holiday. Working age subdued rebellion, not fully committed to the full version. The idea of a quiet life and a reasonable mortgage didn't quite leave me with enough time........ Now, I had all the time I needed and hopefully I could find some place that I could call home on my home planet, and there wouldn't be a soul around to demand tax or require me to fill out a form before I start any building works over six foot. Let's face it, I don't think I'm going to be moving into a place at all, I might, at best find a place that's good enough to be knocked down and reused in some way? Why do I have a sudden urge to play,' Burning down the House' by the Talking Heads. Yeah, why not? Go with it! With extra bass.

What a lovely four minutes of my life that was. Until the line 'We're in for nasty weather' repeated itself in my mind. I instantly took this as metaphorical. In which case I should get serious and put my mind to something more directed towards our predicament. Firstly don't play Talking Heads next best song 'Road to Nowhere'. Then send a message to Ray asking him to bring a brew. There's no point trying to make sense of life without one. Then change the music and the volume. I was told once that classical music helped in firing the brain therefore it helped when trying to be inspired or creative. Well, let's see?

I don't know how long it was before Ray's hand appeared into view bearing a hot beverage. Powerful stuff that classical music.

"Tea, your Nibs."

"Thank you Clarence."

"What?"

"Clarence, first butlery sounding name that came to mind. You were the Nibby one."

"That's true. So how are you?"

"….. Not so different to the last time I saw you, not so long ago. How are you?"

"Better for being here and not around Bernie who seems intent on banging things for the fun of it. Only I can't see where you'd find the fun. Everyone was very glad to know that you enjoy excessively loud music."

"Glad to help. Has he stopped?" I asked and at the very same time tuned off the music completely in order to listen and confirm my own question. He hadn't. Bernie was more than happy being a bit bangy. No wonder everyone was enjoying the music. It wasn't Bernie's fault that banging metal on metal allows for all the annoying harmonics.....I'll have to drown that out with a bit of Metal, a bit of Mercury, of the Freddie variety, with of course a bit of extra volume. What a voice.

"Is that any better?" I inquired.

Ray squinted as though he couldn't hear. I would have thought being a supercomputer would have helped him, but he just looked like any Englishmen being asked anything by someone else of a different nationality under normal hearing conditions, "Err, what, ah?" I turned the volume down and asked him again, "I said, is that any better?"

"Oh yes, turn it back up."

"What you need is a pair of noise reduction headphones?"

"Would they help me to not hear any of your requests for tea?"

"Yes, they would, probably? Along with everything else.... Oh yes, by the power of Brew. Ray, Ray?"

"What? What?"

"Along with everything else..... Ray?"

"What!"

"Noise reduction headphones! They receive a signal and then broadcast it back out which causes oscillations in the waves thus opposing its' intrusion by obliteration. I think, right, right? Something like that?"

Ray stopped me talking anymore with a small half raised hand, which then dived into small bag strapped to his waist belt. He gathered his make-up gizmo and placed it on his own face, there was a small pause whilst Ray selected the look he wanted. I've never seen someone's face look so long. He had given himself two big dumbfounded yet questioning eye-brows and he also lowered his jaw pulling his mouth down at the sides and then, to complete the look he hunched his shoulders and surrendered his palms face up. "Err? And?" he said. I paused a moment thinking I would allow a few seconds for Ray to consider the possibilities of what could be going on in my brain? The only thing he did was somehow raise his eye-brows even further. No, he didn't have a clue.

"If we run the auto bot configures an obliterating wave that destroy the crystals in the engine...... But what if they were surrounded by a wall of anti-wave waves? And then a secondary anti oscillating wave area, namely, your head. I presume you can reverse the signal in your ears and turn them into speakers? Yes? Right? So a wall of speakers around your head, which you can also turn into a wall of sound around the crystals, which you'll have to keep in your mouth."

Ray didn't look so confused anymore. For some reason he looked quite angry.

"So you want to use my head as a muffler? The focal point of a wave disrupter will be burrowing into the very centre of my head seeking its' target and you want to risk my head in the process? I'm pretty sure someone may have considered this in the design? Don't you?"

"I don't know, did they?"

".... I don't know, no."

"And I'm guessing that if anyone has ever tried doing it before they only use the ships computer and the ships speakers to try it with. Which we could also do. So three layers of protection. Do you know if anyone has tried that?"

Ray looked stumped for a moment, "No I don't, however, the problems remains for me that you want to use my head as the last line of defence in that imaginary three layered system. My head. What if it goes wrong and my head blows up? Ey, did you think about that?"

"I thought the material around the crystals was left intact?"

"It is…….. But if it really has to try hard to get through, what happens then? Cos' I don't know, do you?"

"No, I don't….. But if it worked we might be more likely to deliver Don and Pic home to a safe place they can continue to call home……. A place where they can pull up a chair and watch the sun go down whilst holding a hot mug of tea……." Ray paced for a few seconds and then made his way into my bathroom. I heard water splash into the basin. I couldn't see what he was doing but felt that at least one thing he was doing was not talking to me.

"You'd be a hero." I said.

Ray's face appeared in the door way. He didn't look so grumpy anymore, he still retained a hint of, "I don't like you at the minute," but he must have been contemplating the risk to reward ratio at the same time. If his head survived it would be cast in bronze…… I think he may have liked the idea.

"Stay here, do you want another cuppa?"

CHAPTER 13

I didn't even get to the end of the next song before Nelson began pacing up and down and back and forth in my cabin. Upon entering he closed the door behind himself and barred Rays' entrance. He then, I thought either paused for thought or was polite enough to wait for 'Pinball Wizard' to end. I was wrong on both counts.

"I love that song. The film, well that's a bit mad, but I suppose you had to be there. Could you turn that off please?"

"Certainly. Something on your mind," I said knowing exactly what was on his mind.

"You could say that......"

I watched his manor change. He relaxed, his eyes became soft and tender. His moment was his and I left him to it. I wanted to ask him to trust me, as his look suggested a drifting into the land of fond memory, Wife, Mother or mistress? I heard he had a house in Gibraltar, for his mistress, within metres of his moorings. Penalty area distance. Way to keep a mistress, thousands of miles from home and your wife and scoring distance from the dock...... must ask him about that? The quietness settled him and he sighed, exercising the moment allowing his more robust demeanour to reform itself.

"I do not wish to come across as dramatic, I do not wish bias to steer a good idea away, and I do not wish to appear a bit fluffy around the edges, but, and this is going to sound corny, Ray really is a bit of sunshine...... He's been the best friend I've ever had, ok, I've known him for a while now, ages, the longer you live the more you are going to go through. Simple math's really, and, he's been there an awful lot, good times bad times..... So, and this is what I meant about being dramatic, if anything goes wrong, say his head blows up, I'll rip your head off and see if that works as a replacement. Ok?" He smiled....... Oh!

I wanted too lean back slightly. I managed an inch in my plump but compressed pile of pillows. He paused for thought and breath. I daren't say anything and knew there was more to follow so given that I had offered a scenario in which his best mate might potentially sacrifice himself and a relationship that was well over a millennium might come to an abrupt end in a split second, I let him carry on......
I also clenched my bladder.

"You are however in possession of the only idea that could work. Ray explained it, and strangely with a smile on his face," he said whilst his stern eyes bored a small hole into my mind. He stood upright, by which I mean he stopped leaning in towards me, imposing himself and demonstrating his rage. I was quite glad, it was effective, I was very glad of pre-emptive bladder clench too."

"I just saw……" I very nearly got to finish what I was about to say before he raised his arm and revealed his palm. Palm says shut up. I realized instantly he had done me a favour. Whatever I said would not stand as an excuse. Without realizing it I had just volunteered someone else to risk their existence, and not my own. That could be read so incorrectly. I was therefore glad to hear what Nelson had to say next.

"If I had of known of the principle I too would have suggested it….. That's another reason for me to be angry right now, because I know your thoughts are correct and all options should be considered. The longer we leave it the less chance we have. So unless we come up with another idea soon we might as well get on with it. Ray believes that at best, there's a fifteen percent chance that it won't work. And if it doesn't work there's a fifty percent chance there'll be so much resonance in such a small confined area that his head will simply be obliterated. He's already suggested we wear gas masks, just in case, wouldn't want to breathe in a bit of Ray." Sarcasm with Nelson was easy to spot as he always apologized for it within a few moments. There was a bit of a lag this time, due to a couple of harsh looks and one clenched jaw. Which only served me as a reminder of my own bladder. Nelson wasn't being sarcastic, funny, dry, or any other form of happy. He didn't want to lose his best friend…… My idea better work, otherwise, I too will lose friends too, all of them, and I wouldn't blame them.

Part of me was glad to be under Doctors orders and confined to bed, that meant away from everyone, and right now that might be the best place for me, low profile was required. Better keep the music down and ask Smokey to take over tea duty? In fairness I didn't know how anyone else was going to react? I could only imagine other's thoughts. At least Don and Pic should be happy? Should?

Nelson stood proud and took in a deep breath. As he did his eyes glazed for a moment, "You can come in now Ray," he said quite calmly, "I know he's listening." So much for a low profile.

The door swung open revealing a crowd of listeners hunched bunched and looking stupid. Apart from Don and Pic who ran as fast as their little legs could carry them towards me.

Never assume what someone else should or shouldn't like, do, behave like, or most importantly, think. Especially if your name is Colin…. I couldn't have been more wrong, presumptuous even.

"Is that any way to treat a friend? In fact, is he even a friend, are any of us your friends?" Don shouted whilst they poked my legs and feet with their long lemur like middle finger.

"Eh? Eh? Eh?" Pic added with three more finger assaults. They both then made their way to the end of the bed. I thought for a second that they did this to give way to the next person who might want to bully me a bit, but apparently not. With one hand they deftly lifted the bedding slightly and then forced the middle finger of their other hand over into as circular arched position as possible and then they let rip the most painful flick I've ever felt, and on the soles of my feet! I obviously recoiled with this a screamed out in agony, and then in further agony to a now throbbing nose and face.

The collective crowd Ooh'd and Oww'd and both Don and Pic looked over to them questioningly, "What? He deserves it," Don said with Pic adding with a little smile, "and you should see what we're going to do if his little plan fails? Huh?"

"Listen everyone. I'm, I'm sorry…. I just….." I'm not sure if everyone leant in but it certainly felt like everyone's hearing just improved, "…. I just, I visualized it, that's all I did, I, I. We were talking about nothing in particular and then something made me think of it. I visualized a page in a schoolbook and imagined a drawing, a schematic, diagram, whatever, and then I opened my big gob….. I'm sorry…. I'm sorry.

Sam strode into the room and took a seat on the end of the bed and then seemed to stare blankly at the crowd still hovering in the doorway. On reflection he could have been staring directly at Ray.

"The problem here Colin, my dear friend, Oh I see the idea too, I do I do, fighting noise with noise, it's a good it is, it is. Only you saw what, a simple, what, outline sketch, single page, simple straight forward idea? Right?" I nodded whilst a couple of disgruntled grunts quaffed their way into the atmosphere from the doorway followed by a silence gracefully allowing Sam to continue. Before doing so he shuffled in his position and propped himself up on fully stretched arms, clamping down my right foot, smiling as he did.

"The only problem is, and maybe I could make this easy for you to understand in a way you might be able to understand and who knows even enjoy?" My furrowed brow didn't stop him. It may have caused him to apply a gradual increase of purposeful pressure on my already suffering foot too. I must have appeared smug? He continued, "well, not to put too finer point on it. Your idea, he's gone all American on it's arse!"

I wonder if noise reduction headphones could work on silence? I didn't understand, but right at that moment that didn't seem to matter as Sam had propelled himself from the bed with all the gusto he could muster using my right foot as a launch pad. Instead of screaming and facing the pain like any normal person I decided to ride it out and feel my face turn red. I had forgotten I was already a pale shade of harmonica blue.

Ray sprang forthwith deep concern on his face to which I recoiled once more and further still when his hand reached out towards my face.

"You've gone green. Your temperature is ok. I think Colin here might need to rest, he looks more than a bit ill. Do you feel ok Colin?" I was amazed he out of everyone that was there was the first to show any sympathy, and when I say first I should also add only, and when I say sympathy I should say more concern, as I needed to be well enough to be able to play my part in his intricate plan. I then understood immediately what Sam meant by going 'All American' once I finally saw Ray's grand scheme. Which he so graciously and eagerly beamed in a hologram into the centre of my cabin from his eyes. Everyone seemed to stand back as a three dimensional image of the 'Flying Fish' in line form revolved effortlessly in the centre of my cabin. It's entire 70 metre length reduced down to the size of fish you'd still be wary of if you came across it whilst out for a swim one day, about my arm span, just less than 6 foot. Sorry to mix my measurement systems, I grew up in the seventies and schools did their best to confuse everything, 6 foot about 2 metres, there about. Then briefly, but again like a child of the seventies who was more used to Pac-Man and Space Invaders I gawped in amazement and wondered without conclusion how powerful the technology was that could perform such a task. My attention was then drawn to how many rooms, cabins, and areas I had never been in or near. I had no idea what lay inside them. I didn't have time to dwell as my focus was then drawn to several orange glowing small figures that appeared indifferent places and floors all over the ship. They appeared to be randomly placed, but knowing Ray there was probably going to be some method in his mechanics that on the face of it seemed mad. I wasn't wrong.

Ray let everyone take in the view until he was assured that everyone had been baffled once more and me more so as it was my first time. Sam broke the silence, "Come on Colin, ask him what's going on and what all those things are."

Ray smiled, remained silent and by doing so urged I asked the question. In for a penny.

"What's all that Ray."

"I'm glad you asked. May I ask that you leave any questions until the end."

Every head in the room, apart from Ray, turned toward me. Every single face said, "Don't you dare have any questions." I smiled. Some continued to look and intensified the drilling, I think they were adding, "and don't, just don't, give him any ideas."

Ray moved up to the spinning glowing threads of neon-light and touched it with his palm. It stopped spinning. I noticed Nelson chuckle and shake his head at the same time, I didn't understand something? Ray then poked the furthest most glowing orange figure. The image zoomed in at speed and magnified the scale twenty five to one. Mona stifled a laugh and Bernie swore. I didn't take me too long to see why. A miniature Bernie presented himself complete with etched stubbly face and out of bed way to early hair, the size of an action man doll. He appeared hunched over and to be in the very front of the ship. Within the curve of the nose that was the front of the hammer headish front of the ship. In each hand he held what looked like a large spanner like tool, only it wasn't a spanner, or any other tool. It was in fact a massive tuning fork. Something that the bass section in a blue whale choir might use to tune up. It looked as big as the massive arm that was holding it, and there was one in each. The tiny figure repeated the action of whacking them together and the simply placing the ends of them on the skin of the inner hull. Ray tapped each glow in turn. We were all doing them same, just in different floors and areas that seemed to be as far away from each other as possible.

"You will notice that the design is quite simple, beautiful I'd say. You'll all have different size forks dependent upon your own physicality." Ray smiled to himself as he considered his own considerations. Smokey had the worst deal. Although the tuning forks were appropriately sized forks, he was able to able to carry many more being many limbed and having snake like control with those very limbs. Hang him upside down from the ceiling and he'd look like an organic yet industrial chandelier. He was Squid, whereas

Marilyn was a self-altered octopus that was now more human than many humans and definitely more human than her origins and there was no way she wasn't a Monroe fan….. Thus no suckers, that would have been very handy right now with Rays logic so she only had two. The figure of myself, complete with nose padding and slightly black eyes and still bluish in the skin department was performing the same task as everybody else but from the comfort of my own cabin, hunched on my knees and breaching the door threshold reaching out onto the corridor floor, where a floor panel had been removed so that I could reach the structural bulk of the Flying Fish. It looked uncomfortable. Not as much though as Mona, her forks were nearly as big as her brothers, bigger than everybody else's. Something from within told me not to mention that.

Ray then touched floating image and it zoomed in even further than before to show a hoard of rampant rabbits romping around the ship. All floors, front to back. I didn't see them before as they were so small. The more I watched the more I heard what I thought was rain. It was then that I noticed Bernie looking at me with a shriveled up face. Somehow the rabbits were going to be Bernie's responsibility and he wasn't keen. I then realized why? The rain I was hearing, which was weird enough being in space, wasn't the actual result of a shower, storm or down pour. It was the result of every single rabbit having small metal clogs attached to their feet. Four clogs per rabbit, thousands of rabbits…… Ah? Now I see why Bernie could commit Regicide, he was the man with the keys to the workshop, he was detailed by Ray by spend every available minute making mini tap shoes for rabbits………

"Are you having a laugh?" I asked Ray.

"No. This is deadly serious Colin. Deadly. We'll all chip in Bernie, don't look so, murderous."

"Yes Bernie, turn that frown upside down," Marilyn said and then smiled broadly.

Bernie tried his hardest to follow her example but his heart really wasn't into it, neither were his teeth. Like a row of broken gravestones that almost glowed magnolia. He must be related to everyone in Britain.

"It's not the production line that worries me. It's who is going to put them on the rabbits? And by the time I've made the total amount needed there may well have been a population explosion."

"Once more Bernie, we will all chip in," Nelson added and then cocked his head as if to say, 'you understand'. Bernie scowled slightly but then nodded his agreement.

"We need all the clatter, tinks and tonks, oscillations as possible if this is going to work," Ray told the group and not Bernie in particular, and poked his finger into the middle of the ship where at last I finally saw how Ray was intending to turn himself into a hero. In the first instance it didn't look like Ray was doing much at all. His tiny, and I must say, physically enhanced version of himself sat motionless on a stool. His cheeks were slightly puffed out from holding the engines crystals in his mouth, he still had a slight smile, probably because he was looking very much at home with a crown of wire sat monarch-like upon his head, but where he would have had gems and jewels, he had all our communicators equidistant apart.

"I've written a small program that I'm going to load up onto your devices, based on what Colin told me about noise reduction headphones. Let's hope he's right. Essentially whatever I hear I'm going to send back out directly at the sound wave coming my way."

Wow, I hope I am right. Ray then twiddled a finger within the image of himself and I watched a structure form itself around Ray, like a domed cage. Then this structure quickly became covered in everything from mattresses to dish clothes. Like a child's den, but by a child who has too much time on his hands and a well-furnished house. One big noise dampener I suppose. Then I noticed his detached ears spinning on a string directly above the noiseless den. Full grown Ray smiled broadly.

"There, that should work…… and if it doesn't someone punch Colin."

"I'll do it."

"Count me in."

"We can take turns."

"We'll do more than punch him." Don and Pic waved at me with a menacing large middle finger and then smiled.

"There'll be none of that, besides Colin's plan is going to work, right?" Nelson said with assured authority.

Oh dear, it's now my plan.

106

CHAPTER 14

There were more minor details that Ray had considered. For instance, all auto cleaning bots were to have their location chips disabled and the bearings slightly filed down in order to produce bots that continuously banged against walls and doors whilst the wheels squeaked and screamed. All music systems were to play any music that contained harmonics and feed-back, and of course all tracks to be played at full volume. I briefly considered telling Ray about feed-back loops and how easy they might be to reproduce but I feared for my life, as encouraging Ray with any more ideas would only produce more work for everybody else. I stayed quiet. As did everyone else. I thought for a moment that everyone was thinking that silence would be a good way to encourage Ray to stop with his team talk, it was, the plan was set. It would take effect as soon as all the preparations had been completed, Ray estimated about twenty hours. I was secretly glad to be in bed under doctors' orders. I don't like seeing other people work whilst I do nothing, but nothing was probably what everybody else would have preferred me to do, just in case I caused more work.

Nelson finally brought the meeting to a close and everyone left to start their own weird tasks. I then took it upon myself to lighten the mood and become head of light entertainment and play, at a considerate volume, any music that was in a major key and promoted the action of smiling and the feeling of happiness and wellbeing. This was occasionally punctuated by banging, clanging and possibly swearing from the ship's workshop. Bernie was either whacking his fingers or Ray, or, naming every item he made in a hard aggressive language, like a mixture of German and Welsh and the Hic-ups. It was slightly amusing for a while, a short while and then it started to get annoying. Then twenty minutes later I understood why. I also understood that if I were paranoid Bernie had decided to use the corridor in which my cabin was located, as the test track for his rabbit clogs. As with Rays graphics from only a few hours ago I thought I could hear the pitter patter of rain and then saw a family of bunnies sluggishly hopping past my cabin door. Their tiny legs unable to move freely, weighed down by their new footwear. They looked drunk and probably wished they were. One rabbit paused in my doorway and looked over at me, begging me to help or put it out of its' misery.

"Ah Bright Eyes, sorry mate, there's nothing I can do….. It's all for a very good cause." The rabbit just curled his lip and maybe huffed, then surrendering to his fate slowly moved off following his tribe. Bernie then walked by and also stopped in the doorway.

"Oi, if you're looking to offer anyone any sympathy, look no further," he demanded and then strolled off with a snarl and fingers in his ears.

I couldn't resist and temptation took the better of me and in addition I know that a laugh is often the best remedy for stress. I quickly searched for the classic song from Watership Down, 'Bright Eyes' and turned up the volume a notch……

"Plonker," I think Bernie said or indeed shouted from halfway down the corridor and I don't think he was referring to any rabbits that may have just developed the skill of language and insults in double quick time. It made me giggle. It was just a shame I wasn't too stressed, I could have tested my own theory….. I waited until I heard the door at the end of the corridor close and went back to the happier songs that we all needed. Whilst these songs echoed through the ship I tried to think of any hard core tunes that relied on the guitarist playing with feedback. Jimi Hendrix sprang to mind, but I was sure there were better examples at this point I had a problem. I was never a gig goer in my youth and I was always slightly scared to go into clubs where the blokes had longer hair than the woman, the very clubs and gigs where the music played always contained bands that had an amp cavorting guitarist. There must be an easier way. There was, just ask the computer to find one. So that's what I did, it took less than a second to reveal an album released in England on the hundredth year anniversary of the Marshall Amplifier, 'Now that's what I call Feedback.' Jimi Hendrix was the only act I recognized, and after I quickly played through the album in small sections I was very glad of that. This had the advantage of alerting Ray to some very strange sounds that Ray felt he needed to investigate, and as he knew where to go to listen, he also delivered a hot cup of tea. I could get used to this, I thought, but there'd be no point if it didn't work.

"Excellent horrible music Colin, that wasn't what you'd listen to in your time was it?"

"Pardon?" I shouted back.

"I said was that the? Ah I see what you're doing, very funny."

I smiled and turned the volume down and thought about putting the Bangles 'Walk like an Egyptian' on and why if I'm going to do that why not lead into it with 'Manic Monday' it was after all a

Monday and it was now because of Ray more than a bit Manic. Everyone was more than hyper-active, I think I'd call it hyper-hectic. Everyone, apart from me.

This has happened before. I've been laid up and couldn't help..... whilst under house arrest awaiting trial everything happened to enable the escape. All the logistics, happened. Something I easily could have helped in too. I love being lazy when I've earnt it and not before, except when I know or see others are struggling. Ray then spoke and instantly challenged my thoughts on that ethos. I wasn't sure if that was by accident or not?

"I'll have to break your bones more often Colin. You're coming up with some very good ideas from here."

"Mmm, you could just ask me to go to bed and have a nap or something, what's this with the violence?"

"If the accident with your nose hadn't of happened would you have been too busy doing something else instead of what you did and because of that say what you said. I'm not so sure? So maybe it was Fate?"

"Fate?"

"Yeah so, next time we're in a pickle, I'll break something of yours and you'll inspire a plan somehow?"

"No, please don't do that. Plus, it then definitely wouldn't be fate, if I used your head as a cricket ball."

"No, it wouldn't be Fate if you told me about it before if happened, that's the point."

I thought he might not understand. "Yes, I know. That's why I said it."

"Oh, yes, of course, sorry, I wasn't actually thinking of breaking anything, just saying."

"Yeah, I know, but just checking all the same. All cultures have some weird ideas, but yours had a few extra." I pressed play on my communicator and 'Manic Monday' bellowed out. Ray paused before he spoke.

"If 'Walk like an Egyptian' is the next song you play, that wouldn't be Fate either would it?"

"No it wouldn't be would it?" I said beaming like a naughty child already guilty.

"I might break a bone if it is."

We both smiled. I stopped short of laughing once again for fear of angering my nose though. Ray made up for the loss and howled in merriment. It didn't stop me playing the song, who could resist? Ray then went into spinning eyes mode, leading to the earlier projection of the muscular version of himself, it came striding over to my padded nose where upon tiny Ray 'Went to town on it.' I smiled gently and tiny Ray evaporated away and real Ray stopped looking less possessed.

I'll miss him if it goes wrong and what's more I'll live forever knowing that I helped cause it. On top of that the only bunch I consider friends would at the very least resent me for a very long time and if you have forever how long is a long time?

A sigh from nowhere expelled itself from my body. The weight of a bad outcome from an actuality jumped on my back like an Incubus or a morbidly obese wrestler. Only one thing to do when that happens, attack back with a slap of positivity, with severity in context to the situation of course. It's no good saying to a man who has lost his wife, "Cheer up, there's plenty more fish in the sea."

"So Ray, what do you think? We'll be laughing about all this in a day's time when all this is over. In fact we'd have forgotten about it by now, and wondered why we didn't just drive off in the first place, ages ago, why it took us so long? What do you reckon?"

Ray paused for a long time before answering. Sitting down on the end of the bed and smiling at me in a fatherly way before he began prolonged the silence, and maybe his own sense of drama.

"I've reconciled my feeling and thoughts concerning my own death. I did that ages ago. I am mostly dead. I'm really ok with it." He smiled at me a huge wave of reassurance swept over me. At that instant all anxiety left my body. Like an hour long massage in a nano-second. That nirvana didn't last long, "of course if the worst happens it's not going to be me that you've got to worry about, is it?" he smiled before he got up to leave, he stalled his manoeuvre though for more dramatic effect, he then raised his eyebrows very quickly, a cheeky one I'd label it, and subsequently ruined any drama he was aiming for.......

"Ray, if you get a chance you really should try talking into a microphone and standing too close to the speaker. See how that sounds, but do it on an isolated system, don't do it through the ships system, you might break the very things we're protecting."

"That's a good point, I shall try that, my own distortion bomb. Yet another good idea Colin. I'll try that straight away." True to his word he went to leave.

"If anyone asks it wasn't my idea and can you lock the door on the way out." There were no locks on the doors so Ray didn't understand the meaning, I'd better clarify, "Don't want anybody thinking I'm creating more work, especially as I just lay here. Ok?"

For a moment after he left the silence for lack of a Bangles tune had that amazing effect of focusing the mind. How beautiful, we think, how rare it is. We can get to use the oxymoron, "Listen to that silence.". If it goes on for too long though it also, if we choose to let it, give us the chance to calm down enough to be able to judge ourselves and see who we really are, allowing for a self-assessment, back by an honest self audit. Then it's up to us to use the information gained, or not. There is another side effect of silence, the idea that a quick nap might be in order. Which is certainly an idea and consideration made easier by someone in bed and feeling like a patient..... Whose friends are so happy with him. I sipped away on the tea as I thought about what time to set on my alarm and what music I should wake up to. Then I realized that no sleep will ever happen on a full bladder and had to go. It was whilst staring at myself in the mirror, one minute later, washing my hands that I looked quite tired. The exact phrase I used was, "You look knackered.... And why do you have to finish every cup of tea you get?"

Of course, we'll never fully understand why we do those things that we know are in some way just not the best thing. I suspect we do that on purpose most of the time. Avoiding something, burying something else. Sometimes we can do that with sleep, avoid things, put things off, which when you think about it just prolongs whatever agony is stopping you sorting it out in the first place.... Why wait? In this case maybe you shouldn't go for a nap and instead nip something in the bud.

However, if like me you look a bit tired are crusty at the edges and under orders it might be advisable to grab at the very least a nap before you get up and go. This realization made me decide that I shouldn't set any time to wake up from my slumber and that I should indeed play music to accompany me into the realm of dreams via the land of nod. Because then, as we all know, you can say to yourself that you must have at least slept if you have had a dream. Even if it's really weird and leaves you confused for ages, they can be the best, sometimes, at least they make us think about something other than the daily grind. I never managed a lucid dream. I remember a kid at school telling everyone that he had occasional lucid dream and when it happened he changed the dream into a computer game, in which of course you give yourself unlimited lives, great you would think?

Maybe not, think Manic Minor, Jet Pack, nothing compared to what it was even twenty years later, Frogger, need I say anymore. I hope my brain doesn't think I've requested a weird dream or anything?

It didn't. I had your plain old normal dream in which something great happens and you wake to utter disappointment and one of my thoughts did slip in there. In the dream I wore a loose fitting silver space suit but I was clamped into a powerful jetpack, there you go, my thought. I was zipping around the atmosphere of a planet deflecting missiles and bombs, catching them and throwing them back, kicking them away where I had too. I knew for some reason it was dangerous to kick them and so it should only be considered when appropriate. I was like a goalkeeper in a football match. In a game without goal posts and devastating consequences when a goal is scored, and only one goal to score in, mine. I did an amazing job. At the end of full time it was a draw, so it went to extra time. Again I was brilliant and therefore it went to penalties. Being English I knew I was doomed. In my lifetime, up until the day I choked to death it was the norm to feel hopeless in this situation. Especially as in the situation I was in, it being a one-way game. I had to be in the moment though, it wasn't then, it was now. The whole planet depended on me, so I shouldn't be thinking about past failures, and it wasn't the football world cup anyway. I relaxed and then bobbed slightly, ready to pounce. Eyes darting around awaiting the incoming missiles. There was some degree of fairness, they were all painted in a fluorescent pink, so I wouldn't get confused with any passing shooting stars or comets. My jetpack then puffed out of puff, and it sputtered its' last fume of fuel. Oh dear, never prepared, what a rubbish boy scout I would have made, but then a stroke of luck. The first of five missiles came directly at me and I caught it. I had one chance to save the planet. I would wait until the second missile appeared then kick the one I had really hard, I would be blown to bits but, hopefully, fingers crossed, it would set off a massive chain reaction. The second would blow up the third and so on... I had a sense that it worked, a bit strange as I was no more... So I awoke disappointed that I had died, glad that I saved the planet, but worried that it held some truth of the future. Why do we do that, or is that just me?

CHAPTER 15

The best thing about the future? Go on have a guess? You're going to be wrong, so I'll tell you. It's the toothpaste. One of the many items purchased on the space Mall was the most undervalued invention I had ever seen.... Looks, feels, smells like the product I remember only you don't need a brush. Squeeze the tube directly onto your teeth and the paste moves off like a caterpillar, everywhere it needs to go. Once it's done a circuit it makes its' way to the place it started and then you know to spit..... that part of the procedure is still exactly the same. Intelligent, active and hungry it does all the work. That's why it's the best thing about the future. No more fillings. It also allows for best potential taste response to whatever your next meal is. For me, that was a late dinner as I had slept through it and nobody had bothered to wake me. Not sure what it was but it was delicious... I wonder if Ray put some extra love into the cooking as there was a small chance that we wouldn't ever get the chance again. Although there was about fifteen hour's left until then and surely we'd eat again. Either way I was glad for it and the tea that washed it down.

Ray brought my dinner to me and sat in silence on the end of the bed whilst I wolfed it. His silence was unnerving, he would normally be chatting away in an accent that he thought appropriate to the subject, which normally wasn't. This time though just silence. It could have been that he didn't want to look at my face as it made allowances for the bandages and pain. I hope it was that, otherwise something serious was going on and I was yet to be told... Surely Ray hasn't miss calculated and his real percentage chance of surviving is closer to zero but he intends to carry on regardless. No, it can't be that. So what could it be? He really isn't like this normally.

Whatever it was it would have to wait. I was formulating a question as I came to the end of my tea when the door that was already open opened even more. Don and Pic walked in, their heads held quite low. For a moment I could imagine them as children and right now they must have broken something somewhere and then took the brave step of owning up to it. The feeling I had was only strengthened by the pair of them scratching the heads with their very long middle finger and trying to start a conversation with "Umms'" and "Err's".

"Spit it out," I said finally after watching the pair of them fumble around to the point of annoyance. They stopped fidgeting and relaxed. Don coughed.

"I'm speaking for the pair of us Colin. We had a chat and, and felt a bit upset with our attitude towards you in regard to potentially ending the life of Ray here, our very good friend."

"Ahh, aren't they cute?" Ray announced.

"Shut up Ray," I said quickly and looked back towards Don surrendering the floor.

"Well Ray didn't have to do what he's doing and you were just thinking about Pic and me and everybody we love and know and how to get away from the Police Bot. That's all you were doing, and we got angry, we got a bit irrational and shouldn't have. We owe you an apology... So... I am sorry Colin."

"As am I," added Pic.

"Ahh, isn't that nice?" Ray couldn't help himself and I smiled.

"Everyone else still thinks you're a heartless son of a bitch though. Jeb is praying for you," Pic said with a smile.

"For you or some other heathen at least," Don said, not smiling.

"It wasn't all about you Colin, we all got a mention," Pic said quickly and smiled again. I think he was trying to comfort me? He didn't need to if God was battling for me on Jeb's behalf. I smiled back.

"Thank you for letting us say what we needed to say."

"Thank you for saying it," I answered and ever-so slightly bowed my head.

"We owe you one," they both said.

"No you don't," I replied.

"Yes, we do," they both replied.

"No you don't."

"Yes we do."

"This could go on?"

"Yes it could."

"Alright. So, whenever I need a favour I can ask you, right?" I said, to which they both nodded. A real positive nod. They'd do anything right now.

"So, anything, whatever, whenever?"

"I think that's the idea Colin," Ray concluded to which once again Pic and Don positively nodded.

"Mmm. Well I've run out of tea and I really wouldn't mind another one, after such a lovely meal, that's the favour I ask, and then we're quits right?"

Don scrunched his brow and squinted slightly. Pic puckered his lips, not in a kissy way though, more complexed by thought. At least they had different expressions for being confused. They then went through a series of facial manoeuvres that suggested they didn't understand how such a small request equalled their sense of guilt. To me they owed me nothing. I never liked the idea of owing anything to anyone, being beholden to someone isn't anybody's idea of fun, is it? Sometimes in life we have to swallow a bit of pride and ask for a bit of help because things, like a perfect storm, become too much. Sure who hasn't ever asked for a hand in whatever way. However, I wouldn't want to walk around feeling that I had something on someone at the same time. More importantly they, Don and Pic were friends and I would help them unconditionally anyway. By the time I came to the end of my thoughts Pic and Don were still musing over what to do?

"I'd take the offer if I were you?" Ray piped in, "seems to me like that is a very good in your favour. Saves me making the next one too." Don and Pic looked at each other and then Ray. Ray nodded. They then looked at me. I nodded. They looked at each other one more time, shrugged, as though defeated. Don held out his hand towards me and I slipped the mug onto his middle finger through the handle. They left talking their own language. Ray kindly translated once they were out of ear shot.

"They were liking you to a particular mouse like mammal on their planet. It went out of existence as it's only defence was to roll over and play dead. It didn't realize that most creatures considering eating it would take a minute or two thinking about it and that was far longer that the mouse like thing could hold its' breath. Its' insides would explode and cause an internal rupture and they would actually die. One hell of a mess and then nobody would eat it anyway."

"How's that me?"

"Hey don't shoot the translator."

"Sorry Ray," I said, knowing I'd squeaked at him and in a way that suggested it was one of his thoughts. A blank neutral returned stare from Ray was for me to know I was correct so I apologized again.

"Just Relax Colin. We shouldn't let things that haven't happened yet and may not happen at all effect or ruin the moment we're actually in, should we? I'm sure you know that but it doesn't hurt to be reminded and I'm sure you know that too?"

I nodded. Ray went to leave but paused in the doorway, a thought stopping him in his tracks.

"You know, I've been around a long time, and hopefully I'm going to be around for a lot longer yet still, and you'll know this one as well, life is too short."

Well that was a lovely thought to leave someone with I thought as I realized I could hear the silence of space. Ray and I looked at each other as though we should be considering a deep thought. In reality the silence of space turned into a regular awkward silence we all experience every now and then. I don't know if I should even attempt to respond to his statement or even if I'm supposed to.

"Yeahhhh," I said, risking it.

Ray nodded, I had understood, his job was done, he left. I was bemused. Fortunately the confusion was hijacked by the appearance of Don and Pic as healthy a distraction as any. They came bearing gifts, tea, biscuits, a sandwich, crisps and cake.

"We know you only asked for a tea, but we feel a bit more guilty than that, so we knocked this up. If you want anything else or more of the same get in touch," Don said whilst Pic waved his phone. They smiled at each other and then me I smiled back. This went on for a while and for the second time in a few moments I could hear that awkward silence.

"Thanks," I said finally, remembering my manners.

"It's not enough is it?" Pic said disappointedly.

"No, he doesn't like it." Don concurred.

"It's more than I asked for, everything is fine. What made you think it wasn't?"

After some grunts and clicks and weird expressions Don said," You don't seem happy with our presentation." His massive middle finger pointing to the selection of treats.

"I find it quite hard under my nose guard to smile," I said hoping that would be enough. I didn't realize I had to show any appreciation. Pic made the situation clearer.

"For you Colin this might be a matter of us doing something in order to say sorry. But, for us, it's an obligation, a bit like a contract. It's something we have to make equal amends for or an equivalent too. And this, doesn't quite seem enough to us. We thought of you and acted upon those thoughts based upon wrong information, that's dangerous. It was wrong of us, we are sorry."

"The fact that you said sorry is more than enough, really, all this stuff really is a bonus. I can munch away whilst watching some rubbish on television, just like I used to. When would I ever get the chance to do that again. In many ways it is I that should be thanking you. Now go and leave me to an idle afternoon and rubbish shows." They left discussing the situation, I think, it was more clicks and clacks, but I hope they left feeling like they had closure on some contract that I'd never had with them. If anything it was me that owed them anyway, and I'm the only one not doing anything in the final push.

I realized at this point that I could sit quite still and wander off into contemplative mode so instead I made an excuse not to. The situation could change dramatically within half a day, I thought, so what's the point in worrying just yet? Instead I'll catch up on some Planet Earth history. There must be a history broadcast available somewhere? There was, after a quick search on the communicator/computer and a flick of the finger it was ready to view on the main screen opposite my bed. I made myself as comfortable as possible before pressing the play button on my now communicator/computer/remote control. Feels like a Saturday morning I thought and smiled. One last wiggle and the final manoeuvre, reaching and hugging my mug of tea. Are the munchies easily reachable? Check. Are my feet warm enough? Check. Do I need to shift the duvet up a tiny bit and have another wiggle? No, I'm good. Ok, here we go.

'A Brief History of the Third Millennium' by and with Victoria Coren Mitchell. What? I'd seen her on television before, but how did that happen? Turns out she was an excellent poker player and won so much money she could always afford the latest and best of everything going. I was greeted with a big radiant smile, this was followed with by an apology for how depressing the opening would be. She was right and I hit the pause button by the end of Two Thousand and Sixteen....... It was quite a while before I even considered restarting and that thought didn't last long. I was also stumped on the music front as the news of so many performers deaths deflated any of the enjoyment I was looking for from the medium itself. Combine all that with the real events and the politics, and Brexit, whatever that was, Leicester winning the Premiership and England losing to Iceland in the European Championship, was glad to have been murdered. I should consider myself lucky. At the end of the twentieth century I'd gone through a middle to fairing divorce, amicable at the edges. I then had a couple of years of stability and normalness. I would like to think my life was just about to begin again when I died. Just when I was due a second wind you could say..... What I've seen in the last two minutes certainly took all the wind out of my sails. After a thousand year wait in a scientist's morgue surrounded by the magic of the Bakelite coffin I think it might be fair to say that not only was I lucky, but rather, I won the Lottery....... Not the first time I've thought that...... Maybe those storm clouds look like subsiding and turning into good winds.

CHAPTER 16

Yes of, course I went back to sleep, what else was there to do? I set an alarm to go off in one hour. An extended nap, and of course, I didn't go to sleep straight away, I spent ten minutes going through a huge list of sounds that would wake me and then realized the list was so big it could easily take a week to go through them all. Also, I was doing exactly what I hated about people with new mobile phones, although they would choose the bus journey or public space to go through their list of options and annoy everyone around them. Early ringtones weren't pleasant to the ear. So I decided to have a bit of fun and set the song 'Good Morning Starshine' from the musical 'Hair', the title also being the first line. That'll do, I'll try and wake up with at least a smile on my face and hopefully some energy and inspiration. It was also fitting, in a way, a far far way.

I was surprised to fall asleep as quickly as I did and was lucky enough, because I do enjoy them, to have another dream too. One which I enjoyed.

It was a Saturday, midday, midsummer. Sunlight warmed my toes as I lay stretched out on the sofa and a hot mug of tea warmed my sternum as it sat on my chest. As any decent astrologer will tell you the conjunction of the time, day, and month could only mean one thing, 'Match of the Day'. Being a dream it had to be confusing, however the confusion I felt also contained a certain amount of happiness. I recognized the smile on my ace as smugness itself. Why? I was wearing an Arsenal dressing gown that must cost a small fortune, and on 'Match of the Day' past and present Arsenal football players were singing the praises of the new Prime Minister of Great Britain, Arsene Wenger. He had changed citizenship and through public demand he formed an independent party and stormed into victory. Sir Alex Fergusson was made Foreign secretary, Carol Vorderman chancellor. His first act was to make your birthday a holiday for you. Great, I thought, and even better, he was to carry on managing Arsenal whilst in office. Hope he doesn't burn out. I woke with the phone ringing in my ear and instantly understood why my dream was so heavy on the football front. It was blaring out the theme from 'Match of the Day', the ringtone I had set, I might have to change that, an image of Victory filled the screen. That changed into a massive eye as soon as I accepted the call.

"Can you see me?" Nelson asked.

"Yes, but,"

"I can't see you Colin. Is this working Ray?" I couldn't see Ray due to Nelson dramatic extreme close up of his own eye.

"Move the phone away Nelson." How could he hope to see me being so close to the screen? He did as requested. "That's better Granddad."

"Ah, there you are. Less of the lip, millennium boy. I was just checking up making sure you're resting and not tapping your fingers."

Do I answer "Yes, everything is fine, I'm resting?" Or, "I was until you phoned?" I didn't get the chance. At that moment the timer alarm sounded to stir me from the napping that I'd being enjoying, 'Good Morning Starshine' unfortunately the microphone was so near the speaker it must have come across to be excessively loud and rude.

"Ah I can see you're still practicing your disk jockeying skills, but now is not the time, you should really know a bit better than that, Colin...."

"I love that song, good choice Colin," said Ray.

I wanted to explain that it was alarm but couldn't muster the will. I actually found Nelson insult amusing. I turned the alarm off.

"It's not a smiling matter Colin. Now, your orders are to what?"

"Rest, yes. I shall."

"Glad to hear it. Many hands make light work, everything is progressing well ahead of schedule, at this rate we will be ready in eight hours. You may well hear some strange humming noises, no need to worry, that'll be us testing the kit. To ease the time I've asked everyone to visit you to keep your spirits up and to keep cabin fever at bay. Now get off the phone and snooze. I'll be down as soon as I've finished rounding up some rabbits." The screen returned to a picture of the Victory.

How long does it take to round up a load of tap dancing rabbits? However long it is will it leave me enough time to bother trying to go back to sleep? It might not even be worth trying right away as in the distance I could hear tippet taps and dinks and dongs. I could only imagine what was going on. Do you measure the rabbit's foot before making it some metal shoes? Do you entice him in for a fitting with a stick of celery? I imagine Bernie was a bit more hands on than that. He'd probably knock them out with a carrot, or just smile at them, that would be a big enough shock, enough to paralyze them for a moment at least... How did the humble rabbit ever become a pet? A companion for people who can't be arsed to walk a dog or get freaked out by the independence of a cat, and its' claws. A rabbit must be one of the more boring pets to keep, after all. They don't do much apart from look cute, and if that's a reason to get one, why keep it in a tiny hutch up against the garden fence? Note to self. 'Don't hate the rabbits, it's not their fault.'

It only took me a few seconds to laugh at my own brain and the way it wonders. I was even more glad to have heard myself laugh out loud, it's been a while. I then laughed even louder as within eight hours my laugh could be on the other side of the universe and my face the other... I really should stop laughing and remember that nothing is indestructible... It's not as though I'm a teenager, far far from it, even when you take away the thousand years I shouldn't have ever had I should still remember how fragile it all is and how easily it can all fall apart... Well, that certainly stopped me giggling. How depressing was that? Almost enough to get a pet rabbit, so I can laugh at it upon sight if diving deep into dark waters...

'Cheer up Colin, such a long face,' said Nelson as he came striding through the door, he sat at desk. "So what's up with you?" he continued nodding at me expecting an immediate response. Which he didn't get. I frowned, I unfrowned, scrunched my nose, phewed, over pouted, and finally confirmed these universal signals.

"Don't really know. I might just be having one of those moments. Re-evaluating my own stock.... I also laughed at the thought that I might not be around in less than a third of a day. It's only a small chance, I know but it was enough to make me consider, if, if..."

"You'd seen enough to be able to let it all go without fear?"

I let that thought sweep through me and without realizing I gently nodded. He said it as though this thought was an old friend of his. I guess it must have been a constant companion considering.

"Did I live my life? Did I do what I wanted to do? Am I happy with what I achieved? Honestly? No. All I did was find a way to live that suited me with what I had and could get. Nothing much. As a consequence it meant there would never be anything to achieve... I have no achievements. I left no mark. Could I have done more with my life? Probably. I wanted nothing more though than to be left alone, not hassled... Here's my taxes, now go away. That's what I ended up with. Just that... There was always something more to have though, which I never got. A family, kids, grandkids, Christmas dinners that involve going to the shed to get the extra table and chairs out. Sling a tablecloth over it and nobody will ever notice it's knackered and covered in paint. Family so big you need a camera with a very wide angle lens... I would have liked that."

"You idiot. You total buffoon."

"What?"

"Is there any part of that fluffy lovey dovey last bit that you can't still do or attempt?"

There was no need to look so thoughtful as the answer was obviously, "No." There were some obstacles of course. The only human female I knew looked like she had the potential to eat any offspring whilst her brother laid the table. In addition, there was no spark, no twinkle, and no way it would ever happen. She definitely wasn't ugly, but I couldn't have a wife that had much bigger biceps than me...... Likewise, I doubt a petite girl would go for a bloke who had man-boobs that wouldn't fit into her bra. If there is I may wish to meet her in about ten years.

"There are places in the universe where human life goes on. I appreciate it's not as easy as going down to your local pub or club and chatting someone up, sure, it might take three months to get to a club, and any relationship today can by default be classed as a long-distance relationship... Very long. But, it's not out of the question, is it? No, so stop looking so grumpy, every option is open to you, good and bad, it simply comes down to a matter of choice, and that, my friend, is all yours."

He smiled for a few seconds, magnanimously, looking at my face intensely for a sign of recognition. I responded with a shallow nod and a half smile. Then, for a half moment I noticed a shift in his position and an internal thought run through Nelsons' mind. I had the impression that he was examining his own words, maybe for some self-reassurance... So, we're not so different.

"Right," he said, slapping his hands down onto his thighs, "I've got a job to do, you haven't, stay here, expect some visitors and I'll be back later." I didn't have time to respond. He flew out of the cabin at pace only to return a minute later. He popped his head around the door, "Excuse me Colin, I should have asked earlier, but, do you like curry?"

"Hey, I'm British, you should know better, of course I like curry."

"Okay. See you later."

Excellent, looks like Nelsons' favourite pre-action meal was a hot one. Lush. At least it will be a nice one if it is my last one. Hope it's not a korma. One by one apart from Pic and Don the crew turned up with almost military precision every half an hour. First to arrive was Marilyn. I knew it was her before she turned up as I could hear a mass of material being dragged along the floor. She swooshed through the doorway, just, it was more of a two-point turn, came in at an angle, grabbed as much of her garments as possible, changed her angle and pulled herself through.

"Looks like a tight fit."

"Is that a compliment…?"

"…. No."

"You don't like it?"

"Not my thing, plus, I'm really not the best person to be asking. It's a bit big, aren't you hot?"

"No, I'm regulated. It's like sweating, but with without the sweat… and the smell you get with the sweat, and the wet patches… Not all of you. Bernie can be a gusher."

"I'm very glad you didn't bring any food with you as that would have put me off." Marilyn looked at me not understanding what I was talking about.

"I got a bit bored and left to my own devices this is what I came up with."

"Is it Panto season?"

"I thought it looked a bit eighteenth century. Georgian if anything. Which made me come to the conclusion that they must have been the most boring of times… Didn't they have better things to do?"

"Yes. Build doorways big enough to accommodate. We did do that, built in a proportion as to allow for a graceful entrance… and massive wigs. You'd be better off talking to Nelson?"

"Why? Did he wear a dress like this?"

"I don't think so, but the Ladies of his day did, or something similar."

"I wasn't working on a history project or anything. No, it's not that important. I was just bored. That explains why Mona gave me a look of outrage. But it does make you think doesn't it. Why we follow certain conventions or rules or practices that nobody questions even though they are ridiculous and for decades, centuries, more."

I suddenly realized I was close to getting, as some say, 'On one.' A very good blow-out-moan-rant, something massively important to me and thus should be to everyone else. But I couldn't be bothered. As it might also encourage Marilyn to join in. Then we'd both be off.

Instead I gave the, 'what can you do?' shrug.

"Then," she continued, damn, "that made me think about something you mentioned." That got my attention. "You noticed how we wanted to humanize ourselves and copy to a greater degree a similar system. Well, we even developed our body shape to be more human, like you were something to look up to."

"Yeah, I did say that once or twice." I, in reality, banged on about all the human mistakes, quite a lot, trying to point out why they, the Squid, were stupid to want to be anything like us in any way... The only thing I would offer, freely, would be a decent stereo and the ability to make music and play it back. Music, that's mans greatest achievement....... Then the pasty.

"Well, I've decided." Marilyn nodded to herself reaffirming something, "the next planet we find that's suitable, has water, decent fish, or restaurant, I'm off. It's about time I returned to myself, and," she smiled broadly, "swam." I smiled back. Then our smiles got bigger. She was happy that I was happy for her.

"Let's hope nothing goes wrong and we don't all end up stuck here, no more Ray, and a doomed planet formerly the home of Pic and Don."

Once more, bang, smile gone before I know what's hit me. A moment crushed, innocently. Annoyingly innocent, so much so that I shouldn't get annoyed. If I do ever get hitched, just remember not to have Marilyn on my table.

"I mean, let's face it, most humans were, as you would say, 'Like a bunch of sheep', although I'm sure that sheep would take offence at that, but my point is, why would I want to do that, why did we want to be like that?"

"... Because you liked the good bits?" my voice got increasing higher in pitch as I asked the question. I realized as soon as I asked it that I was stretching the argument, a tenuous long shot. It seemed to work though, she contemplated it for a few moments at least.

"...... Some of it, we did enjoy the way you would always ask a Squid his thoughts on world cup results. That would always make us laugh, and totally at your expense. If you knew anything at all you would have recognized that 'Paul' the clairvoyant Squid from Germany and subsequently every other Squid thereafter was actually doing a contemporary dance version of a mating ritual, but in his version he fails and instead of 'getting it on' he was telling you that

124

you could, how could I say this... 'Get off.'" Marilyn looked to be reminiscing. A big smile rested on her face.... "He got his own comedy show years after on the back of that. It didn't last long, you can only go so far on a running gag."

I laughed at the thought that Nelson had asked Marilyn to come down and see me to try and cheer me up. It worked, but for all the wrong reasons... I don't like laughing at people, but I couldn't help it.

"What's so funny?"

"Nothing." I said trying to be as neutral as possible.

"Doesn't look like it. You really are quite odd aren't you? Anyway, one reason why I volunteered to see you first was to tell you that no matter what happens and what anybody else says It was a pleasure being around you and I always liked you, there I said it."

I should have responded with a gracious, "Thank you." Then maybe returned a compliment but only the words, "Volunteered," and, "what anybody else says," came forth.

"Nelson told us all that we had to come and see you, on a regular basis, so Ray made a list. And someone thinks you're getting special treatment, as you're laying here and we've all got to come and see you."

"Who? Bernie?" I didn't get the answer I wanted.

"Ooh, is that the time?" she said whilst still looking straight at me. Ray wants me to make a lot of cushions for, for the thing, that thing we're doing, he's doing, probably should get on with that, yeah. Okay Colin, it's been lovely talking to you, better try and get some rest before, well, just get some rest." For someone who was technically in an alien environment she did very well at moving quickly. How is it possible for something that is out-of-your-hands to cause resentment in other towards you? How? I am not bunking off! You see that? Now I'm getting angry because someone else is annoyed because I've been told, no ordered, to do nothing.

Tut tut, shake the head, that's their problem, not mine. Exhale heavily and blow the problem away. That didn't work so well, the problem came in.

"Hello Bernie," I said, trying desperately hard not to let my thoughts interfere with the situation. I then reconsidered instantly and changed my mind. "What's up?"

"That's a bit last millennium. What's up? Have you been getting nostalgic? And what have you said to Marilyn?"

"Eh?"

"She stormed by like I wasn't even there. It's quite embarrassing to get knocked over by a dress. I'm surprised I had the courage to tell you... Hey, don't go telling anyone will you?" Bernie laughed loudly like he had no cares in the world. Nothing like a man who had small burning cinder of hate smouldering within. Maybe I was wrong? It's someone else who has the hump.

"So, everything is going well? Is it?" I ventured hoping to gain a morsel of information that had nothing to do with the words spoken, probably, unless it was a direct insult which started with my name, Colin, and then the words, "you are a..." Choose your own expletive.

"Yeah absolutely fine, I'm way ahead of myself. It's all tickety-boo, as you might say millennium boy."

"No I wouldn't, say that, I don't know anyone that would. My great granddad may have said it, but I really, really, hope not."

"Okay, what about everything is dandy?"

"No, could have been my great granddad again, I suppose, but yet again, I really hope not, and especially not together in the same sentence."

"I'm afraid my generation could only come up with 'Excellent'."

"Excellent?"

"Yes."

"Excellent."

"Yeah, you have to say it in a particular way. You need to watch 'Bill and Ted's excellent adventure'. Or not... but I'll promise not to tell anyone you got knocked over by a single-minded dress if you promise not to say the word 'excellent' unless whatever you are referring to is actually excellent."

"That sounds like a good deal." He struck out his hand. His handshake was firm, he then tightened his grip and grinned, "Awesome." His grin glinted. The misuse of the awesome was somehow supposed to wind me up. It did, but I saw the funny side and grimaced. This definitely wasn't the action I would expect from someone who really would prefer to be lambasting me rather than making me laugh. I know everyone was asked by Nelson to not bring the mood down, but still, that wouldn't stop some people. We love having a pop if we feel justified, regardless of effect. Some do it just for the effect.

I concluded that Bernie was not the person I was now looking forward to confronting. Whoever had a beef with me could poke...

again I was getting angry when I wished not to be... a third party and my choice of interpretation was causing me to get angry and in that respect it was self- induced... I needed to calm my thoughts down. Time for a leftfield question if only to distract myself.

"So, supposing we succeed in everything, you know, like that," I tried clicking my fingers but failed, then failed again, "Well you know, easily, what plans do you have, any?"

"None. Haven't given it a thought Colin... At the minute, it's a glorious adventure, and far more satisfying than anything I have ever done, ever... It may become the best of excuses to not have a plan too. Take it from day to day, wake up not really knowing what's happening or what you're doing... just keep going for forward. Travel? With no plans... there, that's my plan. Quite possibly the best one I've ever had... What about you? Apart from watering your tea plantation."

"........Just that."

A very long pause ensued whilst we dreamt of our own little nirvanas. Mine of course made me salivate so I broke off early and grabbed my phone.

"I need a tea do you want one?"

"I'd prefer something stronger, but I don't think that's wise."

"I'm sure Ray wouldn't mind a visit?"

"Yeah, he'd be best, he still feels a bit guilty. Don't ask Jeb, he's well off on one. He's not best pleased with you that's for sure."

There you go, and I wasn't even fishing for the information. So Jeb's the one who has some mislaid vitriol to spew... Seems a bit ironic... Shouldn't he be praying for me or something? At least a bit of that before wanting to lay into me... Then maybe pray for me afterwards too. Does he just think I'm being lazy?

"What's his problem?"

"Sam has been winding him up. It's what they do. Jeb bites so easily. After all this time you would have thought he'd recognize it when Sam's winding him up. You only have to look at his face. Everybody else knows before he has even said anything, and Jeb always bites."

It gets worse, I thought. Someone winds somebody else up and then that person ends up taking it out on me and in the meantime, I get wound up... Amazing... Once more I took another deep breath and told myself that it had nothing to do with me and I shouldn't let it dictate how I feel. Easier said than done. Bernie must have seen me thinking about it.

"He's not focusing on you Colin. In fact, I've caught him just staring at the wall, even then he might not actually be looking at the wall as he looked more like he was in a deep trance. The wall just happened to be there. I called to him and got no answer. He wasn't even aware I was there... I've seen it before but years and years ago. One of those emotional moments, the ones that I don't bother with... looks like you might though?"

"I like to know if I'm being a dick... and why others think they can be. You've got to have some emotional self-checking system surely."

"... Not if you don't run the chance of ever being a dick in the first place?"

"... Mmm, doesn't that theory give rise to the chance of a super-dick? You know, if they're not the most honest with themselves?"

"Mmm... It does, however super-dicks are easily spotted."

"Just because you spot one though doesn't mean you can do anything about them? Can you? Listen young man stop being a dick because if you don't one day there'll be enough dicks around to enable you to become a super dick, and who wants that, eh, Adolf?"

"He was a mega-super-dick. But amongst his world full of super dicks he was just a super dick himself... when the norm is dick, super-dicks become just another dick. And then it's only the mega super dicks that become noticeable."

"There must be a gene for massive dicks?"

"That really is an inappropriate thing to say as a lady enters." Mona said as she cautiously entered the room.

I thought it best to explain fully, "Idiot. Plonker, numpty, dicks one and all. You know, people who are at their very best are just obnoxious and nasty, and they need no justification to be so. Far stronger words can be used if required."

"I shan't bother," she said with a smile, which also suggested that I needn't explain any further. I obliged. She then sat down heavily on the end of my bed and then maybe for the first time I saw on Bernie's face a look of concern.

"You okay Mona? Should I ask?"

It took a few seconds for her to even consider the question as she seemed to have drifted off as soon as she sat.

"Yes, I'm fine, now," she paused and then paused some more. Then I realized she wasn't actually pausing, she was in fact drifting again.

"Mona," I said softly as if waking her. Again it took a few moments for her to answer.

"Yes."

"You okay?"

"Yes, I just said so, I am now."

"Care to explain why only now? You don't have too." I quickly qualified.

"Aah, Colin's concerned for you sis," Bernie said with an oversized grin.

Both Mona and I turned our heads slowly towards him allowing us enough time to draw out our imaginary daggers. He just carried on smiling looking between us.

"What was that gene you were talking about?" Mona said slashing the smile from his face with her imaginary weapons.

"The massive dick gene," I said directly at Bernie smiling as much as I could. Mona's laugh was infectious and instantly both Bernie and I joined in.

Mona contorted her back then relaxed it and somehow yawned at the same time, "If you must know then I'll explain. I came down here for a bit of peace and quiet. I've been working amongst the madness of fitting rabbits with metal slippers and building, as far as I can see, a huge 'Den' totally suited to the biggest child around, Ray. Not your normal day on board the Flying Fish yet at the same time just as mad as the last... Right, an hour ago Smokey turns up with all the good intentions in the universe, I'm not kidding, inspired by the rabbits he's asked for the same slippers that he can wear. So I fit him with some slippers let us call them, straight onto an old pair of shoc's..." Mona's shoulders were beginning to rise as she spoke, "... Now, I don't know who Fred Astaire is but that didn't stop Smokey demonstrating how much better it would have been if he had played the part in whatever films Fred Astaire were in, that I will now never ever watch. It got very loud very quickly and I don't know if you know this but it's very hard to be heard over such a clattering racket and I wasn't prepared to risk concussion or worse getting to the door. So I endured. I also realized that someone had forgotten to think that we might need a bit of ear protection. Great minds do think alike, they seemed to forget the same thing... So, blessing in disguise, eh? Smokey is presently making ear-plugs out of reducing seaweed in a pan and adding flour. We reckon it's advisable to have a private fitting... Looking forward to that," she concluded smiling and lying at the same time.

We all took a moment to visualize how that would pan-out. By the looks of it not well. We had a group grimace and now we all need a group hug. Which didn't happen.

"Why don't you have a quick nap?" I ventured.

Mona paused before answering me, but I saw the moment in which she thought 'can I be bothered'. Turns out she could, "You Colin, are the only one with a mattress."

Ahh, I thought, at the same time feeling a mass of blood rush away from all areas that would soon show how embarrassed I was. I had no idea what was going on.

"You have the most comfortable position in this ship. There's not a seat left with padding, no sheets left for any beds, no point worrying about that if there's no pillows or mattresses though. We left two dishcloths as that seemed hygienic. Don't use all your toilet paper, there's no more for a while, don't know why that's not as important hygienically but never mind... Everyone wants to ask Marilyn if she would kindly donate some of her freshly made wardrobe but no-one dares too, or can be bothered, I certainly can't. Some of the flooring has rolled up nicely and I think it's presently being draped over the big mound that is everything else in the cargo bay. Imagine an extremely well insulated tee-pee. Ray has left a crawl tunnel for himself that we block up after he's in. He's built himself a small hat cage thing that he's going to put our communicators in. He's given it a name, the 'Anti-anti-distortion-cage'. Catchy."

"I can see you'll, and well, we'll all be glad when this is over. Maybe then you can catch up on a lot of rest." I said, what else was there.

"Yes, I should," her shoulders slumped.

"You can use this mattress if you want to," I offered.

"Oi," shouted Bernie.

Mona sighed, slightly exasperated and turned to her brother. "Look, it's that gene you were looking for Colin."

"Yeah, I know, I was just waiting for a second opinion."

Bernie answered with raspberry.

"I was just about ask Ray to bring a cuppa down, you want one Mona?"

"No thank you I better get back. There's still loads to be done. Thank you for the offer. It might be advisable Bernie, to a get your ear plugs sorted out and force yourself to see Smokey before he finds you, at least that might stop him dancing, unless someone has knocked him out already, hopefully."

"Such a lady," Bernie joked as he joined his sister in the doorway.

Mona smiled sweetly and then punched him squarely on his nose… I wasn't concerned as the actual nose itself looked like it had dealt with a lot of blows previously and I guessed they were mainly delivered by his sister. It must have happened before as Bernie only shook his head and tutted to himself as though he should have known better. They left in silence but maintained constant eye contact fearing sneaky sibling attack.

I then sent Ray a message asking for a tea, if he wasn't too busy. I paused before sending it knowing that he of course would be too busy, how could he not be, so I changed it too 'if you need a break'.

I was very suspicious of the tea that arrived as it was with me within two minutes of sending the message.

"Hope you left the bag in?" I said looking disappointed.

"Don't you worry about a thing, I can guarantee I've made more tea than you, and the English way. It is probably the best way I must admit. Actually, I needed an excuse to get away from Smokey and happily I received your message as I was pouring the milk in. I was already making it. Perfect timing as far as I'm concerned, I had to get away."

"You're not the first."

"Oh, it's not just me?"

"Fred Astaire routine was it? Performed by a proficient albeit multi limbed mad demented Squid?"

"I had Gene Kelly."

"Oh, he's building a repertoire. I wonder what I'll get."

"I suspect you'll be the only one that doesn't get the horror show."

I held up my hands and showed my crossed fingers, "We can but hope."

"And whilst you're at it can you pray that a more normal sense rationality and state of calm graces everyone. Everyone seems to be getting a bit tetchy, we're becoming a bit short fused."

"Sounds like you need Jeb for that job."

Ray shook his head, "He's probably more annoying than Smokey at the minute."

"I've heard."

"How come you're a hub of information?"

"I must be popular." I said modestly and then smiled to ruin the effect.

"Not with Jeb you're not. But you've heard that, I guess?"

"Yeah, I had."

"You don't look worried."

"No, that's because I'm not. I decided that I'm not going to be as that's all his problem, his concern, his lookout. It's not just me though, is it? He's got a problem with everyone hasn't he?"

"Yes. Including God."

"Eh?"

"He doesn't understand how difficult it is being a God though, he doesn't look at it from that point of view."

I didn't want to upset a partially organic computer android that had a sense of its' previous culture, so I tell him that he wasn't ever a God to begin with. I wouldn't want to make him tetchy.

He however noticed the strained look on my face that displayed my true thinking.

"Only in respect that you have to please everyone and that's slightly impossible. They want everything from you and most of the time they ask for the impossible, I mean not everyone can win the lottery jackpot can they? Because that's was what was mostly asked for, I kid you not, so if everybody wins, what do you get? Your money back that's all... People forgot to ask for what would count and matter, peace and a good harvest. I could do something about peace, but never much when it came to the rains and the weather. I was just a man born into position, and if you tell someone one thing all their lives they'll believe you. I was worshipped, that stood as proof that I must be a God. At the same time I could never get the rains to stop so surely that's proof enough that I wasn't. Add to that the simple fact that I also had to go to the necessary house as often as the next bloke. Come on, what more evidence do you need? The problem with Jeb's God is that you can ask questions but you'll very rarely get a verbal response, I think it might come down to a sense of just knowing." Ray gesticulated quotation marks on the word 'knowing'. I'm not sure I knew what he was on about. There's a small chance he didn't know himself. Well no one can really speak for God can they?

"Maybe Jeb should simply pray to God then?"

"Oh, you haven't heard something then, we've all told him that. Sam doesn't help of course."

"I've heard."

"Heard what?" Sam said as he appeared in the corridor outside my door, hunched over arms outstretched following a rabbit. He then briefly disappeared again in the doorway holding a rabbit at this side.

"Bugsy here is a bit of a prima donna, escaped it's fitting. So what is it that you have heard? What have I done now?"

"Nothing out of the ordinary Sam. Just your normal agitation routine with Jeb," said Ray.

"Oh that little nugget. Yes, I've had him up to scarlet before a couple of veins pumping on his head and a hoarse voice but never beetroot and veins on the neck, that was new."

"What exactly was it you said Sam?"

"Well that's the other thing. I didn't actually say anything too harsh, I said, 'Hey Jeb, maybe out here we might bump into your God sometime somewhere? Something like that?"

"I would say though in all honesty that it was what you said immediately prior to that that did the damage?" Ray added

Sam looked quizzical, cocking his head, maybe too much. Ray coughed and pretended to clear his throat and with a perfect mimic and quote made the problem clear.

"If you know that you can live forever doesn't that also mean that you know you'll never meet God."

"Oooh, ohhh...... Ahhhh...... Yeah... Owww... Just one thing, a bit of a smidge off subject, why has he got a problem with me?" I asked puzzled. Ray answered, still with Sam's voice.

"Colin seems to be enjoying himself, sounds like he's running a club down there, he's only got a scratch on his nose, what's his problem hey Jeb? What is it God says about the lazy?"

"Oh, nice one, marvelous. Cheers Sam."

"No problem, any time Colin."

"And what was Jeb's response."

"That God doesn't like the lazy and neither do I," answered Ray, in Jeb's lovely calming tone. An image ran through my mind of an image running through Jeb's mind; Fire coming out of his eyes, flames engulfing my cabin and bed whilst he screams, "Get out of bed you lazy git... Ahhh!" More flames and probably loads of spittle.

"I think he's got the wrong end of the stick? I'm under orders. Twice."

"It might be because last time we all did the work and again you did nothing," Ray pointed out, too matter of factly.

"I was under house arrest and being guarded at the time, and if you must know I've already had a guilty moment about that one and this one, I'm not happy that I'm here I can assure you. I'd much rather be working like you guys. But as Ray can testify I didn't throw myself into the wall and floor on purpose?"

"No he didn't Sam. Do you want to see, I can show you a replay if you wish?"

"No he doesn't want to see, that."

Sam smiled and turned towards Ray and just bobbed his head gently a couple of times.

"Eh? No, no. Ray can I ask you very kindly not to show Sam anything involving my naked butt flying through the air whilst my face collides with hard things, could I?"

Ray took his time in answering, possibly savouring the moment as he watched the furrow in my brow get deeper and deeper.

"Of course I won't," said Ray assuredly. I however remained in eye contact with them both, darting my focus between the two just in case of a sneaky wink. None came. However as a parting shot.

"Hey Sam, can you do me a favour and ask Bernie if you two are related in some small way. Ask him what he thinks. In a small tiny way."

"What?" Sam replied mostly confused. Good, I thought.

"It was just a conversation we had earlier, we had some thoughts, I'd like to know what he thinks? That's all." I sipped my tea and played innocent.

"No problem I'm going that way now with Bugsy. No one escapes Bugs, no more running, we're all doing our bit." He saluted before leaving.

"What conversation was that?" ask Ray wanting to give the correct answer.

"There's no point telling you as I'm sure you already know right? Just wait and see." Ray looked as mystified as Sam had. Excellent.

"So what sort of curry are we having?" I asked.

"Curry?" Ray inquired.

"Horace not mention it?"

"No."

"Hmm, slipped his mind I imagine, well he's got bigger fish to fry."

"Tonight's menu is already set. Flatbreads and dippy things, as it could be the last time I cook something I thought I'd go for something that reminded me of home, haven't got the exact same ingredients but it's close. Then if everything goes alright and per plan we can have desert, well you can. But I'm sure if it goes wrong somehow and I am rendered useless or worse I'm sure you won't really want it."

"Why? What is it?"

"Jelly and ice cream."

"Oh yeah, lovely… Hang on, did you have jelly when you were around?"

"No but come on, would you need more of an excuse if we're successful?"

"I don't need any excuse at all."

"I wouldn't have thought you'd be in the mood if something terrible went wrong?"

I paused to consider.

"It's not something you should have to think about," he exclaimed. I smiled. I was also saved by the bell as my phone rang. Bernie's name came up as the caller. He couldn't be bothered to change that to a recognizable image. Quite possibly intentionally, not wishing to scare anyone off. More likely to be because he couldn't be bothered, to be bothered. I smiled even more as I got ready to answer with the speaker on as to allow Ray to hear.

"This should be good," I said and tapped accept.

"Ha, ha, ha, ha, ha. Well done," Bernie said with an unhappy acceptance at being a punch line. I heard Mona laughing with Marilyn in the background.

"Yes, very funny indeed but, let me tell you that you'll need to go a long way before you can laugh at me considering how big your genes are. A long way… It might be blue but it's not cold."

"Yahay, good shot," I said, because it was and in a way I deserved it. I hope it lifted the atmosphere at least."

"Well there's no point talking anymore as I'm about to have my earplugs done and I don't want to develop telephone manners, so goodbye. Damn." He hung up.

Ray was still looking confused so I filled him in on the details. He then went on to replay the whole scene and call in his head in real time. He laughed during a moments silence. I had taken the opportunity to clean my ears as he drifted off to watch the scene again. Better get prepared for the moulding.

Ray laughed again and before leaving wished me a good rest before Smokey got hold of my head and packed my ears with mush.

CHAPTER 17

My good rest was completely shattered by a bad smell. At first, with my eyes closed I thought it might be something Ray was knocking up in the kitchen. It wasn't, Smokey, without wearing his new tap shoes had entered my room flanked by Don and Pic. I didn't hear them come in but by the time I stirred and sat up it was obvious they had been there a while as they giggled like little children, completely reinforced by the fact that they are small to begin with. Turned out they had been there long enough to make sure the room was full of a putrid pungency somewhere near to over used damp socks and a month old carton of milk... Turns out I missed something too.

"Does this take three of you?"

"It could do if you want?" Smokey groaned. I had the impression that he wasn't best pleased with the job he was given. I don't think many people would have.

"Right put your big head down here on its' side," Smokey instructed like an order. I did as he said so. From my very side on view I still noticed the Cheshire cat grin on Don and Pic's faces. Maybe they didn't have such a defined sense of smell or something... It turned out to be something. The first constituent part... After placing a polythene sheet over the side of my face something Squidged was eased into my left ear, the polythene acting as a barrier. I then felt something gel like settle over the whole of my ear and just over it. Maybe the spread of a hand in total. I couldn't hear a thing, but maybe my smell improved instantly or the stuff was simply closer to my nose.

"What's that smell?" I heard my ask muffled through the one ear that lay on my pillow. Smokey said something which I couldn't quite hear and lip reading really didn't help, as he didn't have any. Don smacked Pic on the back who fell into my bed causing Don to laugh even more. From my position I couldn't see Pic's reaction. I certainly didn't expect to see him fall back the other way into view laughing even more than Pic. Smokey remained motionless and held up the end of a tentacle still, suggesting I should do the same.

"What is that smell?" I asked once more. Again I couldn't hear the answer and Don and Pic almost went through the same routine. Smokey mouthed something over and over. I didn't have a clue what he was on about so I didn't attempt to understand or say anything further. It was obvious all would be revealed when I could move or take the first earplug out. That took what seemed like a long time during which Smokey finally conceded to the joke, me, and joined in with the other two jokers. At least they didn't point. Then finally Smokey nodded and gave a close thumbs up. Finally. I sat up, half deaf with a giant muffle over the side of my face.

"So, what's that smell," I said with a grimace already on my face.

"Rabbit poo," answered Smokey without batting an eye lid, which he did have.

"Sorry, I'm partially deaf. Did you say rabbit poo?"

"Yes, I did, that, seaweed and flour," Smokey replied, this time enjoying the moment, he went on, "Now, give me the other side of your head, leave the other one in, but don't put any pressure on it."

That made the whole procedure very uncomfortable indeed. I held my head off the pillow for the duration and by the time I could sit upright again I had a niggling ache in my back and I was rendered completely deaf. For the next few minutes I had the pleasure of being insulted and made fun of, but I didn't give a damn as I was in complete silence, I tried singing to myself and couldn't hear a note. At least it momentarily stopped all joviality elsewhere. Smokey then glued in a soft metal strip in-between the two moulds and finally, and I'm quite sure too long, my personal earplugs could be removed. I made an obligatory suction sound as Smokey did the honours. Amazingly having my ears back didn't prompt me into using them in anyway and ask what they were mumbling on about. Instead I gazed in silence at the creation that not long ago nestled itself in my head... think of two murky brown breast implants that resemble earmuffs. That should do it for you. They also really stank.

"What the heck have you been feeding the rabbits?" I inquired.

"Seaweed mainly. Washed and dried of course, too salty otherwise." Smokey replied.

"Yeah, of course."

"Anyhow, I can't malinger. Things to do, things to do. Come on you two. Where's Horace likely to be?" Smokey didn't look back or offer a goodbye. Don and Pic followed behind but stopped to offer a raised hand, as ever it looked offensive but I knew it wasn't. At least this time.

I was glad that they did leave as it gave me a few moments to do a few stretches in order to get rid of the ache in my back. I was back in the bed within the minute as something cracked somewhere else that shouldn't have and it felt worse than the niggle I was trying to get rid of... I was beginning to feel old. I could dwell on that thought and annoy myself endlessly or, laugh, as in reality I was a very old man in the body of a man who was due a midlife crisis sometime soon...... I've always had the thought that we grow old by major event, trauma or crisis and not birthday. Apart from the big ones of course, the milestone ones. I was a teenager until I fell in love and then when that ended I was in my early twenties, but it was only then that I grew up. I was a man, a young one. But I almost instantly could look down on teenagers who were actually only a few years younger than me... Then you fall in love again and you consciously decide to be an adult and lose all those years... You know what it's like when you occasionally bump into an old friend in the supermarket and they have their kid with them. You always stop to say hello and leave thinking time must be getting on and you're definitely older based on how much the child has grown in height alone. If it happens too much you could make a measure of it. A death of someone automatically makes us recalculate our own potential remaining life expectancy. A thought I no longer had to contend with. Not only because my life expectancy now was excessively long but because I was hardly liable to bump into any old friends or their children. Something I was very glad of with most of them. No, all of them... A joke that became a saying in my day was the good thing about other people kids was, you could give them back. I'd go one step further and far safer, never take them in the first place... I even shaved for some of my friends' kids as I noticed that a big hairy face hardly ever got a smile, more often than not it achieved the opposite. I stopped bothering after a while. Grow up, get a life, we can't all have baby soft skin, think yourself lucky, you big baby.

I instantly told myself that I could do with a shave. If anything was to go wrong later at least I would be looking good. Or at least as good as I could get. However, the only problem would be I wouldn't be able to shave the centre of my top lip as my nose guard rested there... I could leave the guard there on purpose so that when it was removed I could reveal the 'Hitler' tash. I wonder if that look ever made a comeback? Like the name Adolf that faded in popularity after the beginning of the second world war. Did it ever make a comeback? I doubt it and hope not. Fortunately, he didn't have a more popular name, Steven or John or similar, and in that respect it's a shame Adolf wasn't named something we could all do without like Bernard or Neville or Dick..... Even my name wasn't the greatest I'll admit. Colin, not very exciting is it? Doesn't leap out in anyway as it sounds like an accountant's or a data crunchers name. My favourite Doctor Who was a Colin though, and not because we shared the same name but because he looked the part and had a scarf that no one in their right mind would ever choose to wear. Rebellion against authority through un-trendiness. He, Colin Baker, I think may have contributed to the worse dress sense decade the planet ever knew. Oh no, every decade in the eighteenth century was the worse. Georgian pomp and enormous wigs and Beau Brummel. If you have to build rooms big enough to accommodate a dress and a hairpiece then there's something wrong with societies logic... someone should have said, "No" or even better, "No, if you want it then you build it, I'm not being mugged by a mug in a big wig. How about I build a bathroom instead because actually, everyone really stinks around here."

There you go, once again, I think about some nonsense and only succeed in convincing myself to have a bath. So that's my facial hair and hygiene taken care of. It is always a great way to relax. Is that the right thing to do before our second escape attempt? On the other hand it's a great way to relax and waste a load of time....

The bathroom was nothing special. Practical would be the word used by the designers. Polished metal everywhere with no noticeable joins, broken down by small white moulded bathroom units. The bath itself was longer than the normal human bath by a good metre. The Squid must have replaced the original ones, which must have been tiny in comparison, and had the good sense to have them big enough to actually stretch out in. Have you ever seen a bath long enough to lay flat out in, I don't think so? In such a brilliant place to relax in, why do we deny ourselves the full potential of the very thing we seek. It's a bit like going to a big gig somewhere and leaving when the band say they've finished.... They haven't, they want you to ask for an encore, you want to ask for an encore... so why leave? There's a bit more you can have, don't leave yourself short... Now I definitely need a bath as I've wound myself up moaning about baths being too short.... Worst of all I've got one in front of me that's too big... Never happy... So I decided to have one. Why not I thought? I do have the pleasure of Jeb's visit to look forward to and I'm going to need to be as relaxed as a sloth during a massage for that.

It's good to know that some things don't change and that small idiosyncratic eccentricities carry on regardless. I always whistle

139

whilst getting ready for a dip. It somehow settles me. Always a different tune that I've made up. Add to this the minute spent getting the right temperature of the water, which sometimes leads to the whistle having the occasional 'Ooh yeah' or 'Ow oww' jazz stab. It can all lead to a moment in which we can choose to reset and re-sync to ourselves and not what the universe wants us to be... Sometimes it can backfire. With all the noise around me I didn't hear Jeb come in. He must have waited a few moments before coughing.

My whistle suddenly included a Tom Jones yell, the force of which caused something in my nose to crack so I yelled again. Jeb's stern expression didn't budge... Great, I thought, the very person who shouldn't have heard or seen my attempts at relaxing probably now thinks that I've taken laziness to an art form...

"Hello Jeb. You okay? You look deep in thought there."

"I........."

"Am," I answered for him.

".......... Yes."

Maybe I should bite the bullet and ask why he has a problem with me, explain it from my point of view and ask him kindly to remove the growling scowling look from his face. It doesn't suit him and it concerns everyone else and as I seem to be the reason for your high blood pressure it concerns me a lot more. He's wasting his anger and all the energy that involves. Put it to some use... I really should say something. How about the Little Birdy tactic? Maybe not. A more mature approach might be necessary... It's not like Jeb to hold back normally when things annoy him. It only takes a small turn on the crank or a tiny red rag to set him off. He must have been asked, told or begged not to lose his rag and say something... I didn't ask to be here. I am not being lazy and skipping the enormous task of rearranging the ship that everybody else seems to be engaged with... I smashed my face already don't you give me any grief.

Jeb's face softened and then a look of concern crossed his face. He then pulled up the chair to the side of the bed and sat down.

"Are you okay Colin? You're grinding your teeth."

I broke my thoughts to check the status of my mouth. Jeb was right, I had been grinding my teeth as a consequence of the thoughts running through my head. The angry ones that were building up. Jeb leant forward and put his hand on my forearm.

"Whatever it is, it's going to be alright," he said a smiled.

"... So why are you so miffed and think I'm just be lazy?" there I said it. I didn't make me feel any different, I thought some sort of weight was supposed to be lifted. It didn't help that Jeb only looked mystified.

"Excuse me. I recall a conversation in which I answered 'Yes' I don't like lazy people. But it wasn't in context to you. Someone else may have put it in that context? And they may also have taken my mood as being angry, I suppose?"

Now I was confused. There was no reason for me to think that Jeb would lie. In fact I knew he wouldn't. In which case, not only was there a massive misunderstanding that had repercussions and mostly mine but no one had considered Jeb's mood and the reason for it. If he had the same face then as he did a few moments ago it would have been very apparent that something was on his mind... could he have been facing away to hide it at the time? So nobody noticed?

Protocol required me to forget about my own frustrations, that needn't exist anyway, and ask what was running through his mind and causing his manic features.

"So why are you so wound up Jeb?" Sometimes a straightforward question is the best and easiest approach. Hopefully it gets respect and a straightforward response. Although I doubt Jeb's answer would be anything but. My hunch couldn't have been more correct.

He shuffled and settled and a restful smile penetrated through. The use of those muscles was a rarity. I smiled back.

"You are going to be the first person I'm going to tell but, it's something for everyone to hear... I let them know as and when I bump into them... I said you were going to be the first person right? Meaning?"

"Meaning that, I, was going to be the first person," I said with no confidence. Jeb shook his head.

"Meaning I've told something non-human already, prior, before." He shook his head again and continued, "It's G...."

"God!"

"No, it's Greg, it's Greg. I've asked him if he would kindly like to reside somewhere else. I thought that would get your attention." It did, so much so that not a single thought crossed my mind. I could sense a load of questions trying to get in but it was as though a bouncer had appeared and asked for tickets to get by. I said something that wasn't even a proper word, just a sound, if anything just a one syllable unintelligible utterance. An 'Uuuh' moment. Jeb

141

tilted his head and pondered something and then nodded to himself. He must have agreed with himself.

"Yes, yes, in a way I suppose I was angry with you, in respect that you instigated all this, I wouldn't be here, and I mean, free, if you hadn't come along. Once I had my life back in my own hands I realized that my life could continue as I should. If I can't die then how can I get to heaven? I can only get there through Him, and dying first..." His voice trailed off and his gaze ended upon the floor. He was smiling though. He then regained his energy, springing upright and catching my eye.

"When we get home, when, then Greg has agreed to help fertilize an area big enough to be comfortable. If that's possible? There might be a place that's suitable? Earth is a big place there must be a place? And then, I'll just get old a die. And hope God judges me good enough to open the doors and let me in?"

There was a very long pause before I answered. Unfortunately I mumbled as before, I used different vowels, but I still looked like a numpty, again. Jeb noticed and laughed. I nodded repeatedly allowing Jeb to continue.

"I'd like to travel as I did before. I know it's not hospitable, but I'm kind of used to that. The desert was home for me for many a year. I'd need a vehicle that's sealed and has air but I'm sure there's something to be found."

"That's very," I said hoping something would come to mind. Nothing did, or nothing halfway appropriate, "natural, of you." I grimaced at my own choice of words.

"Yeah. You're not wrong," he said but had his own look of self-confusion as though he possibly didn't understand himself.

"Brave, is that the right word. It's very 'Brave' of you? No, that's not quite right. I'm sorry, I'm not happy with 'Natural', there's something far more correct than that. It's not 'Brave'. Courageous?"

"Sacrificial?"

"Eh?"

I was glad to see him laugh before he repeated his suggestion.

"Well, you know, I'm bringing it on. This is the beginning of the end for me. I'm effectively killing myself... slowest suicide in history."

I laughed and because of the known infrequency of his quips I laughed again.

"What's so funny?" he asked with his normal knocked expression. Which of course made me laugh again. One of those laughs you have to control with heaving breathing for fear of damage or pain. It took me a while to calm down enough to explain that what he said sounded funny. 'The slowest suicide in history'. He didn't understand why and only squinted.

"Please don't get me wrong it's, great that you are making a choice, I'd be scared, right now I'm still scared, but I haven't had my whole life yet, mid-forties for someone from my era was nothing, it might not even have been mid-life? I also saw myself retired, small place by the sea, simple life, daily walks and feeding my neighbours cats... unfortunately I'm scared enough to want to avoid old age and I can... That's why it's 'Brave'. Yes it's brave. That makes me a coward."

"That makes you human."

I hated my hair being ruffled as a kid and now I can say I hate it as an adult too.

"I'm an old man, I can do that," said Jeb as he stood, "is there anything I can get you? Anything you need? Apart from God?"

"Well if you're offering I would love a cuppa.... Marilyn has decided to do the same you know, be herself when the environment suits. Sounds like the old gang splitting up?"

"Old gang?"

"Well okay. New crew."

"Yeah that sounds better. Especially as you're in it. Back in ten." He span on his heels and left.

CHAPTER 18

Ten minutes can be an awfully long time if you're deep in thought. Maybe Jeb was right and I should do likewise? Go grey and get old gracefully? I neglected to think that with Greg's help it could be a lot easier. Especially in old age for sure, but, I'm sure he'll help anyway in either case? So that really shouldn't matter, it's very nice to know though. Greg is also like an onboard antibiotic factory. Who would want to get rid of that benefit? Right now, not me... I'm glad he's plant material and not a worm.

Of course, the problem with deep thinking, especially when concerning your future, is that you are seconding guessing things that haven't happened yet... So is there any point? Right now for instance my thoughts took me to a place that involved a sunset, two chairs, an umbrella, and a lady with long flowing hair, hand in hand and looking towards the horizon. Not forgetting a table on which is placed a tea pot and two cups and a milk jug. My future. I don't think so, somehow? Who is that lady? Let's face it, I didn't see a face, I haven't really had the chance to meet anyone just yet.

How does anyone meet anyone these days anyhow? It's not like I can pop down to the local bar and then go onto a club. Too old for a club any way. It doesn't matter so much as I won't be finding one soon... I couldn't hang around in one of those Malls and wait for a woman to come along, that it in itself could take ages and unfortunately I'm also the sort of guy that can take ages just to pluck the courage just to be able to smile a someone I might fancy, and that's only the beginnings of a hopeful spark. Then there's the slow courtship, I'm keen on respect. No one is going to have time for me in a place where you need a spaceship to go anywhere... Please let there be a huge settlement on Earth. A place where the only vehicle required was a bicycle. Maybe for the second time I should do as Jeb would do and pray?

An overriding thought flooded my mind. I wasn't going to ask Greg to leave my system, no chance. No further discussion required... Not until further notice which I doubt will arrive for thousands of years... Or, extreme boredom or depression smacks me sideways if that's sooner? Even then I'd still be tempted to carry on, time is a great healer after all, and I do have an awful lot of it. So, technically, all things should pass. Eventually.

What I might want to consider is the fact that everybody else has their own plans and they may well want to go it alone. That thought might come quite easily for most onboard as they've been cooped up with each other for over a thousand years. A change of scenery can easily lead to a change in company, it's what the scenery requires sometimes. Getting away from it all might not be enough. You might need new voices to hear and listen to as well... What do they all want to do?

I suppose, considering the situation were all in it's a good time to be thinking about your long-term plans. At least for those who like to plan things out... It's much more fun being spontaneous though, not all the time, and not just when you're young enough to be able to deal with the consequences. I'm talking about unexpected nights out and impromptu parties mainly here. They can be good fun but everybody knows of messy stories that should be a deterrent, but aren't. It's only when you hit forty or so that you start to consider the morning after, before the obvious fun and laughter to be had that night... All that's different of course if you're married... especially if the other one can have a lay in no matter which day of the week a party is on, because they don't work, and as they don't normally drink they're obviously entitled to drink as quickly as and much as they wish, and in any case it wasn't them that was driving, and because I had to cut it short for work the next day they had to start early and drink quickly anyway, so shut up...... Good to see my issues with the Ex still cropping up every now and then and when you least expect them. She would then always be ill with gusto. Where her guts would go. Vomiting with such force she could put out fires, made the little girl from the 'Exorcist' look like an amateur. Yet somehow, she never hit her shoes, everything else, but never footwear. Sometimes she would slip of the shoes before any attempt was made to even get close to a basin or bowl or bucket. I should have put shoe racks on the walls because she managed to hit them okay... I wonder how much time will pass before those issues pass? Not as long as the stain on the wall...

I was glad to have my thoughts broken by what sounded like a stampede of deranged five-year old's at a beginner tap dancing class, and just then not to be disappointed, a shuffling enraged troupe of rabbits scuttled passed my open door down the corridor. I wanted my ear plug mufflers as they went by. Ray followed keeping up the rear, when he got to the door he nodded, I nodded back as though it was an everyday event. It was a good few seconds before I recognized that I wasn't satisfied with what just happened.

"What you doing Ray?" I shouted.

"Rabbit distribution. I'm presently a Rabbit herder. Sam's doing the same on the lower decks. It's all going very well." He may have easily said something else but the thunderous chorus of tiny tip taps drowned most things out. I heard the door open at the end of the corridor, that was followed by a moments silence, Ray whistled and barked a hopeful order and the rabbit storm moved on. The door then closed with its' familiar clunk. Then, a lone tip and then a tap followed a shuffling scrape. I imagine 'Stomp' rehearsal sound like this on a slow morning. Eventually a what must a been the equivalent of a teenager rabbit stopped, probably out of breath, in my doorway. It looked at me opening its' eyes at it did, maximum cuteness. It must have asking for help? Take these ridiculous items of footwear off me please, or, kill me now? It decided on a cross species plea of help and slowly fumbled its' way over to my bed. It maintained eye contact all the time not letting us notice its' plight. Then to make sure I got the point it tried jumping onto the bed and failed miserably ending in a heap. Undeterred it tried again with the same results. The rabbit then, resigned to failure sat motionless, after hunching his back, and gave up. It looked like he wanted to give up a whole lot more than just his attempts at some comfort and company.

"Have you been talking to Jeb?" I asked. If twitching your nose counts as an affirmative it was enough for me to feel a pang of sympathy and pick it up and place it down gently on the bed at arm's length, as to not get hairs or worse anywhere near my pillow. The last thing I needed right now was a sneezing fit. I didn't know that I would get one but just in case, not worth the risk. The rabbit looked at me with thanks so I went one step further a slipped of his metal slippers. Overjoyed with happiness it hopped once towards me and nestled itself under my arm supported by my chest. It then sniffed a couple of times and laid its' head down on my forearm. I smiled, only for a few seconds as I soon realized that I was unable to go anywhere or to even make myself comfortable. Pinned down by a two kilo cutey. I smiled again at my own stupidity and situation… It must have felt secure in its present position as it didn't even acknowledge Jeb's arrival with the promised tea.

"You've got one friend then," he said placing the tea down on the bedside table, "the bloody things are all over the place you very nearly didn't get your tea and I very nearly attacked a rabbit that couldn't move. I hope they're a bit more active when needed. They all look exhausted. Just look at your best friend there?"

"Yeah, poor thing, I think being man handled by Bernie was probably enough for this little one."

"Oh yeah, if and when you get to the kitchen whatever you do don't open any cupboards, if Ray asks you to. He thinks it's very amusing watching your reaction to discovering a rabbit where the plates should be."

"Yeah, not my idea of fun."

"It's nobody's idea of fun. Apart from Ray's. He says it's good for keeping up morale. If a hat was involved I might find it slightly amusing, at best."

"I'd still struggle," I said and gently stroked the rabbit."

"Well don't let Bernie see it without its' footwear."

"Don't Bernie, what Bernie?" said Bernie as he strode in bearing tuning forks. One small normal size one, something you might expect to see and consequently have a go yourself, and, one the size of my lower arm. Elbow to finger-tip.

"She looks like a beaut," I said impressed with his handy work, and trying to keep him from looking down beyond the rabbit to his other pieces of metal work, presently not on the rabbit under my arm. He didn't respond to my praise.

"You know we might have to eat that so don't go giving it a name or anything? And why have you taken his clogs off? What was the point of me doing it in the first place? Well, have fun getting those back on. It won't be the cute little bunny you now think it is, I can tell you."

That explained the many plasters on his hands. I simply thought he was a bit slapdash in his work, and nicked himself a lot. By the sounds of it they were indeed angry rabbit wounds... I hadn't considered that side of the equation... It was only going to be the one, I really should be able to handle that? He waved the tuning forks.

"Right, do you need a lesson in how to use one of these babies?"

"No, I'll be okay I think?" He handed me both with ease, to my one free arm. It dropped instantly to the bed.

"Watch out, they're heavy."

I pulled my arm free and picked up the normal sized fork and whacked it on the side of the bedside table and then placed it single end down on the tabletop. The whole thing hummed and resonated. The rabbit bolted upright and scanned the room for threats. It saw one, Bernie, it then curled up under my arm again and hoped the big ugly man wouldn't bother it further. I put the tuning fork back on the bed next to its' bigger brother.

"And I'll just prepare the area you're in. Give us a hand Jeb?" Jeb got up to assist. Between them they managed to lift a two metre floor section of the corridor, and heave it out of the way, revealing the support structure beneath. Then carefully walking along the struts they re-entered the room. Bernie grabbed the big tuning forked and hopped down into the sub-structure. He turned and smiled in anticipation of the upcoming throng, the inner child about to enjoy the moment. The resulting boom was like a wall of bass. The room hummed the fixtures rattled and the bed wanted to glide around on micro oscillations... The rabbit didn't move, I presume it thought its' days were numbered and gave up, the trumpet called. Bernie clambered out and returned once more, and only now he decided to wear a smile that said I'm happy with my work.

"Nice bit of work Bernie," I said.

"Yeah, I know," he replied losing the grin and all sense of fun. Jeb smiled for some reason. Possibly spotting the obnoxious attitude exuding from Bernie for no good reason. I think he thought I needed saving.

"Come on Bernie, I'll give you a hand."

They both left me in silence and not wanting to negotiate anything right outside my door.

I was very glad to have ironed out my misunderstandings with Jeb. I wonder how different our relationship would have been if I let myself believe something that never happened... He certainly wouldn't have helped usher Bernie away as he just did.

CHAPTER 19

"Don't worry my big eared friend the big ugly hairy man has gone away," I said whilst gently stroking my new buddy. He twitched his nose which I took as a thank you. He twitched again which I interpreted as "you forgot he smells." I took the opportunity to giggle. I stopped moments later when I noticed something spooked the rabbit. Its' ears sprang up and around to face the door.

"What's up dish head?" I said to the rabbit.

"What are you calling me? I've never been called that before. It's not even that offensive, as I sort of do have a roundish head," said Nelson in a strained voice from the corridor. Negotiating entry into my room was presently a small obstacle course that needed concentration, flexibility and maybe some muscles you might only discover climbing.

"I was talking to my new friend here," I answered as Nelson finally got his feet securely fixed to the floor safely on the door threshold. He straightened his clothing before going any further. Once done he looked up smiled and noticed my new friend.

"Hewo wittle wabbit," he said advancing towards the rabbit raising his arm as he did in preparation to stroke it. Both myself and the rabbit looked slightly shocked for a moment. The rabbit mainly because he was nervous, so much so he took to opportunity to leap off the bed and hop off to the bathroom in hope of an escape route, I guess? I looked more in shock because of the cutesy voice Nelson had used.

"I've had pets before," he said, obviously instantly understanding my look, "Not as scared as that one and only ever cats."

"I had a cat. Well more a cat moved in and never left and somehow, we, then just me looked after it, fed it, took it to the vet.... I wonder what happened to it?"

"What? It moved in somewhere else. They're not so stupid you know. Best fed animal on a ship. They mug everyone with their big round eyes. Never met one that liked water though, odd that. Water, water everywhere and all the boards did shrink. Water, water everywhere my cat needs a shrink... You can thank Coleridge for that one."

"Should I be feeling nervous or excited, because in all honesty I feel nothing at the moment apart from a tiny bit bored," I asked Nelson.

"You mean because of the next few hours and any potential, losses? I used to get a moment of calmness before any engagement but it was part of contemplating the negative outcomes. A sort of planning for un-foreseen's I didn't want. Is that what you mean?

"... No... I just want it to be over and I've been in bed all this time, that can't help."

"No I guess not. Don't worry though everyone seems to be, off, in their own way. I told them all to see you at regular intervals of half an hour. Not everyone within half an hour. They'd make for a rubbish bunch of sailors back in my day.... but what can I do, it's not as they are getting paid, is it? However, the one bonus is that we're not too far away from getting started. Ray is double checking everything and then, well, we'll be ready to go."

"Or go nowhere."

"We'll be fine." Nelson obviously heard some concern in my voice as he quickly added, "I promise."

"It's not as though I've got a better place to be."

"... You've been thinking about what you're going to want to do next?"

"Yeah. Jeb and Marilyn have made some decisions and, they're big ones. You know, the ones that will affect everything that happens in their everyday future for the foreseeable ever. Everywhere to go, but, nowhere to go."

"Beautiful... everywhere is home. Right now here is home. If home is only ever one place you can always turn around and return. What's the problem? Of course in our case it's a completely different place."

"Shall I scrub that thought then?" I smiled.

"You know what I mean?"

"I did have a thought of finding the exact location of my house and putting something there. Park a ship. Put up a tent, a big one, it just wouldn't be the same though. The view would annoy my senses. I'd be out of whack with myself. Memories of noisy neighbours and their crap parking, the flickering streetlamp and the noise of bin night. The noise of students forgetting bin night."

"Doesn't sound like it's something worth missing?"

"... Familiarity?"

"It's just nostalgia now, but, if you like the place so much why not find the exact spot and do something? Got something better to do?"

"What about you? I can't imagine you want to settle down. That has to be the last thing you would choose to do?"

"You know me too well Colin."

"Well no, not really, it's kind of obvious. There's no home, no, Lady at home."

"The same situation separated by just choices. Destiny on a this or that, a yes or a no... Well if you choose to settle down at least I'll know where to go for a decent cup of tea."

"I'm going to need a big cupboard for a lifetime supply of tea."

"Just as well you have a lifetime to find one."

"I should check but I might as well ask. Do you know if at any time someone genetically altered a cow, and made a micro cow, something that could stand on the edge of a coffee table and not tip it? That would save a lot of hassle, like getting a full-size cow and a regular size shovel. Imagine that, just picking your cow up from the table and holding it above your cup. One squeeze or two? Could be on to something there?"

"No. Someone did try that very thing but unfortunately it failed, when they 'Moo'd', because of the pitch change they sounded like all manner of alarms and warning bells. They only moo'd more when they saw panicked humans. Which strangely enough could lead to a stampede... The remaining stock was sold to a planet where ears didn't bother to evolve. Marketed as "organic lawn moo-wers.'"

I shook my head at how bad advertising can be at the same time thinking what else could you do with a product like that. I preferred my idea though. Employing it as a tabletop fresh milk delivery service. I giggled to myself thinking of how you'd have to coax over it with some lush looking grass to get a squirt.

Before I had the chance to explain my extra thoughts to Nelson, whom I sure wouldn't mind one himself now, just for tea, we were interrupted from distance. Ray from somewhere in the corridor was tutting at volume. Nelson smiled expecting something designed to be culturally insensitive was just about to follow. A harmless banter bout opener.

"Tut, tut, tut... tuttertut... Miles from anywhere and anyone and two Englishmen are talking about tea. I thought it was me that normally talks rubbish."

"It is," Nelson answered for the both of us just in time for Ray to appear in the doorway looking perplexed as to why he had to negotiate a floor without flooring.

"That really should have been done last," he complained.

"Working with purpose. You should understand that Ray?" Nelson said.

"Especially when that purpose is your own life," I added as though I knew anything.

"Well it appears that whatever it was it has worked we should be ready to go in half an hour, even less at this rate. Can you go to your cabin to have your muffs done and can you put the rabbits boots back on? I'll announce the Go's over the ships tannoy."

"What are the Go's?" I asked in all innocence.

"Well, when I say 'Go', you do your thing. In position, muffs on, tune away at will. I let it all build up for a short while before getting Smokey to go to phase two. Driving away at speed and shoot the auto bot if it looks like it's about to do anything. So only two Go's, and you only need worry about the first, and I'll route your screen onto the bot so you can watch to see how phase two goes. You can just about see the screen from your position."

I wanted to reply in a sarcastic manner as Ray barked away but as it was he who had the most to lose right now I simply answered with a nod and a thank you. Nelson smiled noticing a demonstration of humility and then quaffed.

"Ooh. Look at Ray getting all General.... That's how you answer that Colin." He laughed stopped immediately and stood. "Earmuffs call loudly," he concluded and left with caution.

"Phases and efficiency. Might appear as abruptness to an untrained ear," Ray answered back with increasing volume to allow Nelson to hear. Nelson's response came in the form of a chuckle. Ray simply smiled. A hearty smile that suggested something genuine...

"He loves me really, now don't forget the rabbit's footwear, please." he said flapping his eyelids and half smiling, being as offensively inoffensive as he could be. He couldn't hold it for too long before he broke into a giggle. I laughed loudly. Then the thought that I shouldn't really be having this much fun at this particular moment wondered into my thoughts, so I stopped.

"Yes, I'll sort out the Rabbit right now. Another tick on the checklist."

"There you go, you know what I'm talking about."

"Any last words of advice Ray?"

"... Hmmm... next time ask Nelson, but, in my experience all I'd say is, make sure you go to the toilet."

I wasn't expecting that as an answer but from his look I knew that he meant it as a serious thing to do. You wouldn't want to be fidgeting about busting for the loo whilst operating a weapon that had sights, I thought.

"I'll make sure I do that. I'm going that way to catch the Rabbit anyway," I said.

"I'll give a standby before the go. Please don't ask for an explanation."

"Standby, fine, got it."

Ray noted my muffs and industrial tuning forks, then moaned again as he worked out the easiest route over the missing floor section outside my cabin door. I followed his advice and then delicately put the rabbit's clogs back on. After the first small struggle the fur-ball surrendered to his fate, I think I caught I look saying, 'I thought you were on myside'. I could have made that up though. Something in my brain again told me to be sensible and remember that this is not the time to be enjoying myself. I then took the Rabbit to the door and lent out as safely as I could with him and placed it gently on a safe section he could easily move from. He turned back to look at me. He may have said anything in his twitching nose but I'm taking, "Thank you for your room, but why do I have to wear these ridiculous shoes... I pooped in your bathroom." He then half-hopped off to the open door at the end of the corridor...

As if by instinct I took a deep breath and seemed to focus. I only had one thing to do but I was going to do it with gusto and vigour. I was going to concentrate and do it right. My face had obviously caught up with my internal feeling and had decided to become ferociously stern. I felt furrows that I never knew existed. In an attempt to balance and neutralize this facial feature I tried to look surprised and then unsurprised very quickly and repeatedly. This was only effective as a temporary measure it lasted no more than five seconds before I felt it beginning to drop and wanting to curl, so for the next couple of minutes I made highly exaggerated facial expressions in a further attempt to nullify too much furrowing. The last expression I made, one that contained shock as well as surprise, happened whilst a very relaxed feeling was in motion. Ray's head appeared suddenly on the screen which I was only inches away from.

"Oiii," I proclaimed falling back onto the bed.

"No time for napping Colin? Standby. Get into position, don't put your muffs on yet, wouldn't be able to hear your 'Go', would you? Give me a couple of minutes to crawl into position I'll give the go. At that moment put your muffs on and let slip the dogs of tuning. I'll wait until, until, whenever it's too much and give Smokey his 'Go'. All clear?"

"Yes, all clear."

"Don't forget to let the rabbit run wild."

"The rabbit is roaming already."

"You'll go far Colin... I'm changing the channel on your screen and the next time you hear me, go for it." Ray's head disappeared and in its' place perfectly framed appeared the bot.

How could something so small cause so much damage. Which pales into insignificance next to the damage the small biological device presently sailing its way to Planet Crrrrk could cause. If you're a policeman you don't stop the husband driving at speed his pregnant, and in labour wife, to the hospital, do you? You give them an escort and radio ahead... Maybe a small reminder on the way out that speeding is still speeding though. If you want to get your face in the paper just smile and walk away. This little bot is reaping havoc right now and it's not even aware, just when we need the police assistance with a smile bot. If only there were papers for bots?

Tools on the floor, shuffle into position along the struts. Sat on one, banging the one in front of me. Place the muffs around my neck and the tuning forks on the strut that's getting the pounding. I would be watching the screen from a very tight angle but it will have to do. If the bot was going to do any damage it would be over pretty soon so in effect watching the screen was a pointless exercise anyway. Just concentrate on the job, not the view, I thought and then vocalized a moment later as a reminder. It worked as a warm rush of blood spread across my body causing a cold sweat. On instinct I picked up the massive lumps of metal in front of me, they were heavy. Numpty, I thought and should have said out loud, how am I going to get my muffs on? So I replace the forks and decided sitting quietly until the 'Go' was given was the way forward... Silence. Familiar furrows and now a dry mouth. All easily attributed to the present situation, even without the explosions. Turning my attention to the screen might help. It didn't, instead I saw the bot, motionless, merciless, and looking second hand, innocently standing in the way of us trying to save a planet and everything that lives on it. My mouth was now so dry I couldn't swallow.

"Ladies and gentlemen of the Flying Fish would you please, go. That's a go go. Go on the go. One for Colin, Colin that's a go," said Ray sounding like a holiday camp announcer.

"Plonker," I said to in response.

The Muffs went on and all I could hear was the sound of my own heart beating, quite quickly at the moment and my breath coursing its way around my sinuses and nasal cavity. That was until I smacked the heavier of the two forks onto the strut and placed the single end down onto its appointed position, the middle of the cross section. My hand felt like it had pins and needles as the fork shook itself into a spasm and vibrated everything around me and a deep boom wailed out as the hull felt it. The second went down, slightly lighter but the effect exactly the same only the pins and needles running around my left hand tickled more. I counted thirty seconds before I felt the first waning. So I repeated, paused and then did the same with the second fork. The sound was massive and I was very glad to be wearing the muffs. Poor rabbits I thought as one bounded into view at the end of the corridor freaking out it, it was soon followed by another who was even more buoyant. They clattered into each other and pogoed off back through the doorway. I wanted to laugh but needed to concentrate. Ray must be near calling phase 2? I began to feel a static hair lifting sensation with the hairs on the back of my head and became aware of the rubble of noise coming from behind me above and below. The ships harmony had been brought to life and it sang. I was beginning to think we needed bigger muffs, even a suit. I swear my position was being shifted by millions in micro bumps shuffling me about on a microscopic level, easily readjusted as I ban the forks down again any moment. I managed two more hammerings before I recognized the ships engine being switched on. My head swivelled to the screen. The bot twitched, but nothing happened, it then began to look very flustered, shaking and convulsing, a tiny whisp of gas shot out the top. We edged forward gently, the small jolt before the zoom. Then zoom…

The last thing I saw of the bot was of it beginning to spin, following its' last gasp of force, its' own momentum carrying it off powerless as its' mechanisms finally gave out. It may well have completed its' purpose and fired its' disruption charge? We could be disabled and now we're drifting at something over light speed? Should've found out when to stop banging? Can I stop? Mmm? I don't know the answer to that or much else so best not to stop then, I thought, so carried on. I watched my hands and now wrists vibrate away, I was losing the sensation, finding it hard to recognize the strength of my grip. On the screen stars were now just streaks of light that couldn't catch up with themselves. I could have been watching an episode of Star Trek. The stars then caught up with themselves. We've stopped. Nelson's face and his thumb joyously appeared on the screen. He was laughing and ducking his head as an arm slapped him on the back and tried to hold on for a squeeze. Nelson sat up and gave another volley of thumbs up and a huge job done smile. He then pointed to the muffs suggesting I, like everybody else left them on, but, at the same time I could definitely stop banging. I realized too that I had no choice as my heart must have been going as fast as it has ever been in its' long life and that, although I could go on it was probably best to stop... I was beginning to look like a madman who couldn't control himself or a blood thirsty nutter who needed to quench. In reality, I just lost it for a moment, something of myself disappeared and left me with only the facilities required to perform the task I had, which, let's face it, was tiny, so a lot of me was able to leave. Thus I perceived myself as a crazy man. I had an urge to watch 'Apocalypse Now'.

However, a stronger urge to disregard the ship's computer doctor eased its' way into my thoughts and shouted at me, 'Go to the bridge, idiot!' I extracted myself from the sub-structure and with a hop in my step made my way. Every rabbit I came across appeared very annoyed, wide eyed and frantic. I stopped for a moment and slightly lifted my muffs. I put them back almost instantly. It sounded like Big Ben had a hangover and he wanted everyone to know about it. I came across one frozen in fear and tried to pick it up, it bit me and then came back for another go. I held up my foot to keep it at bay. This was no obstacle, the little thing bounded over it, landed on my knee, which he used as a launch pad to jump from and kicked me where no man wishes to be kicked. Hearing my response, I presume he took off and hid amongst the crowd, blending in. I wasn't able to tell much as I was doubled over with my eye-lids clenched because my eyes wanted to fly out. I also took the opportunity to swear like I'd never done before. I knew no one was able to hear me as we all wore head muffs... All apart from Ray, who tutted and handed back my communicator, on which a message very soon appeared.

"Does your mother know talk like that?"

I messaged back," She taught me." To which the reply came.

"I'm not wearing any ear protection."

"Ah yes. She taught me," I said again for some reason and then called him a bad name.

He giggled whilst typing another message.

"What happened to you?" I explained the scenario which he found very amusing. He also took great care when walking near any of them. Which I found very amusing.

"Oh yeah, glad to see you're well," I said as nonchalantly as possible and then hugged him. It felt a bit impulsive and I wouldn't normally extend to such a welcome, but, I was genuinely happy. He in return broke the embrace in order to grab my cheeks between his thumbs and forefinger and shake my Jowls whilst shouting something, I quickly lifted a muff to listen.

"You beauty!" he shouted.

"No, no, no, you the beauty. All yours my friend. You could have taken a hit there. The worst that would happen to me is what? I remain motionless, and have a massive sense of guilt over ever suggesting the idea in the first place. Pic and Don never speak to me or of their home world again and become the last of their kind? You'll go down in history Ray, you'll go down in history... Actually, how come the British Museum had none of your stuff? Never Discovered?"

That question certainly wiped the joy from Rays' face. I heard as much when I finally removed my ear protection.

CHAPTER 20

He wasn't disappointed for too long. As soon as the door to the bridge opened the cheer went out. Ray was hugged, slapped, applauded, high fived and proclaimed. Sam offered me his flask as he grabbed me and forced me into the huddle. Nelson shook my hand. Smokey from his chair gave me a thumbs up whilst lighting a cigarette, pouring a drink, plotting a new course and fist pumping the air. Pic and Don broke off the mass and started a little jig. Marilyn and Mona joined in. I took a brief moment to look around at the smiles and happiness and as a result shouted, "Come on." I was very tempted to join the dance but saw the flailing arms of Mona and decided against it. I should also add that I can't really dance and that may have had some bearing on my decision.

"So what's the plan now?" I shouted over to Nelson, who was looking very tempted to have a quick spin.

"Join in," he shouted back stepping forward and doing so. I pointed to my nose as an excuse. Jeb went halfway and clapped along. Sam added a clap and an enthusiastic foot stomp. Bernie looked to be recounting his part to Ray possibly to avoid the scene. An improvised tune soon became the overriding sound. Quite well done too as it seemed to be in tune with the wailing ship. Then, as always, the tune got faster and faster until a natural crescendo took over finishing at the exact same time as exhaustion, the physical exertion finally becoming too much for everyone, leaving just enough energy for a last cheer.

"Then what do you think happens Colin?" Nelson asked breathing heavily.

"Off to save the day?"

"… How about a cup of tea first? Come on."

That wasn't quite the response I was expecting. None the less that's what happened. Nelson placed an arm over my shoulder and lead the way. We all were soon gathered in the canteen. All apart from Ray and Smokey who were left in the bridge to plot a difficult course. One we weren't told about before because we might panic a bit.

"It's like space surfing. Only you start at lightspeed and then get catapulted. Imagine being on a surfboard and you're riding a wave, a big one, and then, you turn on a jet pack and hoist a sail….. Stalling the engine at the exact moment the gravitational pulled takes over and then restarting it the exact moment we gain speed again. That's

158

the only, the only, moment when there's any potential for, for, well, obliteration of some kind."

"Is there more than one?" Sam pointed out.

"We have to make up time now. That's the objective. We don't know what we're up against. We can't say for sure anything apart from one thing... They are closer than us. Simple. If they get there first why bother going on now?

"How long is a moment?" Bernie asked.

"About five seconds." Nelson answered.

It didn't take that long to turn the engine on and hit a button. It could be controlled automatically so in most ways there didn't seem to be a problem. Jeb soon put an end to that.

"We only need to be a metre out at the wrong moment and we're imprints and star dust. I shall return to God, but I'm not so sure about you lot. So at the same time, I'm happy to do it."

"Hang on, one metre out and you're happy to do it?" Sam asked.

"Yes. Plus, the Admiral is right. The only way we can be assured to even just get there first is to steam ahead, and then, and only then will we be in a position to help. Right?" Jeb looked around the room and brought us all under his gaze. In turn we silently agreed with him. No one asked any further questions, of anyone... I got the feeling instantly that we were all amazed and shamed that it was Jeb who had to convince us of the requirement.

"Hey, what are friends for?" I said smiling trying to encourage a lighter mood. No one joined in.

"Can I take it we all agree?" asked Nelson who left the silence lingering before adding, "I'll take that as a yes." He looked amongst us as he tapped his communicator.

"Admiral, what are your orders sir?" Ray asked officiously.

"When can we go?"

"Just waiting for an asteroid wave to clear and we'll be ready to go. Wouldn't want to smack into one of those. Ooh, that would be terrible."

Nelson grimaced slightly. Not the sort of thing the troops should hear. He tried smiling reassuringly.

I thought about playing with the words 'ship' and 'wreck' in a statement but quickly thought better of it. Instead I asked how long we had. Nelson relayed the question to Ray.

"Mmm. About four minutes for the next window of opportunity. I reckon. The next after that is ten days."

"Is there any need for a red light and the call to stations?" asked Nelson.

In perfect synchronicity and silence we all stood and left the canteen. Our stations in a moment like this were already defined, they were the same for nearly all light speed travel. I was on the bridge, with Nelson, Ray and Smokey. Everybody else was in the travel cabin. A room full of first class travel seats with almost full body seat belts. Better than the one I had from my gunner's chair.

It occurred to me as my chair descended from the ceiling that I must still be running on adrenalin. I wasn't sure if enough questions had been asked? I found a few concerns creeping in. Mainly, how can you tell what's happening light years away? I was slightly consoled by Rays' smile and Smokey's reclined position and slightly disturbed that I didn't try and get an answer to my thoughts. I just strapped myself in and went dry, again. Nelson turned from his chair and asked if I was okay. I nodded back. Which was a small, well big lie. I couldn't verbally answer because my lips had nearly stuck together and I couldn't swallow any longer. Nelson turned back and I noticed him grip his arm rests.

"Ray, whenever you're ready." Nelson said gripping harder.

"Good day Ladies and gentlemen of the flying fish. My name is Ray and I'll be your captain for this flight. We'll be flying at an altitude of no consequence and at a speed of really, really, fast. With a flight time of twenty minutes before sling shotting around a black hole hopefully we'll arrive at our destination before we left..."

I could only look over to Nelson's chair and hope he would turn around so he could see my concern. It was easy to spot at that moment. I looked like a statue. A statue of a very scared person. You could say petrified... He didn't turn around. I don't think he wanted to. No one had mentioned a black hole in the mission statement...

"There'll be absolutely no need for an inflight safety demonstration as any problem will probably lead to......"

"Ray! Just press the button." Nelson ordered without regard for the anger in his voice. I was glad Ray stopped his chat but noted Nelson tone. I'd never heard him speak like that. Especially as it was Ray. He of course noticed his folly and apologized instantly and returned his attention to his control panel. He'd probably checked it a thousand times but used another check to keep his head down and his eyes away from Nelson.

"Initiating in five, four, three, two, one."

Once again the stars of the universe whizz by like fireworks leaving a flashing trail of themselves. A barrage of light engulfing our view. Ray's fingers worked his control pad the same way I would furiously hit button on early arcade games. The only difference being Ray wasn't looking at what he was touching. He must have been making minor adjustments as he went. Not a reassuring thought at all, but at least he was making the changes as and when he needed to. I was beginning to confuse myself with mixed positives and negatives so I naturally applied my normal holiday flight method of control, falling asleep. Let's face it, if something happens, by which I mean we crash into something, at this speed I'm not going to know about it. So, my thinking is, if I wake up, I've arrived... Yay.

I always found it very easy to fall asleep in anything that was moving. All forms of transport. Now was no different. It may have even been quicker than other times? Once I recognized the sounds around me and they seemed normal I could relax and use them as a white noise background hum that lulled me to my subconscious destination. I wondered what I would dream about?

A train guard asked me for a ticket. I didn't have one. I was going to be fined. The guard pulled out the form and began to fill it out. Somehow he knew my name? The fine could be paid now, now, now, Colin...

I'm awake, it's not two thousand and four. I'm awake. I know that's a good thing for some reason. Ahh yes, we didn't crash and Nelson is telling me everything is fine, repeatedly. That makes sense.

"I can't believe you slept," he went on to say.

"I can't believe I went along with that and woke up."

"Reasonably easy if you have a Ray," he answered very sure of himself.

"How long was I out?"

"Four hours. How did you do that?"

"I'm not so sure."

"Well, the good news is we're ahead in the game and now there's only three months of travel at a more normal speed."

"Eh?"

"Before we're in communicational range."

"Eh?"

"Space Colin... It's a big place. You didn't think we were going to pull up outside a customs control and walk in did you?"

"... Yes."

161

"The hardest part is yet to come. Well, it starts now. Limbo time in which anything could happen and all we can do is wait."

"Can't we do sling thing again?"

"Not if you want to get home... My advice, take up a hobby."

His words didn't inspire me that much. Three months? That's three months without being able to open the front door. No porch to loiter in, no garden to escape to, no shed in that garden to hide in... not even a letter box to peep through... in addition, I'm already staring at walls.

"There is one conciliation Colin. If you'd like to step forward and look over to you right you will notice a big thing that looks like a cruise liner. Which is handy because that is exactly what it is. Same shape only fifty times bigger than the ones you're probably used to. Stupid design for space, just an iconic design I suppose? Well we've just ordered a load of everything and it's going to be here any second. Everyone else is in the canteen banging cutlery on the table singing songs waiting for it... I'm surprised that racket didn't wake you up? Anyway, are you a korma or a vindaloo sort of man?"

It took me a few moments to answer as I was contemplating what it would be like booking a cabin and having a holiday instead of everything that was going on here...? Still wouldn't be able to open the front door.

"How is it you could pull up right outside this thing and not the customs office?"

"Simple really, it has a homing beacon and, it delivers curry!" Nelson said as wide eyed as possible reinforcing his point.

"The universe just got a bit smaller," I said observing the dozens of smaller ships buzzing around the liner. Occasionally darting in and out of cargo bays fulfilling their own daily missions. Amongst the swarm a tea chest size box made its way directly towards us.

"At least we don't have to tip the driver," he joked.

CHAPTER 21

I've never liked the words 'over' and 'indulged' next to each other. If I've indulged then surely, I've over-done it too much already so no need over emphasis. Over emphasize, see what I mean? In this one case though I think I'd be justified, and that goes for everyone. Apart from Smokey and Marilyn who steered clear of all sauces just in case. They enjoyed the nan breads and washed the sauce completely from some fish. Bernie and Mona didn't mind consuming the extra portions. We had things that tasted like chicken but weren't chicken and vegetables from planets I couldn't even pronounce. Desserts and sweets made from fruits and berries I instantly wanted to have more of and harvest. The silent bliss at the end of the meal was only broken by clothing being loosened and quiet groans of pleasure.

"I'll get the kettle on. Hands up for a cuppa," I asked.

Only Nelson responded. Everybody else looked exhausted, all they wanted to do was sleep. It had been a very long, adrenalin fuelled, busy and at times confusing day. It was also the first time we could afford to relax. Obstacles had been over-come, more may follow but there are none at the moment, so don't stop yourself enjoying the now. By the looks of it enjoying the thought of sleep seemed to be looming over everyone. Not so much myself, I'd done quite well earlier. Nelson seemed to have a bit of energy left too. He gave me impression that he was taking the moment to reflect on the day's events in order to consider if anything could have been done differently or better. He nodded to himself every few seconds going over something intersected by a couple of frowns.

Slowly people cleared away their mess and tidied, then they surrendered to the call from the land of 'Nod'. Some offered a 'Goodnight' as they left, they were the ones left with energy, as others just looked around nodding with a half raised hand and then shuffled off. Smokey was the only one to say anything understandable.

"Everything is on auto. I'm off to bed."

There was a prolonged moment of silence in which time I made a second cup of tea and Nelson reflected. He must have liked what he saw.

"It's been a good day Colin. A very good day... Did you enjoy yourself?"

"I'm not sure if I would call it enjoyment.... Massive excitement and then absolute relief. I smiled very little, do you know what I mean?"

"Yes, but when you did, it was a biggy. Right?" he replied nodding wanting me to join in with him. So I did.

"Hey, I almost forgot to ask. I put Ray out a bit when I asked why he wasn't represented anywhere in the British museum?"

"I took out the French ship all his artefacts were on. Stuff that was destined for the French Museum. I was the difference between him being spoken about in history lessons at school and displayed to the world or, well, just a voice somewhere that you may once hear an echo of... He then saw how history treated people, especially in films, and was glad to be only known by fish just off the East African coastline. A pile of carved and painted building rubble on the seabed. He accepted it as fate. Besides, what could he do about it? What could I do about it? What could anyone do about it?"

"Not a lot I suppose... A lucky find by an archaeologist at some time?"

"Everything would have been worn away. All the information which is on the surface of the stones would get smoothed out. Then add to that the fact that I probably demolished half of it. Luckily nobody has found it or worse, filmed it. Imagine if somehow they found out that a statue of Ray clearly had its' head blown off by cannon fire? Imagine watching that episode on the discovery channel, with Ray?"

We both remained quiet for a few moments to contemplate that scenario. I then realized there were many outcomes so I decided not to think about it at all and change the subject.

"So it's plain sailing from now on then, that's good. Leaves us plenty of time to formulate a plan for the next problem. How exactly do you stop a bunch of potentially genocidal Squid with the will and power to do so actually becoming genocidal.?" I instantly realized that my change in subject was probably not a good idea.

"You want to start that discussion now?" Nelson asked, surprised by seriousness of the question and thereby giving me the chance to decline.

"No, maybe not right now."

"And don't forget, we're now fugitives from the law, and we've Police equipment, their stuff... They're really not going to be happy with that."

"They'll understand. Once we've explained. Won't they?"

Nelson replied by shrugging his shoulders and blowing his lips.

"I kind of hope that's you wanting to practice the trumpet, but I don't think I'm right, am I?"

This time Nelson shook his head. "We might not get the chance to explain ourselves. You should watch an episode of 'Space-Cop. Camera. Spaceship.' Then tell me what you think?"

"Maybe I shouldn't? Is there anything else I should be aware of?"

"There's going to be a lot to understand and things to know about Colin. For all of us. There's good guys and bad guys and there's the worst kind, the ones that want to tax you. Look at it this way, if you live on a planet with a government you're going to pay tax at some point. If you live on a planet without a government you're not going to pay taxes but will at some point, I imagine, wish you could..."

"I was always happy to pay my taxes. As long as they left me alone.... I was self-employed once and just found myself correcting their mistakes. Taking days off work to work for them unpaid. Then of course there's always a minister who tells us to pay our taxes and do the right thing and forgets to tell us he keeps his all his money the Cayman Isles... in the interest of fairness other tax havens do exist."

"Isn't it in our nature?" asked Nelson, possibly hiding something.

"It wasn't until the first guy did it. And then slowly everyone cottoned on. Of course you need enough money in the first place, but if you're willing to hide it, I'm going to want to know how you got it in the first place? Especially if you have anything to do with the way taxes are formed."

"So if you had a lot of money you wouldn't be tempted?"

"Well that's the point isn't it. If I had so much money I was thinking about a tax haven then I've probably got too much money already, so what am I worried about? Greed isn't healthy. Banks lend my money to the poor keeping them poor and competition drives down wages keeping the poor poor and having to borrow from my huge stash, making my stash even bigger... Where's the fun in that? Great for me but not much for the masses who make up the equality in the formula of that mechanism."

Nelson looked at me with a taught frown and a distressed shake of the head. "No, please don't bang on," he requested.

"... Yeah, you're right, sorry. That's all irrelevant now anyway I suppose."

"Everything is different. Apart from one thing. Getting up in the morning, applying yourself and going to sleep at night. Everyone needs to do that. Also have a plan, of some kind, or at least chase something. Whatever that may be? We all seem to be wanting to do things. Jeb relinquishing Gregg's capabilities I find, mmm, brave. Marilyn wanting to just swim and return to her greater self I find admirable…Things. The things we do. And we have to do them too. Smokey wants his own tobacco plantation that might be a bit different but you know what I mean. You'll have to find something to do. You'll only get bored otherwise. I could always use a gunner? I could also do another cup. You having one?"

Of course I was. I passed him my cup as he stood. No need for words. I then drifted off for a moment and saw myself looking like David Bowie's character from 'The man that fell to earth', in the scenes from his home planet. A desolate and barren sandscape, no water and his family dead or collapsed. He's forced to take drastic measures in order to simply survive and has to leave everything he knows and everyone he loves… Okay, my problems might not be that severe, it was the sandiness of those scenes that popped into my head as that was planet Earth now. A bite of a truer reality that awaited me when I finally get there. Not the gilded image that comfortably sits in my brain where everything runs smoothly and I spend most of my days drinking tea and gazing at the horizon. I might as well add a few songbirds I'm dreaming that much…. Maybe the harsh truth is I'd be better off staying exactly where I am? Become the permanent gunner of the Flying Fish? Everything is here after all, including the best doctor I've ever had. There's company, even though that looks like dwindling. There's also a really loud sound system and that might seem inconsequential, but it's actually a vital part of life as every now and then you have to go all Spinal Tap and turn it up to eleven. I could get one for wherever I end up but herein lies my first problem and it's a small one, which doesn't bode well for the future, that of, where would I actually get one, and where would I get any music to play on it? I very much doubt secondhand vinyl shops exist anywhere near. Maybe I shouldn't have even escaped in the first place as I had my stereo and my music there. Forty albums, fifty cd's, even more music on tape. The last time I played any of the tapes was ten years before my assignation. I doubt they even move now, the tape has probably melted into itself around the reels. At least the cd's will work, they're indestructible, right?

The art of drinking tea you realize must contain leaving your brew to cool down. Remember, the thinner the vessel the hotter it will be and the longer the heat will last. This time should be used to either offer banter and fun if in a group situation or if alone to contemplate recent events and think about life. As Nelson had done with vigour only three minutes ago. It is possible to be in a group situation and take an alone moment because you may need to and know the benefits of the alone tea moment. They are quite easily spotted amongst your tea peers. One sign would be the glazed, seeing through the wall or thing in front look. The other would be the concentrating yet confused face. Nelson noticed this one.

"Something on your mind Colin?"

"… Nothing unfortunately, and I mean no thing. I've been struck by a bolt of moron and I'm feeling empty of, something? The power to think about the future. To make a decision. I know I have the perfect opportunity to do something, but I have no idea what?"

"What are you waffling about?"

"Waffling is all I'm good for at the moment," I began to feel myself looking through the wall.

"Why don't you go to bed? Sleep on whatever it is?"

"I'm not tired," I answer in a tone that suggested I wished I was.

"Good, cos' I'm exhausted and off to bed."

He finished off his tea and washed his cup delicately. Respect to the vessel. He might also be allowing himself some time in which to formulate a question or have a suggestion. Sometimes best saved making for Special tea moments. It doesn't have to be poetic or prophetic. Sometimes candid and blunt works more effectively as they are the one that feel like you've been smacked about by some flat wielded by someone bigger than yourself. For someone who has done that much sailing Nelson didn't have much knowledge of tact.

"You've got a couple of years and more before you even see Earth again. That's a lot of time to do a lot of thinking. So take it and don't panic… As you're up you might as well take the night shift then, eh? I'll see you at, tomorrow," he said with a very cheeky smile. I don't think he had much intention of setting an alarm of any description. Leaving me no option but to laugh heartedly.

"Goodnight."

"It certainly is Colin."

It remained that way. Nothing happened. I watched space from the drivers' seat. Occasionally regressing to a childlike state when the reality of why things were whizzing by so fast became too much to comprehend and I felt nothing but an abundance of amazement. Life is simply easier when you feel the beauty of things and not know why they are that way, and, there's no reason to find out. If Jeb was here right now he would be claiming that the beauty only proves God's existence and I should thank Him for it... Maybe I should? The sky was beautiful from any angle though, from anywhere, in my opinion, however it all got there? I would certainly congratulate God for his work if I ever got to meet him... Jeb would be happy with that.

Throughout the night I had the regulatory tea breaks every two hours and being alone and on nights a sneaky tea every other two hours. Equating to a lot of tea. I wondered aimlessly around the ship several times needing to stretch my legs and un-stretch my bladder. Way too much tea. I also relieved as many rabbits from their bonds as possible as I went. Fortunately for them I went a lot. I did contemplate leaving the rabbits with their big metal clogs because at times, when a few of them were gathered together and were moving about it almost sounded like rain hitting the ship. A nice moment to drift off to and pretend it was a late autumn Friday evening and the rain has come again to say hello and clear the air... At times the rabbits made it sound like a storm was kicking off but I won't go into that. I'd only depress myself.

Instead I distracted myself by giving the canteen a good clean and then making a mess again after an early morning breakfast and tea. So I gave it another wipe down. I must have then got carried away on the energy of the cereal thingy we call breakfast as I decided it would be a good idea to give all the communal windows a wipe down too, including the screen in the bridge. No doubt Nelson would have told me that I should have been following computer docs advice but neither of them were around so it was easy to ignore that thought. Plus, I needed something to do. I knew I should be considering my many futures but now was not the time. I didn't want to think about these things so the mundanity of cleaning gave me a moments rest from my restful mind... thinking too much at four a clock in the morning was never a good idea no matter what you did, or were doing? For instance, at about half three in the morning I considered taking manual control of the ship and trying a barrel roll. It must have been a serious thought as I considered it for a moment and then decided that if I was going to do that I might as well add a loop into the mix. I even looked at the button that would allow me to do so.

Ray turned up ten minutes later and proved to be a handy spontaneous distraction. He needed to press a few more buttons and alter the flight path. He then reset the ship to auto and offered me a cup of tea. I escorted him to the canteen.

"I did consider creeping up on you and shouting boo, you know?" he admitted. He chose not to just in case I clobbered my nose again. For some reason I thanked him.

The conversation soon developed into the very subject I was steering clear of, the future, and where we were in it. I wasn't even at day one or even looking ahead just yet. Things, ideas, possibilities were merely wisps of thoughts, not even mists yet. Ray spoke with some wisdom.

"I suppose you are new to this." Ray nodded to himself very content with his choice words and I sat back and nodded in agreement. He was right, there really was no need for me to be rushing into anything just yet. I should in fact take all the time I need. Had Nelson asked him to have a quiet word with me?

"I, on the other hand…"

I leant forward waiting for him to continue. It took a while.

"… Have no reason to settle. No reason, no desire. You need food and water, sorry, tea. I don't. I'm not human in that respect. I can go a decade or so without recharging. More if I shut some systems down. So my feeling is I should journey on, understand more, learn new things, see what I've never seen. Take it in. There, that's the phrase, take it in, you understand that one, right?"

I nodded. "Well there's certainly a lot of it, so I imagine you'll have a lot to do."

Ray half smiled. Some of it had a tinge of sadness however. Some thought wouldn't allow a full one.

"More importantly, so much more importantly, what am I going to do without my friend Horace? I don't know if that means I'm scared of the thought of being alone or I would miss him and our friendship if I settled down and watched him sail off."

Yet another good point. We all need friends. There's another subject I'm going to shove into the 'Not Now' compartment in my brain.

"We have fun. Why would I stop myself from laughing? I'd end up alone, sad and miserable. That would have been from my own making. Doesn't make sense, so I'm going to drive on Colin. I'm looking forward to it."

"Makes sense Ray. Let me know if you find anything interesting," I said with a grin knowing that he would and everything is interesting to him. Even the mundane. He couldn't help but know things and want to understand more. He would get excited about watching a documentary on paint drying. So as Nelson said, it wouldn't be good if there was one concerning Ray. Fortunately for me Ray gave me the perfect excuse to avoid any further discussion on anything.

"You look terrible Colin. With those tired eyes and your blue skin you could have easily been an extra in Brave Heart. I'll take over, you go and get some sleep."

I didn't need to be told twice and at that very moment a wave of tranquility ran through my body, even my nose felt better. My bed beckoned and with every step I took I slouched and slowed. This meant I had enough time from my cabin door to the bed to undress, breathe and sigh heavily once and aim for a spot to collapse on. I was left with seconds to spare to fidget under the duvet before my lights went out. That night I dreamt I was drunk by a cup of tea.......
No idea?

CHAPTER 22

Not too much of note happened over the next three months. Two birthdays, one Christmas and a new year. It was a strange thought that I had breached three millennia. Though that thought didn't last too long when I put it into context of well, everything else.... Smokey became the freshly inaugurated table tennis champion, as he cheated. He stood on the table. It was the only way he could play the game but maybe he should have just been the umpire. We offered him a highchair but wasn't having any of it. He also became champion of the backgammon league... because he cheated. He'd leave a tiny bit of goo on the dice. They would stick instantly displaying exactly whatever he needed. You've never seen so many double sixes. We all let it happen as it became quite funny and just accepted whoever was second in the league was the actual champion. Which was me, and now you know why I protest too much.

Nelson must have given the same advice to everyone as he gave to me... Take up a hobby, find something to do. None of us became spoon whittlers but we all took up something. A new skill or something educational. Ray offered classes in anything we wanted. Bernie became a horticulturist. Mainly with the intention of growing trees. It turned out he was a bit of a tree hugger and may well have wanted to whittle some spoons after all. Mona joined him in these classes and took a more practical brief, that of growing stuff you could eat. It looked to me like they were after an easier, simpler, something they were used to, sort of life. Then later I discovered that Mona was also practicing the art of being a club D.J. and that Bernie was looking into building a club. The sort you dance in and not hit balls or people with.

This was excellent for all of us as we got invited to nights in a pop up club. Something of a practice session for Mona and her bouncer barman manager brother. Marilyn would provide the scenery and Ray would project amazing light shows. At some point in the evening Nelson would timidly ask for a particular track and Mona would oblige. She'd add her own mix to it which worked every time and it was amazing seeing Nelson rock out to the Starsky and Hutch theme. That's what he was doing all this time when left alone in his cabin... Practicing his moves, and to be fair he was good, better than any of us. It had been years since I had danced and somehow I think I may have missed dad dance style stage and prematurely hit grandad style instead... Terrible. It wasn't long before I stayed mainly out of sight and just tapped my feet and nodded my head. Not always in time. Sam wasn't much better, every dance he did had to happen with his thumbs in his belt loops. Marilyn danced to every tune. From first to last. Everyone interpreted in a different way but always with a smile. I must admit, I was jealous. I saw in her and those moments a sense of freedom I don't think I'd ever experienced. Maybe my English upbringing meant I wasn't ever supposed to... Morris dancing, need I say any more?

Jeb became somewhat of a fitness fanatic. Reasoning that without the aid of Greg he should try and get fit and stay that way for as long as possible. I tried getting the nickname Rocky into everyday usage but it didn't catch. Everyone actually admired his decision and that gave him a respect that disallowed casual jokes. This also meant that the secondary nickname attempt of The Teflon Kid also failed.

Sam looked into all forms of brewing and distilling and offered his services to Bernie and his night club. He had been making moonshine of some description for centuries but admitted he never liked it. It served a purpose for him and that was enough. Now he had the chance to experiment with taste and he spent many an hour with Ray in the kitchen discussing herbs and spices and the chemicals that they contained, how they reacted to each other and what conditions were required trying to acquire and extract the same. The best storage and even the best sort of vessel to drink the results from. Because apparently there are...

For longs periods of time the ship was amazingly quiet. If you weren't busy doing something as part of the crew then you were probably asleep eating or reading. All of which require no sound. Jeb's running through the corridors the only noise at times and the longer the weeks went on the faster he got and the longer the sessions lasted.

Nelson took a more sedate route and took up the pen and wrote poems and then the sketch pad came out. With Rays help he manufactured some paints, brushes and constructed an easel. Unfortunately, he also made some canvases out of some sheets and a covering of a traditional treatment made from a solution of boiled up and reduced rabbit bones. The stench was horrific. Smokey begged to open a door whilst we all begged Smokey to smoke more. The air conditioning got rid of the smell in seconds but it returned even quicker. It was like a ghost had farted and was so embarrassed he couldn't show himself and was afraid to say 'Boo'. The pot he used to make this foul formula was ejected into space where I used it as target practice. Everyone came to the bridge to watch and we banned Nelson from making any more. A couple of days later when Nelson had an unveiling of his new work all memory of the pungency was forgotten. We both complimented and laughed as we recognized ourselves aboard the Victory in naval suits standing in rank whilst saluting the viewer. I saluted back.

Marilyn became very industrious and we lost more sheets. This time to the fashion industry. Which was a shame as I refused my new outfit of a Hari Krishna alike copy preferring my now worn in Adam Ant ensemble. I doubt even he would have worn it though, not enough frill... over the weeks everything got reused or just got shorter or ended up as a cloth. Here best work was on paper, and I'm not being patronizing, but on paper she could let her imagination go and could, on paper, use materials and body shapes that weren't available within a zillion miles. Then every other day or so new soft furnishings would appear. Cushions at first, then seat covers, pillow covers, tablecloths, napkins... Napkins! A few more cushions, now scattered, randomly of course, in the Mess room ironically Then curtains. What we, at least those of us with real feet needed was socks. Did any of us ask? Did we hell. We daren't ask for something so mundane and uninspiring and menial. Bernie responded to this by making himself look stupid whilst trying to make some rabbit fur lined slippers. He'd been making Huggy style boots forever and somehow Marilyn forgot that and instead got so irritated with his groans and yelps that she grabbed his attempt straight from his hands and finished them in half an hour. He wore them the second she was finished and then showed them off as much as possible. "Ooh, feels like cramp, better stretch my legs a bit, here from my chair, at least I have toasty feet eh?" His pomp didn't last long. We all had a pair by the next afternoon. I darned a sock that developed a hole.

That however, was about as much as I did do in those three months... I darned a single sock... my only practical act helping my future, the warming of a single toe... I did other things, but nothing to write home about. I watched a lot of films. I watched a lot of television. I bathed, ate and slept, a lot. There's tea of course, but I do only have a regular size bladder so don't think I did too much. Is twelve a day too much? I sat in on other people's courses, not really participating or even listening. I just wanted the company or to hear a voice in the background like a white noise... I stared into space way too much. I couldn't resist. Just as well I didn't have a fish tank? Lastly, and I shouldn't take credit, because it just happened, I returned to my normal milky complexion. Night shift graveyard grey to be more precise. The pallor most English people settle on in February. I could do with a holiday I reckon? In a sunny place.

Together we continued with all our normal duties and jobs. On top of that Nelson threw in some surprise battle station drills. At four in the morning. Obviously we were pathetic. Nelson laughed as we staggered onto the bridge yawning, stretching and some of us swearing. We knew that a drill was coming up, so none of us figured to panic. Maybe that was the problem? I'd guess so as the second time it happened we weren't told in advance and cut the time in half, and Nelson only laughed again.

Pic and Don spent most of their time contemplating what their home world looked like. It had been thousands of years after all since they had seen it and they'd had no news since the day of the accident and the Squid took over. They had signed up as youngsters expecting to return and never did. They had an extraordinary long-life expectancy as a species but Greg was aboard to help out. They had probably outlived everyone they knew.

No Squid ever became a plumber and as a consequence they needed Don and Pic's natural and cultural heritage skills to maintain their own ignorance and lifestyle and clean limbs. Plumbing on planet Crrrk was a primary school lesson. It started when plumbing fees simply became too much and everyone ended up doing their own. It didn't take too long before it simply became the norm and then it appeared on the curriculum. Unfortunately, so unfortunately, they'd never bothered to have a centralized water system from the start and everyone just laid their own pipes wherever they wanted, one for the stuff you want coming in and one to get rid of the stuff you want nowhere near. Sounds like mayhem? Is was, the environment became perfect for algae and other underwater plant life to grow rapidly which meant more plumbing, this time with filters and cleaning chambers with expansion tanks and other stuff I have no idea about. All of which requires, more pipes. Which led to even more algae. A sea of green, Don described it as. Getting on a Star Ship and flying off for a few years sounded like a nice get away from all that, at the time. Now, they were almost as new to the planet as we all were. You included. Pic spent one evening worried that everyone had left the planet and now algae was the dominant life form and who knows, the whole crew might get eaten by a carnivorous plant that could have at one point in its history been defeated by a good net and a current. Their conversations began to follow a pattern excitement for the return, apprehension for what they might find, a sadness for what they never knew, excitement and a resigned whatever to the future. They always went to bed happy. "It's all good" became their own nighttime mantra. Everyone always agreed.

CHAPTER 23

There was standing room only in the bridge an hour before we were due to even see our destination. Most people were there, in my opinion more to see the reaction of Don and Pic than the actual planet. The screen was on maximum magnification so we could get an early view and to see it in all its' glory. Everyone had a smile on their face, apart from Nelson who was waiting for the unexpected, and also myself, who may have to deal with the unexpected. I sat in my gunner's chair, suspended above the others and observing the view via my screen's graphic interpretation. So naturally an hour later when I could see a single pixel I believed to be Planet Crrrrk and I heard nothing from anyone else I began to wonder why?

"Ummm, it should be there?" Smokey said. He then tapped a few buttons.

"Where is it?" asked Don.

"What's happened?" questioned Pic his voice raised a few tones, panic rising.

Smokey tapped again, this time faster and more of.

"Is there a problem?" asked Nelson wanting an answer promptly.

It seemed only right that I should pipe up. "It's here on my screen. It's only a dot but it's definitely there."

"Hang on," said Ray and then tapped some buttons that Smokey must have missed. "I think it's simply changed colour and from this distance it's hard to see against space. There it is. It's certainly not blue anymore. I'll just put a filter on that."

"What...?" asked Dom, without finishing his question. He tried for a second time but failed again.

At that moment I leant over in my chair to have a look at the truer image. The planet seemed to be murky, like a dark coffee with a small splash of milk yet to be stirred. Pic and Don were looking between themselves and the screen with a concerned frown beginning to show. That's probably how I will look when I see Earth again for the first time. Unsure if I actually would want to travel any further. I felt Don and Pic's concern. I think everyone did. A silence consumed the bridge. We were all waiting for something good to say and completely avoiding saying something negative. Not a good time for jokes or meaningless banter or flippant remarks. Something like, "there's plenty more planets in the universe, just look for another one." Ray was the first to break the silence.

"That's not the actual colour. It's should look more like…" Ray tapped a few more buttons.

I was hoping to hear an, "Ahh that's better" but I all we got was an "Errr, looks even worse." It now had a dark earthy green hue, the shade of a vegan health drink, still waiting to be stirred."

"Is there any chance that it just the lens that needed to be cleaned, you know, it's a bit dirty?" Pic asked hopefully.

"I don't think so. But your idea that there may have been a massive growth in vegetation stands as the best possibility. We're too far away to detect what life is down there," concluded Ray.

A tiny speck of light came from the planet.

"I think that whatever life is down there is perfectly capable of launching a star ship though. Either that or a missile," said Nelson without flinching. Ray and Smokey tapped away like Fred Astaire and Ginger Rodgers.

"Should I?" I started to ask.

"Yes, you should Colin," Nelson informed me.

My sweat glands decided to work only within the confines of my palms. Every few seconds I would unconsciously wipe my thighs and return my concentration to the screen and the dot that had just appeared from the other dot. Only this dot was moving towards us.

"Smokey get ready for evasive actions. Everyone but Don and Pic should go to the departure room and strap yourselves in, just in case," added Nelson. They left without question

"It's not a missile," said Smokey.

"No, you're correct, it's a ship. With many missiles," Ray answered.

"Bring us to a halt Smokey but stay ready."

"Aye Admiral," replied Smokey.

"Who's having my chair?" Nelson asked of Don and Pic.

From my position I could see the Back of that chair. Don stood to its' side so I presume Pic took the option. Nelson made his way back to me stood to my right. He looked up towards me and smiled briefly and then turned his gaze back to the screen and asked Ray to hail the approaching ship. There was no response.

"Try again," demanded Nelson. No response.

"Here let me try," asked Pic and then added, "Umm which button is it?" Nelson stepped forward and obliged. Pic coughed a couple of times before pressing.

"Ship of the planet Crrrrk. Hail. Please don't shoot. I am Pic Gur Gur Aahchtact Hehe Errkch. Hailing you from The Flying Fish.

177

Consular shuttle of the Star Ship Ventura One. I'm a Filtration technician. Payroll number...." There was no need for Pic to continue. The light became brighter in the Bridge as the screen became a monitor and a small reptilian lemur like face appeared. I had to lean over substantially to see. I then returned to my more correct and sensible position satisfied and before Nelson could notice.

"Hail..." said a voice and then nothing for a while, although you could hear shuffling and rustling of paper, the taps of buttons or keys, or both. Different voices in the background asking, "how's that possible?" and "I thought that ship was lost?" and another voice answering, "Obviously not!"

"Hail, again," said the original voice.

"Hail," replied Pic not sure if that was the correct response as he had already said it.

"Uhh, err... Are, are, would...? Do you want to land?"

"Yes please."

"If you could disarm we'll send over coordinates and an escort."

Nelson tapped my ankle and nodded to me when I looked down. I hit the switch and my targeting console disappeared into the ceiling.

"Thank you," the voice said and I immediately heard a beep.

"Thank you," answered Pic and added awkwardly," I'll see you in a minute." I heard a slap. I think it was Pic's palm hitting Pic's forehead. Don started to shuffle his feet and a couple of steps later added a swing of his hips, then let out a flurry of "la la's" and "doo doo's" and "biddely bop's". I'd never seen him so happy. Seconds later Pic had joined in and they linked arms swinging each other around in circles. Of course, as these things always do they went faster and faster until the laughing made it impossible to move and breathe at the same time. Nelson giggled as he retook his chair. I giggled as I left mine. Both Pic and Don grabbed hold of me and the whole jig started again. Fortunately, for me, Nelson asked for quiet whilst he switched on the ships' speaker and spoke to everyone.

"Hello crew members, unbuckle those belts, have a wash and get your glad rags on. Be ready in twenty minutes. No longer."

I knew I didn't need a wash and didn't have any glad rags but I left the bridge all the same. I whistled on the way to my cabin. No tune I recognized, I was simply very happy. There was also a sense of comfortability emanating from within. A satisfaction that work had gone well. It was a good day at the office, you might say.

I had a wash regardless and put on a clean shirt. I wasn't the only one. Although we no longer looked like a bunch of makeshift escapee pirates something didn't quite gel. Most of us looked quite similar, something you might see on dress down Friday aboard the Jolly Roger, all of us apart from Ray who had decided to wear something very reminiscent of a simple Egyptian tunic but somehow pulled off a regal look. He'd used his make-up machine. Marilyn however took the crown by appearing as though she was off to a ball room dance evening. It wasn't only paints that Ray had been making. He'd also dabbled in dyes and Marilyn had asked for pink. I'm not going to say it was shocking. However, it shocked all of us, even Ray. Where did she get that much material and where exactly did she think she was going? Then as we entered the atmosphere and the happiness disappeared from the faces of Don and Pic as they scanned the view, Marilyn removed herself from the bridge only to return minutes later in a much-toned down skirt and jacket combination. During those few minutes everything became quiet. Once again we felt the unease, sadness, frustration, whatever it was, coming from our Crrrrkian crew mates. I've never seen iridescent brown before, I don't think many have, but that was the colour of the swelling mass that used to be the blue sea of this planet. Its shade changing as it rose and fell and in the moments that a wave breached the surface a hint of white as clean water hit daylight. In the distance hills and mountains the only sign of land but because of the vegetation there, it was hard to tell one from the other, where one ended and the other began. No cities or towns in sight. No industrial landscapes. No nothing. Even the clouds had a hint of green. The place felt, dare I say it? Damp, dank, dinghy... mouldy. We cruised for another couple of minutes and then at last a sight that might allow us to say something jovial to Don or Pic. Brilliance shimmering through the horizon. The clouds disappeared and a Sun broke into view, which one I don't know but it looked stunning and its' light had warmth and beckoned us forward. The sea turned from muddy brown to muddy green then to a murky green and greeny blue and finally just blue. I can't speak for everybody else but I certainly salivated. I instantly wanted to swim. I'd have to see if that's possible?

Then within seconds on the new fresh horizon something geometric to shape. From here it looked like a disastrous first four Tetris blocks, the last one completely upside-down length wise with one block hanging out over to the right. That's a very bad game score coming up... As we flew closer I realized first impressions can be correct, even the colours were similar... The blocks became bigger blocks with no sense of logic as to their lay-out and we still had a couple of miles to go. In that short travel time the blocks just carried on getting bigger. The over-hanging block seemed to be our destination and once we were slightly closer to this gargantuan structure we could see it had sheer sides that cut into the sea. Probably all the way to the bed. The top of this particular block did seem to have some sense to it and to give you an idea of size it was like a big grey car park, only there were no cars only massive shuttles and ships. Hundreds of them and maybe as many empty spaces left.

The escort ship we were following as it travelled spun one hundred and eighty degrees in a controlled slow manner suggesting we had arrived. A large blue light from a very empty area flashed every other second and a voice came through the speakers.

"That one there. You have it?"

"Yes we do, thank you," replied Pic. He then turned to Don and embraced him.

"Come on my friend, we're home," said Don.

For the first time in a while we relaxed and enjoyed the delight. No one left the bridge until Smokey had like a chauffeur brought us to a standstill without a single judder. Then still no one moved until Nelson suggested that Don and Pic should lead the way. He also pointed out that we shouldn't really leave via the more normal flight door as it looked too official and we didn't have passports, and that we were far less liable to be shot if we left as a group via the loading bay doors at the rear. Smiling was a good idea and wave with both hands in a friendly no guns in these here hello hands... Now that's good advice.

The hinge in the floor section that lowered itself down creaked heavily, mainly because we we're all stood on it. Pic and Don leading the way. They didn't bother with the grin and enthusiastic waving. Everybody else did, I started before even knowing if there was anyone to wave to. Everybody else joined in as soon as they heard the many clicks of switches being hit from the other side...

"That's one way to make sure you buy a parking ticket," I said waving salutations. Which is very difficult to do when faced by hundreds of two and a half foot tall cute looking reptiles, with guns.

"Hail, hail, hail," exclaimed both Pic and Don. I was certainly it wasn't someone with a gun. Pic then in a calmer manner hailed once more holding up his right arm which I suspected was a national salute. After a nervous second or two a Crrrrkian standing at the front with a bigger gun and a uniform suggesting he should have it, returned the salute and lowered his aim. The others didn't follow suite, just kept a steady aim. The captain or whatever he was stepped forward saying something in his own tongue. Don and Pic turned around to us and told us to wait exactly where we were and then stepped off the ship meeting the captain. After a quick exchange we were told we could stop waving.

Nelson very slowly turned to Ray and without moving his lips and very, very, softly said, "What are they saying Ray?"

If you knew what to look for at that moment you would have noticed Ray ever-so slightly flinch. Maybe tick is more appropriate. When that happens something is booting up, or clicking in.

"Prisoners, escaping. Far run running…"

Ray seemed to be struggling. There seemed to be far more words spoken than Ray was actually translating.

"The language has changed significantly since I first spoke it… Everyone dead, big catastrophe, all dead. Ship taken over. All change, all change. Now working prisoner. Then new prisoners. Wait, wait, wait, long long time. Escape. Zoom, far run running…"

The captain seemed to be captivated by the story being relayed by Pic. Every now and then it would be punctuated by Don nodding or saying, "Uh ha." Ray continued his translation as best he could.

"Oh no, problem. Stop. All stop, wait. Enemy zoom. All behind, no go, fifty fifty. Must go, urgent, big urgent. Hero. Big big hero." The captain looked over towards Ray who couldn't resist waving.

"Phut, all good, go, super zoom, ahhhh, ahhhh, ahhh. Here. Here. Enemy zoom. Sun, sun, moon, moon, enemy zoom Boomboom." I'm sure the original didn't rhyme? Pic then mimicked being strangled demonstrating something airborne. The captain understood but looked perplexed and paced to and fro and then turned to his troops and said something that Ray couldn't hear. There wasn't much need for a translation. A group of a dozen or so Crrrrkian soldiers split off from the mass and made their way towards us, then half of them surrounded us and pointed their weapons up at our faces. Down in the case of Smokey. The other half of the group continued into the ship, they seemed to be looking for people and not stuff, at least for the moment. The captain shouted again and began to walk away followed by two others who politely suggested to Pic and Don that they follow him. Raising a weapon works wonders when needing a yes. The six guards surrounding us opened up and made a way clear. Our route was different though. We looked to be heading straight to another ship. Along with another twenty or so armed guards who joined our party. Pic and Don were being led to a smaller ship in the opposite direction. We remained silent for a few steps and then Nelson broke the silence.

"It's certainly a shame no one speaks their language isn't everyone?" there he was trying to steal an edge when all I was going to say was, "Not the welcome I was expecting." I guess that's why he's the boss.

CHAPTER 24

I was amazingly disappointed with the transport. Reminiscent of a nineteen fifties single decker bus for an interior, itchy seats, and the finesse of a b-52 bomber on the exterior, rivets everywhere, I wouldn't have expected rivets. Just as well we weren't really going that far because it looked like it was made at the same time. As it turned out our destination was an old compound designed for taller visitors, normally dignitaries from other worlds. Visitors who might like a cliff top view with an easy reach beach, for which you need land and the sea of course. So unfortunately, we headed back into the green soup and out of the sun light towards a once renowned headland with hotel stuck on top of it. They haven't had visitors or even local tourist in hundreds of years now since it became somewhat of a giant dirty pond but they kept the place going just in case. Fighting the algae here was an on-going daily event that required a dedicated team. The air smelt fresher but you knew something lingered in the background. Other staff appeared occasionally carrying this and that and something else but disappeared as quickly as they came. The rooms we had were basic. Holiday camp wooden huts that if we wanted to kick down we could. We weren't going to, just yet, we were still trying to be friends and at the same time save their butts. Should be their butts we're kicking? I hope they know how to apologize in English?

It would have been pointless trying to cause a problem or escape as we really had nowhere to go. To prove the point no doors were locked, no one shut us in, nothing was slammed. No one actually bothered to give us any rules to follow. We followed the end of the barrel not the words they barked at us to find our way. They shuffled us into what must have been the reception area and left us to it. We even had to look for our own keys. Which didn't take long, they were behind the reception office door and hung on the wall within easy reach of the service desk. It's what I would have done. Maybe they keep the keys to the shuttle behind its' sun visor?

We congregated in a conference room at the end of the corridor beyond the bedrooms. It was the size of four bedrooms with nothing to confer around. Just stacks of chairs up against one wall. We took one each and without saying a word formed a tight circle. Okay, there was a few seconds where we all shuffled back a bit as we couldn't get comfortable with so many legs. Once settled and some gruff looks were exchanged Nelson opened the floor.

"Did you get anything else Ray?"

"Well, from assessing all the language I didn't understand and the construction rules of their tongue I believe I've been able to deduce that they are very confused and very upset at the same time. Mainly because until a few moments ago they just had a vegetation problem and now they have an extinction problem. Unfortunately Pic and Don were part of the crew that caused the original animosity so are in some way to blame."

"But they had nothing to do with it. They weren't the powers that be and decided what to do? That's ridiculous," I added in defence.

"We all know that, but they don't," Nelson pointed out.

"Look, Pic and Don will provide them the history and then we'll be taken somewhere nice and then someone will shove a big drink into our hands and ask for forgiveness," suggested Sam.

"I agree," said Jeb and then continued," It's the only outcome. And it always has to end in forgiveness." It's hard to argue with a religious man when you know they are right or at least should be.

"We still need a plan and a contingency," Nelson said.

"Overpower the natives and steal their shuttle in order to re-re-steal ours," said Sam as though we had all done that before.

"I agree," Nelson said without hesitation.

"Oh, shouldn't we wait at lit…." I didn't have time to finish.

"Of course we should, and will, but at the first sign things are going wrong we need to know that we at least have an intention, and half a plan." Everyone nodded their agreement including myself. "We might have to improvise without notice so if I shout 'Victory' knock someone out and grab their weapon head for the shuttle. Everyone?" Again, everyone nodded in agreement. Even though in all honesty the plan was very sketchy, if you asked me. Fortunately nobody was asking. Most were having their attention drawn away by the sight of small armada of ships, each looked far more superior than the old bus we turned up in. For starters they had guns and several of them and looked like they do more than fifty. One ship departed from the swarm and descended. It then flew overhead and landed nearby out of view.

"Obviously now wouldn't be a good time to try and knock anybody out," Nelson said staring up at the armada minus one. He then turned around, his eyes twitching with a plan. He then huffed and sighed. His plan failed whatever his thoughts were. He noticed me looking at him, studying his face,

"Just thinking of a massive switcheroo," he said smiling and at the same time shaking his head.

"I think I should go for a walk outside where I can listen to the wildlife and any loose lips," said Ray standing bolt upright.

"Good idea, I'll come with you. Bernie, Sam, Mona I think you should come too, just in case," Nelson suggested, but ordered really.

"And what should we do?" asked Marilyn.

"Look innocent and relaxed and happy, nothing is wrong. There's nothing going on. Got to go," he followed the others out of the room.

It's quite hard forcing yourself to be all the things asked of us. I know this from working customer service every now and then at work. Having to deal with customers who actually believe the customer is always right. For instance, 'Can I get my money back on this? '. 'Yes you can if you take it back to Tesco's where you bought it. We're not them.' 'But....'. But what? You can't tell them what's actually on your mind and instead you're asked to smile through it all. However, now is not the time to be grumbling about something I'll never experience again. Now is the time to pretend to be happy, like nothing is out of the ordinary. Life is good... If it was that good I can't understand why I suggested we play Charades? Neither could anyone else. Smokey just laughed and then suggested we play Call My Bluff instead, how he even knew of that game astounded me, but because it seemed more apt he laughed again and Marilyn joined in. Then Jeb suggested that an even better game would be Hang Man. No one found that funny, but that itself became funny. Too funny to contain and the bug caught us all. It was seconds before we were howling.

We didn't notice the door open. Personally speaking, I was wiping the tears from my eyes. We did eventually notice the small squad of small armed guards looking at us shaking their heads in confusion. Especially when they made their way over to us and some of them started poking Marilyn and Smokey with the barrels of their guns. They both protested but moved as required. For a split second there was a moment when I was ready to pounce and at least take one out. Do I shout 'Victory'? Standing just inside the doorway and arriving just in time Nelson shook his head. He had spotted the wide-eyed look and my stance readying itself, ready to release an instant of rage and anger. He then smiled softly and somehow reassured me that he knew something that I didn't.

"Will you stop poking my friends?" shouted Nelson in a full gusto voice I'd never heard before. For a second the guards stopped, a couple actually stepped backwards. Then a guard, who must have been in charge of this bunch stepped forward and approached Nelson. One word Horace, that's all we need.

"… Yes, stop that," the guard shouted to his men whilst maintaining eye contact with Nelson. Go on, I screamed inside my mind, one word. Nelson remained calm and ever so slightly bowed his head in respect to the new orders. The small creature in front of Nelson just watched him and then moved off. Smokey, Marilyn and the rest of the guards going with him.

"They're just following orders, don't worry, don't fight," Nelson shouted down the corridor to our friends. He then either waited for the front door to close or he was composing himself for what he wanted to say next.

"… At least we know they understand English… Okay, here is the situation, from what Ray could gleam… Marilyn and Smokey are being taken to another compound for visitors whom they suspect of something or just don't like. Pic and Don must have expanded on the story. So taking Marilyn and Smokey sounds like something a lot of people would do? We've been listed as refugees, but as strange as it sounds we haven't any documents or, a passport. As though we would have? Come on? Further to that, we should have declared some weapons and technically we were in their ship. Which one could argue was theft. Again, ridiculous. Then to top it all off, they had already been notified by the police that we are wanted for trashing an auto bot," he sighed then tutted and then, took a deep breath. He hadn't finished, "Try and do someone a favour! I rarely swear. Damn… Now, the only reason we are not in the same secure compound is because they are considering sending some of us up in the Flying Fish in the first wave of attack to cause as much damage as possible but to also act as cannon fodder. Unfortunately the first wave comprises of us…" Nelson stopped, we thought mid-sentence, then soon the meaning became clear. He remained quiet until we all got it.

"So, a suicide mission?" suggested Sam. Nelson crooked his neck.

"Unless we win," then again remained silent until I asked.

"Are you saying we blow them up? It's them or us?"

Nelson could only sigh. We looked to each other in desperation. Hoping that someone would be inspired with something. There must be something?

"That's millions. Some of them my friends," I said feeling a change in my colour, "I think I might be sick?" I ran to the window just in time to open it and half throw myself out of it, to maximize the distance and therefore chances of not having to clear it up later. I then noticed hundreds of bugs coming along to have their fill. The thought of which only made me hack again... and again, then twice more. I do apologize to those of you with a sensitive stomach. It all disappeared before my eyes. If I do die and then come back in a next life scenario that's one creature to avoid if I get the chance.

"Sounds like you're getting a devil out Colin?" Jeb shouted over.

"I think you'd feel a bit sick faced with that thought Jeb? Just as well you're only the pilot for the day?" said Nelson stone faced.

Jeb joined me at the window a few seconds later. You can guess what he did?

"Just as well Ray can't be sick and my stomach eats news like that for breakfast," Nelson concluded and thus informed us of the skeleton crew that would board the ship. Leaving the others, our friends, as pawns, and the reason we couldn't just fly off and blow a raspberry. "Na na na naa na, sort your own extinction problem out."

It wasn't going to be that easy. Far from it. For the next minute or so people around me spoke but absolutely none of it registered. My mind wasn't quite processing things right now. The only thought going backwards and forwards in my head was the phrase, 'Friends for friends', numbers meant nothing, the friends themselves dissolved from view and just became a mist that ended up swirling around in one big friend fuelled fog. I couldn't separate the two sides, and the different elements of the role in my immediate future. How am I going to feel afterwards?

"There must be another way?" I asked, begged.

"We can put our minds to it Colin... But do it quickly."

The enigmatic silences that in the last twenty minutes had become prevalent with Nelson's delivery of bad news was beginning to annoy me by now.

"What is it?" I asked myself. "Silence."

CHAPTER 25

Four in the morning was simply a time I watched go by, as I questioned what it was I'd be getting up for, at that time anyway. That was at midnight, one, two and three in the morning. At four and finally, I simply got dressed and had a breakfast that looked like something I fed the bugs the previous day. Which I tried really hard not to think about as I ate. I needed a coffee, but we had none. Instead we had something a health food shop might call a tea, but, no, it really isn't. One of those packets you keep on display suggesting to anyone who notices that you at least try and be healthy in some way. It stays there for years.

Unfortunately I was so tired I looked like I had already died, my goodbyes to everyone must have seemed negative and remorseful, when I was simply very tired. It dawned on me as I followed behind Ray, Nelson and Jeb that everyone remaining kept on telling me to, "Cheer up. You'll be alright. Everything will work out." I was already having a bad one, leave me alone. That's what I looked like all the time when I did night shift. As for everything working out, yeah, toss a coin, some side will come up… Ah, there's coffee on the Fish…

"Can we have a quick, what the hell is happening meeting, in the kitchen where I can make the strongest coffee I've ever had. Please?" I asked.

"That sounds like the beginning of a beautiful plan. Of course we can. As is the custom of a quick chat, before you kick off," said Nelson and then yawned.

On a normal day coffee really wasn't a problem. If we were left alone to get on with the job. However, today we had an escort. Whom I think was probably, technically, in charge of things? Only one, a very slow moving, hunched, aged and robed Crrrrkian. He introduced himself as a previous Admiral of the fleet. Now retired, bored ever since, and there's not long left to go for him now, anyway. The wife had gone, along with the kids. All together to a holiday ship, which he forgets the name of, where they all run a wind surfing school. He was on board to watch everything and to make sure that we only did what we had to. Definitely no running off then. The first sign of any sign would result in a large explosion caused by a small electric charge being backfired into our engine drive. Plasmarized, was the word he used as he explained the physics. The very same thing would also happen if his communications stopped for any...

"What happens if our communications go down?" I asked as petulantly as possible.

"What happens to yours is your business, I've got my own," he replied sharply, smiled thinly and continued, "and I have a life-ball in my pocket. Just in case I need it."

Ray, seeing my puzzled expression explained that a 'life-ball' was like twenty first century air bag that enveloped you rather than cushioned and allowed five minutes of being in space before the air ran out. You could extend this time if you also had compressed air in another small device... of which he had a few in different pockets.

It did occur to me right then to jump him and get Ray to do an impression of him when needed. I noticed Nelson twitch a little, but the moment passed.

"Have we got one of those?" Jeb asked.

"We're not going to be needing one Jeb," Nelson replied with conviction.

"That's the spirit," said our guest. Nelson took one step towards him.

"A wager sir?"

"... What could I possibly hope to win?"

"I'll wager you that I can win and if I do you apologize to my friends and, who should be your friends, Marilyn and Smokey."

"And if you lose?"

"There'll be no one to left to apologize to."

"... So..."

"So you haven't got much to lose, and you have everything to win."

"All I have to do is apologize?"

"If you have to apologize, I'll get everything."

"Bosch!" I said, out loud too. I surprised myself, and others, although Nelson did grin as he turned and led the way to the kettle.

Nelson did offer the admiral a coffee, probably knowing he would say no, maybe not thinking he'd get a few tuts along the way, it didn't deter him making an excellent cuppa, very strong, I woke up on the smell alone. This was also my first in a while as many months ago I half promised my share to Marilyn. She wouldn't mind, plus whilst she's not drinking it, and the amount we're having won't dent her stash so much. She'll have more than enough to celebrate with after that apology she's going to get.

"To Marilyn and Smokey…" I said raising my mug.

Everyone who had a cup agreed. The admiral sniffed the air.

"Yaauh. That smells disgusting. Doesn't surprise me, you and your friends have no desire to enjoy what you consume. We gave, Marilyn and Smokey the finest foods, better than what we get, and they declined it, and to show absolute disrespect they ate the muck covering the ponds. Don and Pic said you all had strange habits but really? What's that you're heating up?" he asked me as I'd stuck a pot of emergency stew in the oven. A thirty first century old school microwave, same stuff different design. It even went ping.

"Stew, you want some," I replied as dully as I could muster. Quite difficult with the amount of caffeine presently coursing its way through my system.

"No, I don't. I was demonstrating yet another disgusting thing you're going to consume. It smells awful."

"Then why don't you wait on the bridge until we get going?" I said unconcerned at the anger in my voice. I'm getting good at surprising myself.

"Oh we can get going whenever you want, everyone else is leaving tomorrow. When you're ready… I'll wait in the bridge." He left slowly only turning his head once trying to discover the source of a ping sounding from the oven and I opened the door as quickly as possible to release the pong he disliked so much. At least it made him move faster than he may have done for a while. Healthy then, even when you don't eat it. We didn't wait for him go before we hurriedly ate. It helped settle some nerves and gave the coffee something to work on before it ate me from the inside out… Once we knew we were clear to talk Jeb opened the bidding.

"I didn't come all this way just to get blown up on the first volley. I need five minutes, fifty minutes with Smokey. Or communications, something, I need to go through some of his more extreme manoeuvres. Can I do that?" Everyone remained silent hoping he could answer his own question. Jeb's eyebrows only raised themselves. He didn't know.

"Like you Jeb, I don't know," I said and looked to Nelson.

"I don't see why not. Not if we have the chance to leave when we want."

We didn't load the dishwasher correctly as we suddenly had haste. Did anyone load those things correctly? On the bridge we discovered our small friend sat in the driver's seat. He got out when Nelson and Jeb both coughed loudly.

190

"Where can we find Smokey?" Nelson asked.

"In his quarters."

"And do these quarters have accessibility?"

"Most days."

"We want to go there right now, right now?"

"… what for. Shouldn't you be busy elsewhere?"

Jeb broke in clenching his eyes, giving himself something of the Rasputin look. "You take the best pilot and replace him with an inferior one. I need advice. Five minutes isn't going to hurt is it?"

"Is it?" added Nelson within a fraction of a second.

"Makes sense to me," I added seeing the admiral struggling to think of a reason why he should object.

"We have warp drive?" concluded Ray and tutted.

"Alright, alright?" he said, exasperated. He then said a few things into a little communicator abruptly and with same friendly tone turned to Jeb. "Okay, take her up and go that way." He pointed east. Two minutes later we cleared the smoggy haze and then it was just a matter of a bit over there, to the left, watch out for upcoming traffic, slow down and speed up. We arrived at our destination, safely. On top of the same block we departed from. From there we under guard transferred to a smaller shuttle the size of a limo, with driver, and then off to a smaller block and a few levels below. From a lower street level it could have been Lego City only the pieces were the size of shipping containers. So, in fairness maybe you could have called it Shipping Container City? I don't think it really mattered, I just noticed, that's all.

The buildings, structures whatever you want to call them soon became the same everywhere, uniform, smaller and smaller blocks within the even bigger outside a big box. Boxes everywhere. Lines converging into the distances, up and across. To make you want to either throw up or scream. The traffic seemed to follow a similar pattern. Changing lanes meant changing our altitude by twenty feet.

We stayed travelling on the same route for another few minutes, until the boxes ran out and we entered what seemed like a small park with a soft security prison camp site smack in the middle. It actually turned out the park was an attempt to save some endangered plants and wildlife and to filter some wastewater. There were several other places like this but only this one had more boxes in the shape of huts. We parked alongside and clambered out. We arrived at the right time, the sun was high enough to be shining through the gap in the nearly-planet wide haze. We all closed our eyes and took a slow breath. When I reopened them I felt a surge of energy and saw a small disconcerting shake of the head from the Crrrrkian Admiral. Tuff I thought, and as everyone else, including Ray was still soaking up some sunshine I re-joined the group and obscured everything from view again, closing my eyes. I heard a tut. I only reopened them when I heard a gentle cough from Nelson. He then went on to bellow our arrival and in a loud voice called for Marilyn and Smokey. Without being asked we started knocking on doors. Their rattling being the only answer. Then we heard Marilyn singing loudly.

"Follow my voice, you'll find us over here," she sang and repeated as we followed. They weren't behind doors. We followed a small dusty path around a few bushes and stumpy trees to find them swimming around a pond looking euphoric and content, very content.

"Hello boys."

"Hello Marilyn, you look, happy," replied Nelson. There was a hesitation in his response, and the end of his sentence finished with a high inclination. The way an Australian might say something, leaving you unsure if it was a statement, question or sarcasm. Because, although Marilyn did look happy, she did have a smile, she also had at the same time, a head covered in algae sliding down her face as we spoke. Smokey looked the same only he was gathering the algae on his chest, squeezing it into balls and then eating it. He held one up and offered to throw it over for us to try. If I was a vegan I might have given it a go. Turns out none of us were and we all declined, quickly.

"You want to come in for a dip?" Marilyn asked as she swam over to us. No one bothered replying.

"Smokey, Jeb needs a while with you. Piloting issues?" Nelson said with a sense of purpose.

"What's the problem?" Smokey asked and popped in another algae ball.

"I hate being the one who brings down a party," Nelson started and then went on to explain the very very bad situation we were in. The happiness soon disappeared and they both fixated on the admiral who shrugged unconcerned.

Smokey did point out that he also had never experienced anything like this and didn't really know if anything he conveyed to Jeb would actually help? He did also see the dilemma we were in and went with Nelson and Jeb to his cell hut for a briefing.

Presumably they went through the process of spacial reverse J-turns, barrel rolls and evasive manoeuvres.

Whilst that conference occurred the admiral took advantage of Marilyn's swampy look and her munching on some of the algae balls that Smokey left bobbing around to complain of his disgust at other creature's habits. She did look like she may have stepped of the set of a fifties B-movie, so he did have a point, a small point, and in another way, no point. I wonder what he'd make of Stilton cheese and its' blue veins.... Veins, in a cheese?

I took the opportunity to see if she recalled anything the Maniac Fred, television show congenial happy presenter host and dictator idiot may have had planned. Marilyn shook her head and then dipped under water disappearing for a good five minutes.

Ray took the opportunity to test the water. He dipped a finger in and had a taste. "Yuk, why did I do that? I knew I shouldn't had done that." He tried to spit but nothing came out. Some of the guards looked a bit ill. Others just shook their heads. The admiral just tutted.

"One man's pleasure, one man's poison..." I said but needn't had bothered. Ray spoke before a silence swept over.

"It's good enough to swim in, wouldn't want to drink it though."

"We try not to, but at least on my planet we have some to drink," the admiral replied with either a grimace or a smirk on his face, followed by a tut.

Marilyn surfaced close to some guards looking like a swamp monster.

"Boo," she said very softly and then slowly drifted back out. "He did start a countdown clock for a new show he was planning. His biggest ever show he called it, but he's bound to say that isn't he? About a year ago. I don't really watch shows like that. I think I read about it or it was on the news. I don't even know what it was called." Once again she descended to her world of slime and disappeared under the water.

"Don't you remember anything Ray?" I asked him.

He paused to think but shrugged before answering. "He was always on. When he wasn't on his own show he was on a new show he was now on, or someone else show that he'd turn into a show about him. Do you know what I mean? Think of him as say, Noel Edmunds, a Noel Edmunds who actually harboured dark evil thoughts and desires of absolute control and genocide."

"..... Mmmm. Okay," I replied frowning heavily. Ray must have noticed.

"Stephen Fry, Terry Wogan."

"No, I get the idea. Someone so well known that you just wouldn't suspect. But none of those people were as slimy as Fred. Fred's ego was bigger than Fred... You wouldn't have a countdown clock unless there was a major event coming up? It could be connected?"

Marilyn surfaced at the edge of the pond bedraggled in plant life. She massaged it away from her face as though it was the latest Product. "I think the strapline was 'The slowest, quietest spectacular event in history...' That and a clock, counting down. Any help?"

"Not really, possibly, maybe?" I replied shaking my hand.

"You may as well chuck in, probably?" Ray added.

"Could do."

CHAPTER 26

My thoughts were broken a few minutes later when I heard Smokey's splash from a dive bomb into the pond. I had my back turned at that moment. I heard a large splat and span around. Smokey clicked his tentacle and tutted. He'd missed me.

"Hope your instructions are better than that attempt," I said.

"So do I," he said and then spiralled amongst the algae to ensure complete coverage.

The admiral coughed. Nelson raised his eyebrows. Jeb raised his higher and added a smile. Ray and I looked to each other and nodded. We left Marilyn and Smokey to their delights without saying any goodbyes. Which was strange as it might be our last, they didn't seem too bothered. Maybe they wanted to enjoy the moment just in case it was? I frowned most of the way back, thinking of things to ask either admirals. Was there anything we needed to know? Of course there was, we just needed to know what questions to ask, surely? It wasn't until the moment we took off that one of the questions I needed to ask finally formed itself.

"Admiral, what sort of thing can you detect coming from space from the surface?" Everyone turned to hear the answer.

"We have an array of detectors for everything. There's not much that could get through."

"What would that not much look like?" I continued.

"Well, something natural, small, something…."

"You'd spot a missile?"

"Oh yes."

"You're sure?"

"Oh yes… a projectile that's obviously manufactured, absolutely, no question."

"But not, maybe something small and looks like a small rock? A meteor? You would let that burn up in the atmosphere?"

"… Probably. We normally do, if they're small and harmless."

"… And what do you consider small to be exactly?"

The admiral threw his arms around briefly looking like he was at a rave. "About that big."

"About the size of my old television. Old school tube style… Could it be as easy as that?"

"As what?" asked two admirals, Jeb and Ray and then Nelson again after a silence that went on for too long.

"Well, call it a hunch, but, from what I know, from the scraps of knowledge I have… I'd say we should look for the slowest moving object in the area, which is on a direct course with the planet and see what it's made of? A small meteor looking thing that's been hollowed out and stuffed with a bio bomb, or, a fishbowl full of gas and no fish? A moment for history delivered in a slow fashion, devastating effects, something that could be filmed and used by an egotistical maniac. Build up, he anticipation with a clock that goes backwards… It's worth a shot, right?"

Nelson asked Jeb to get us going whilst the other admiral said something into his collar. He then pursed his lips seemingly waiting for someone to answer him.

"Hold on everyone, take your seats." Jeb recommended. Thirty seconds later I was strapped into my gunner's chair. Nelson took his seat Ray sat aside Jeb and the admiral took the communications seat to my left. We rose vertically at tremendous speed and within seconds the planet vanished. We came to a halt abruptly and the stars stopped tracing and stood still.

"Where now?" Jeb asked.

Whilst he waited for any response I primed the guns and set multiple scans through my target screen. I whipped the sight around with a gentle roll of my control tracker curser, blindly hopeful of discovery, the object would appear to me as simply as winning the lottery. Looking at all things in all directions working out which was the slowest might take some time. My plan was failing me and everyone else already.

"If they were on a direct course from where we last met them and launched something…?" Nelson didn't get to finish. He didn't need too. Ray, like a twin brother, the one who was better with maths, and a keyboard was a fraction ahead of him.

"Bingo." He tapped a button and all screens including mine changed into a black nothingness.

"Are you sure your man is working correctly?" asked the guest but kickable admiral.

"What am I looking at Ray?"

"I'm glad you asked admiral." There was a small pause. I couldn't see Ray but I'm guessing that he turned to the Crrrrkian admiral and smiled momentarily in anticipation of a moment soon to come. I wasn't let down. Ray continued.

"… What we are looking at here, but not seeing, is the slowest smallest moving object within sensor range... It also happens to be made mainly of graphene and silicone with a small amount of lead, and Squid ink. It is very, very, black. No explosive inside. I think it's been designed to slowly disintegrate upon entering the Crrrrkian atmosphere." Once again there was a pause in which I hoped Ray was fist pumping. Nelson certainly choked on a chuckled.

"Say when," said Jeb.

"Any ships nearby? Get ready to bring us along-side but go in steady. Standby Colin," responded Nelson to all of us.

"No ships."

"Ready."

"Standing by."

"……. When," said Nelson.

Nelson must be busy thinking. Ray must be computing and Jeb must be getting sticky palms piloting us along. Probably knowing we could get blown to pieces each and every second… Maybe that was the reason for the silence, we all knew that? I certainly did. If that was the device and someone was just about to discover it, well it only figures that we could get attacked whilst finding it and taking a close look? How far is close in space?

A crackled noise from the Crrrrkian admiral croaked from his collar. He hummed and mummed and then gave his verdict. "There's nothing else that would fit the bill and there seems to be an old model satellite of ours not too far from here that just shouldn't be there, and it's working."

"Standby Colin. Get us ready to shift right out of here if I say Jeb."

"Yes sir," Jeb replied. I'm not sure he meant to say 'sir' but the moment caught him.

"Standing by and I've got it on my screen. The satellite, it's tiny, is that, is that a camera? I think there's a camera in it and I'd say it's looking straight at the black fish tank bio bomb thing. Yeah, I'd say so."

"I'd agree," seconded Ray.

"It was an observer satellite. It would have a very good camera on it," said the Admiral who knew, proudly.

It can always be a challenge pointing out the obvious, or what you believe to be the obvious. Because if you are wrong you'll end looking like an idiot, a big idiot as the obvious should be singularly obvious and simple. I couldn't resist.

"Can I simply blow it up, vaporize it?" I said hesitantly fearing I'd prove myself to be an idiot and a big one at that.

197

No one answered. We all looked to Ray for an answer. He however paused. I saw his eyes flicker as he computed something. Maybe he was considering how much of an idiot he could prove himself to be. He looked towards Nelson and shrugged. Nelson also remained silent hoping for some guidance from Ray.

"Or put it in a sealed container and return to sender?" I added after another round of silence.

"Is there any sign of their ship?" asked Nelson.

I couldn't see anything, Ray answered, as did Jeb.

"Wouldn't it make sense that they have taken a position miles away and that's why they are using a satellite to watch everything on?" asked Nelson rhetorically. "I think it might be," he answered himself and then added, "Give me a minute."

The obvious thing to believe at that moment was he was nervous or had drunk too much coffee and needed to empty his bladder. I was glad I didn't say as much as I would have proved myself to be wrong, although not necessarily an idiot. Who would have guessed that the next time we saw him he would be outside the ship in a space suit carrying the container our curry was delivered in heading for the bio bomb.

"I couldn't ask any of you to do this could I?" he said over the intercom. "Jeb, get ready to whizz off if anything happens." He then proceeded to glide alongside the bio bomb and give us a thumbs up and the observer satellite a tiny wave.

"Get ready Jeb, and remember, at the first sign of anything coming our way, shift," he said and opened the curry box and very carefully let the bio bomb land itself inside. He then closed the lid and gave the satellite another wave and slowly made his way back to the Flying Fish.

"I've had a few curries like that could cause that much damage," I said and chuckled.

The Crrrrkian admiral said something into his collar.

"Find the biggest ship in the system and destroy it," Ray said translating for the benefit of Jeb and I.

"I thought that was going to be an apology?" I piped up.

"Not yet," the admiral replied.

Nelson joined us a few minutes later, out of the space suit but now wearing a big smile instead. "I've left it in the delivery hatch."

"I believe that if we cooked it to a super heat we'd neutralize the bomb," Ray said. He seemed convinced. "And we could do that in the oven."

"Can you do that?" Nelson asked of Ray. Ray left without a word.

The main console beeped. Someone, from somewhere was trying to get through.

"Shall I open a channel?" asked Jeb.

"I think you should, it's only polite," Nelson responded. Jeb flicked a switch and a familiar voice hit the airwaves. It was Doctor Sandra.

"Well done Horatio, we're all so glad you did that. However, may I ask you to ask the Crrrrkian's to step down?"

"And why should we do that?" replied the Crrrrkian admiral.

"Because the mad Squid Fred has been led away to a cell. The same one he had me locked up in and I've been given temporary presidency until further notice. And I'm not bonkers."

She went on to tell us that Fred was so convinced of his own superiority and destiny that he promised that if his televised adventure failed in any way he would step down immediately and recommend that Doctor Sandra should take over, he was so convinced his plan was fool proof. The whole event was being watched by the anyone within view of a screen. It was the only thing on as Fred demanded as much. It turned out to be the biggest anti-climax ever and everyone just cheered at the failed attempt and laughed at Fred himself. No one else wanted this attack to happen. Fred was using it as a way to secure complete control and authority. Too much control and control of the media... We're so stupid, and sorry. We looked the other way... He was taken away instantly, stripped of power along with a few generals who propped him up and his plans.... Everyone cheered when Nelson appeared and commented on what a lovely smile he had.

She then went on to play a recording of the event to prove what had happened and begged again that the Crrrrkian fleet stepped down. The Squid would defend themselves but why risk anyone's life because of one idiot who only had his own interests at heart.

The Crrrrkian admiral mumbled into his collar.

"Thank you," Sandra said, many times, and then suggested that we pop over for a cup of tea and a friendly chat.

"Mmm, tea," I said. "It's been ages since I had one of those."

The two Admirals looked at each other and without a word something was agreed.

"Put the Kettle on, we'll be over in a minute. Send us your coordinates," Nelson said and probably with a smile on his face.

Another beep beeped from Jeb's console and seconds later we span around and zoomed off.

"Shouldn't we be whooping and cheering, opening the bubbly or something?" I asked.

"It's not over just yet Colin," answered Nelson.

"You're very trusting. What makes you think they won't just blow us to smithereens," the other admiral said.

Nelson tutted before answering. "Didn't you hear the lady? She said pop over for a nice cuppa, not a fist fight."

"And we're both English. Tea first, fist fight later… Maybe biscuits?" I rounded off leaving our Crrrrkian friend tutting, shaking his head and leaving the bridge.

I sighed involuntarily and my shoulders dropped, all the muscles in my neck went weak. A great rush of satisfaction swept over my body and then I became still and relaxed. We had just saved a planet. Was it really that easy? Really?

"… Well, I've got to say that wasn't quite what I was expecting," I said questioning the ease of success

"What were you expecting?" Nelson asked.

"… Don't know exactly… whizzing around at a great pace, flashing lights and firing lasers. Zap zap, kerpow?"

"Sounds like last resort stuff Colin. If there's something you can do before a shot is fired then, you really should do it. Look how much hassle and grief it's stopped. And it only took a couple of minutes. Drinking a cup of tea would take longer… I think you could join us down here now Colin."

My console disappeared into the ceiling and the chair descended to ground level leaving me feeling like I 'd have to pay a barber. Certainly wouldn't be leaving a tip, my hair was a mess.

Jeb turned in his seat and told me, "I'm glad you were disappointed Colin. I would have been a disaster getting us out of there. Besides, we are whizzing now, I can do this bit all day long. Although for some reason I want to do a victory roll."

"Not now I'm out of my chair."

"Tempting though, eh?" Nelson said through a mischievous grin flexing his eyebrows.

"So, what happens now? When do you think we could get going home?"

Both Jeb and Nelson drifted off for a moment musing on something form the past. Jeb remained there whilst Nelson drew himself back from his thoughts and smiled at me.

"When everything is sorted, fine, cool, fixed, done, finished. When you can leave knowing that you don't need to think about it anymore and give yourself leave to enjoy your home."

I found myself nodding in agreement. He made perfect sense, but I still asked when that was likely to be to which he giggled and then suggested we had a cup of tea before that other cup of tea. That too made perfect sense.

Jeb pressed a few buttons and joined us for beverages. In the canteen we found Ray had found a small audience, the Crrrrkian admiral sat at the table wearing a napkin around his neck and a tomato sauce around his face. Small grunts of delight from him, confirmed with lots of positive statements from Ray, who was wearing an apron and just about to serve the next course. Which looked like the same thing as before but with a cream sauce instead. The admiral couldn't wait to get stuck in so much so that his slobbering put me off my dinner, whatever it was going to be? Hopefully not rabbit.

"I've got to get one of these?" our dinner guest said.

"A chef or a rabbit?" Nelson said with a little hint of sarcasm.

"You turned your nose at it earlier," I added.

He just looked up and chewed enjoying the moment and then after swallowing said "Rabbit" half a dozen times, just to make sure he was saying it right.

Every Englishman can make a cup of tea whilst contemplating something else, it's a very second nature activity. So whilst I waited for the tea to brew, I suggest four minutes, I asked myself why we couldn't just go home instantly and what would make everything fine and dandy? Nelson was right of course, everyone had to be satisfied, maybe something had to be signed? Only, you'd only sign something if some action or instruction needed to be carried out. Something needed to be unlocked? So what was it?

I was stirred from my thoughts and tea with a glutinous gurgle of delight from the small admiral. Which considering he was indulging in something that looked like scones, strawberries and clotted cream sounded fair enough. He was on dessert. Ray sat close by observing the delight adding small nods and smiling widely. He twice wiped the admiral's face for him.

"You're going to need a tca to wash all that down," I said to the messy diner and proceeded to make him one. He didn't say no but that could have been because he had his small face full and couldn't. He finished just in time for me to place it in front of him. His first slurp produced the inevitable "Ahhhh" and I saw him slowly sink comfortably into the chair he was already slumped in.

"You've got to get you one of those too," I said smiling.

"You're certainly not wrong," he replied and smiled back.

"It could be arranged," added Nelson. I had the impression he was looking at a way into a much bigger discussion... setting up a trade of some description always seemed to be involved in a peace deal. Everyone seemed to profit. Or hoped to.

Maybe I could become the owner of a tea plantation? A Rabbit farmer? On earth there is all the land you could manage, after a lot of work transforming it. I had to say something. Just not yet. I'll run over my thoughts and maybe tweak them a bit. Wait for the right moment for maximum impact... Although supplying tea and rabbits wasn't the biggest thing in the universe. I began to back away from my own idea. It wasn't big enough.

CHAPTER 27

It occurred to us all that we could just be arrested and marched off at gun point as soon as we landed. We weren't that stupid. Maybe Jeb had prayed and we we're all high on faith? Or that we all believed in Nelson and his belief in himself? Either way we walked onto the deck of Bay One without too much concern. Doctor Sandra met us with three others, all of whom looked serious and business-like, but before any greetings happened she knelt and bowed slightly in front of the Crrrrkian admiral in act of humbleness and sincerity. The three others remained standing but their heads hung low. Almost with embarrassment.

"On behalf of us all I beg your forgiveness," President Sandra said and lowered her head a notch further. "May I welcome you with an open mind and heart."

Nelson stepped forward, not allowing a possible break-out of uncomfortableness and silence.

"Hello doctor. How's my ship?"

Doctor Sandra stood up and shook Nelsons' hand and then everyone else's.

"Your ship is fine. It hasn't sunk at least." She then extended an arm in the direction of an executive buggy and once inside we drove off to the nearest large enough lift.

On the way we passed many happy looking Squid. Some cheered as we drove by. Some shouted my name repeatedly like I just scored a winning goal in a world cup match. I must have gone a bit red in the face. I looked over to Nelson who was smiling directly at me enjoying the moment.

After a few more of these moments we turned into a wider boulevard that was packed with onlookers eating and drinking from many different bars. More cheering and large banners welcoming the Crrrrkian's began to appear. The only Crrrrkian around noticed them but didn't smile. I wondered for a moment if he couldn't read or his military training didn't allow for it? He was definitely taking notice of things.

We had to accelerate to the lift as we were beginning to attract too much attention. The crowds began to encroach from either side narrowing our road. Happily skipping, bobbing out of joy... couldn't call it dancing really. Something like the cup win dance all football clubs perform when raising the cup. All of them, you know the one.

It was safe enough to speed up a bit as there was only a slight chance of anyone getting run over. No one got run over.

After a few more doors, twists and a turn I had the impression we were heading towards bridge. I was wrong but close. The Rest room adjacent to the bridge had an adjoining smaller canteen. Less formal than I expected for something so military and so close to the bridge. Nelson knew the place already and made his way to the stack of cups mounted next to a machine that dispensed hot beverages.

"Anyone else?"

Only Ray remained tea-less. He did however get to take the best seat in the room, right next to the large window. Which he ignored, along with the view and instead pulled himself close to the table and scanned the room with a smile on his face. I then noticed that the tables themselves were set in such a way to allow a conference. Everyone looking in, seating in the round... I sat next to Ray and gazed outwards making use of the window and its' width.

"Aren't you going to pay attention Colin?" Ray asked. I took a deep breath and exhaled through a smile. What Ray didn't know was I had a plan and had been paying a lot of attention... It had only just amassed itself as something tangible. Nothing like working under pressure. I turned and sat as correctly as Ray. Just to reassure him.

Doctor Sandra, her entourage and three newcomers with peaked caps all waited for the visiting admiral to take his seat before sitting themselves. This he noticed, and for the first time I'd noticed, he cracked a very small smile...

"Are you able to speak on behalf of your planet?" Doctor Sandra asked and his face returned to sternness. He waited a few seconds to respond, not because he was thinking but because he was getting a squeaky voice giving him instructions from his collar. It went on for a good while.

"Yes," he finally responded and after quickly looking at Ray added, "I've been asked to remind you that you're in our ship."

"We didn't ask for it," came the response in a flash from the acting President.

"Have you come to return it?" she was asked.

Doctor Sandra didn't respond. She hadn't. In fact, the only reason the ship was this close to its' home planet was to destroy it. That particular problem had been resolved with all good intention. Yet the small canteen we were crammed in suddenly got closer and several seats creaked as several occupants shifted slightly. Doctor Sandra didn't move, she spoke instead, matter of factly...

"Yes, one of us came here to use the same biological matter that your kind were already using on us. "Again the room got smaller and the silence got quieter. The admiral didn't flinch and he didn't get any word from his collar. Nelson stepped into the breach.

"We've all done wrong. Some more than others and others only less and others less than some." Nelson's voice was slow and deliberate. A tone or two lower than normal. He instantly grabbed the room and the thoughts as the focus centred on him... Good move I thought whilst everyone waited for him to continue. Then he looked at me. Long enough to make me nervous. He stood and continued.

"We all just want to do one thing. One small thing. And what is that small thing Colin?"

"Eh?"

"That one thing? What is it? What's the one thing, most overall, that you want to do, Colin?"

Could have warned me, I thought. He knows what my answer is. What it will always be. It's universal anyway. It's the truth, which helps.

"Me, I just want to go home. Have a cup of tea. Choose to do something or not. Even though I have no home or place to make a cup, I'd still call it home and like to go there... I." I didn't get a chance to continue.

"Thank you Colin. I share your sentiment, as I expect everyone here does. We all want the same, we're all thinking the same. There's no need to think that we all can't be satisfied. Right?"

"And what exactly do you suggest?" asked the admiral.

"I'm sure we all agree that firing any weapons won't resolve a thing, so there's no need for a fight. Right? I'm sure the Sandra would say that all she wants to do is depart and to not be seen again. Right?" Nelson looked toward her nodding, assured she would agree.

"That's exactly what I'm recommending. I would like to have some good news for the public. Some treaty, some agreement. There's every opportunity to change things here for ourselves and with you. To be open, no need to hide anything," she said.

The collar squeaked something.

"Every gun on this ship is loaded, all pointing one way."

"All of your ships are surrounding us and pointing there's on this very spot."

"Yes, that is correct. All trained to my communicator... Couldn't be in a better place."

"What!" I shouted, trying to stand up but not managing being too close to the wall and window.

"Colin, please..." Nelson said. Asking me to calm down, and maybe sit too.

I chose to re-arrange myself as squarely to the room as possible. Being slightly hunched with my head tight to the wall didn't allow for much movement and I had to raise my eyes to see the faces opposite, but I didn't sit. Instead I placed my hands on the table and leant forward. Much more comfortable, and slightly menacing too. Even Nelson paused.

"Can you not see it? Did you not hear Horace? I think you did, I think you did? I'm not wrong, am I admiral? Your planet needs help. It's covered in slime, it's taking over, eating the space you need. You need something to fight back, something to eat back. Invite the inhabitants here down to your lovely planet and let them graze and swim, take a break, stretch their legs and arms and limbs, and eat. The admiral here thought it was disgusting that Marilyn and Smokey could even consider it a food, and maybe in the way they ate the stuff, but, but no more than the way you enjoyed Rays' rabbit. Right? If rabbits like the stuff, maybe dried, then the planet could be clear in what? A few years? Two years goes by in a flash, a few years, not much more. Admiral, you could be the planet wide sole rabbit farmer, wholesaler, fast food outlet emperor... Also, I know an awesome builder who could with a small army totally centralize your stupid pipework system. That would certainly help the problem. Ray, if Smokey and Marilyn were an army of a million how much space could they clear in a day?"

Ray smiled at the thought of being useful and smiled even more at the answer.

"In one day, three meals a day, light snack late evening, about something the size of Wales... The country." Amazingly everyone seemed to know that that was as a measurement.

"Do you all know what that is?" No one said no, some looked shocked that I even asked the question. I shook my head in disbelief but took the chance to hammer home. "So why not become the best of friends and help each other out? Surely that is what life should be about?" I looked around eager to gather the smiles of at least optimism and some of absolute affirmation. Even a stern nod of complete agreement. There were none. A few faces looked for the same body language hints. I hoped they would be the joiners and wait for someone else to start. The Crrrrkian admiral gave nothing away. I wondered if he even got the huge hint at a massive market he could have and control of. East India company style diplomacy and tactics, and probably beyond… Nelson didn't bat an eye-lid. No one else did either. Battle on.

"And don't forget about the information you could all share, the science, knowledge of other planets, different places… Set up some trade. Some exchange. Language classes, I don't know? But let's not sit around and bicker and let's not wait to get to that point!" I looked around hoping to find faces now nodding in singular agreement. None were. Instead they had all backed off slightly and had similar wide-eyed stares… oh yes, I must have raised my voice a bit too much and gone a bit wide eyed. I instantly settled back into normal English mode by going slightly red in the cheeks and apologizing. I sat down only stopping to add, "sorry, I just want to get home, and sooner the better." I spent the next ten seconds smiling through the silence, hoping for someone to break it. Nelson finally coughed. Phew

"… This has certainly been a strange voyage and I have to admit that I was expecting a lot more in the way of support and thanks in light of how far and how long and why we ever came here. Considering what could have happened as to what is now happening. It can take years for two parties to ever get to a table to discuss mere possibilities after a bust up. At least a few months… and look at us, we've skipped all that and gone straight for the table and tea. Amazing. No loss of life, no blood not a scratch. Straight up cards down candid conversation. With the offer of help for your overgrown planet. I don't know why you already haven't shaken hands and aren't transporting hungry passengers? Sound advice Colin. There's always a way." Nelson slapped me on the back hard.

"Ow."

"Oops sorry," he said continuing," Human history is littered with conflict and we never learnt the one important lesson of living in peace before you start. Our history wounded us before we understood anything else. And then generations pass down systems and mechanics that sustain the scratch, hoping it acts like a reminder and inoculation. But it only promotes continuation, more conflict, bigger wars. Has there ever been a generation in human history when someone wasn't slaughtering someone else Colin?"

I screwed up my face in thought. Deep thought. I couldn't answer his question.

"There, so normal was it for us to be fighting somewhere or other Colin couldn't answer... And all because from day one, someone heard that someone else, was beaten up by another person so you better buckle up and get a gun. Imagine if that first bloke just heard a funny joke and he wanted to share it with someone else instead. How things would be different I don't know? All I'm saying is it doesn't have to be aloofness and paranoia, daggers at dawn all because that was what it was last time."

The Crrrrkian admiral bent his head to listen to the crackle in his collar. Everyone else leant in to listen even though it was only Ray who would understand. The admiral then stood and extended his arm in the direction of Sandra and raised an eyebrow and announced, "Would you like a tea at my place?"

"Sounds lovely," she answered whilst firmly shaking the Crrrrkian hand." He then turned to Nelson. "I've some friends who wish to apologize, and, thank you. They too then shook hands. Then everyone shook hands.

Nelson stopped me asking my next question by answering it in anticipation.

"No, we can't go home just yet. But it won't be long."

He was right. One month isn't too long in a lifetime. We would need to restock and pick up some friends anyway. I could in the meantime watch Nelson accept a lot of thanks and be amazed at how much algae the Squid were clearing every day.

The next day, the first day on planet Crrrrk dignitaries met. They smiled, shook hands, appeared in front of cameras, smiled even more then sat down in a room and came to arrangements and partnership deals, financial trade mechanisms, joint education and scientific conferences and organizations. Partnership ventures of various endeavors that would benefit all. All this seemed to happen very quickly. At the first break Smokey and Marilyn demanded they all try the algae slime before they did anything else. They had prepared some and it disappeared in seconds with looks of disappointment there wasn't any more immediately available. However, they were led directly to it during the next session's break and got stuck in. They were late getting back, even President Sandra. The Crrrrkian's didn't mind and just smiled thinking how brilliant it was. Diplomacy then seemed to work even faster.

By the end of the week every vessel available was ferrying passengers down to the lush algae fields begging to be devoured.

Half the population of Squid had visited the planet by day seven just to try it. Millions were staying to do nothing else but eat it.

In between meals, snacks and munchies they engaged the locals making as good an impression as they could. Many Crrrrkian's took them to be extra polite as they never accepted any food not knowing they were far to full already and needed to walk it off before they could start again. For many old Squid swimming in an ocean was a very old memory, for many others it had only been an old tale heard from those same old Squid or from what they'd seen in footage in an old film, so for millions it was the first time in a real sea so they never came ashore. For that reason, the population of the planet didn't see how much algae was disappearing from the oceans at the same time from the land reclamation they could see. Then a few images started to appear and for the first time the locals realized how much work was being done and the Squid became very popular. Locals boated to the algae's edge to offer support by way of singing traditional songs and banging old drums, wearing simple cut but ornate tunics, decorated with leaves, feathers and shells large and small.

Ray designed new centralized waste plants that extracted every nutrient and morsel of energy if could Pic and Don approved the plans themselves. Ray was certain it would control any future algae attack. It would take twenty years to build but the Crrrrkian's volunteered with such enthusiasm it bought that number down to four. Everything was good, going fine, the future would have something good to write about history.

Day nine was different. It was explained to us that the entire crew of the Flying Fish had to be arrested in order to fulfil some paperwork issues due to the arrival, finally, of the police. Nelson listed himself as a sailor with the name Horace Nelson. It meant nothing to the police questioner, a hairless orange oily humanoid with no eye-lids but very long eye-brows, ten centimetres at a push. He seemed more interested in form filling and getting home. He did manage to raise one of those eye-brows when Ray listed himself as minor royalty. Once he got the full story Ray was listed as an android much to his annoyance and he let out some Scottish words of choice. Once everyone had been through the same set of questions and the everything was signed, an abridged version of events was explained to him during which time he received a message ordering him to allow for the lowest possible punishment. A two hundred credit fine for not stopping, twenty thousand in damages, the police bot, and three points on Smokey's license and a further fine and three more points to Smokey as he didn't have a license. The Crrrrkian government had contacted the people they needed to and applied some pressure. They paid the bill and paid for Smokey to take his test. Then we all jumped on that one and did the same.

The good will didn't end there. Before anyone even asked the question the Flying Fish was bought from the original Crrrrkian fleet through charitable Crrrrkian donations and donated to the us, the crew. Just in order to tie up any paperwork. The Flying Fish's' Crrrrkian mother ship, now home to thirteen million Squid was paid for by employing the Squid to do what they were already doing, charge one hundred percent in tax to pay for the acquired home. This was seen as so fair that numbers and munch hours rose dramatically and the Crrrrkian's themselves gave time in lieu. Then a famous Crrrrkian lawyer pointed out that if anyone wanted to become a citizen their wages would quadruple. Over half a million Squid became citizens by the end of the next day. Their smile and the delight in their eyes, was very infectious and that number trebled by the end of the week. They described the place as a dream destination. Another million became Crrrrkian by the end of the weekend. The bill for the ship would be paid for within half a year.

Could things get any better? Yes, they could. After clearing up a couple of queries from a lot of computers on both ships, giggling at something only known to himself, the orange copper, with local aid placed Fred, two generals, ex-president Crabbe, his wife, her daughter and the daughters' hairdresser. The hairdressers were a centre of intelligence, secretly installed microphones and cameras. Fred and the producer, also arrested, and the hairdresser planned everything from gossip lead intelligence. It only served the wives of the government and councils and the like. They had all the best gossip, so once salon customers chatted about television but seemed to ignore or be negative about Fred and the shows he did for mass consumption the more paranoid and determined he got, to be seen more, to be regarded as something special, to be spoken of as great, in some way. He wanted to be king. A thirst to be dead centre stage, of everything, it took over. His hair became more the talking point and that wound him up. Greatly...

There may well have been one or even twelve more that could have been arrested and taken away somewhere unimaginable, a hell hole that only Vin Diesel would attempt to stand on, but the police ship wasn't much bigger than the Flying Fish and didn't have the capacity. Cold storage units would help cut down on food costs and any chance of rebellion. No one saw the condemned leave, and no one spoke of them for a very long time. It felt good there was no one out there willing to trash so much for so little. Their name on the wind was all they wanted. Fred will no doubt smile at some point when he realizes how much material there will be for future generations to make a documentary or film about it all, and him.

What he probably wasn't told was that the police ship had offered the Flying Fish an escort. After realizing fully what we had done the orange copper informed Nelson that the offer was open for two weeks only, whilst the very cold prisoners would, Settle, as he put it. It wouldn't be a quicker journey, but, we would be far safer, ships changed course regularly when a police vessel was around. For some reason some things don't change. The chance of getting attacked was low to begin with but with an outrider flashing his lights the chances were practically zero. He could take us for half a year and then we might, if someone else was free pick up another copper, after that, approximately decades at light speed, we'd have to play the escort by ear. He went on to add that if he had his way he'd take us all the way back to Earth before dropping of his cold storage, but he'd probably be dead by then and he'd promised his wife he'd sort out the house and garden as soon as he returned from duty.

Ray thought we should hold off on the escort until finding out what plans President Sandra had. Would she want to return to planet Earth? If enough Squid demanded it would she be obliged? In any of those cases it might be wise to return with them and hitch a lift all the way. It might be wise to do this simply because there was a vast amount of space to walk around, much more to do socially, and I did already have a house there.

It turned out there was a call to return to Earth, from the Crrrrkian's, keen to learn how not to trash you own planet. Their own algae scare was enough. They realized how close they came and saw the need for more information. Earth was a brilliant place to examine, because the damage happened in a relatively short amount of time, half a millennia or so. A joint working partnership easily set itself up and was eager to get on with the business at hand, getting to Earth.

After another week some estimates of a departure date began to be heard. They varied from two weeks to four years and everything in between, so I paid little attention. Although after another week and more speculation I realized I could just ask the boss. So, I did. I

211

invited Sandra around to my place, for tea. I placed two kitchen chairs outside and looked upon Sam and Jeb's homestead, the peak of Ray's miniature pyramid behind it and the lake in the distance shimmering, with a small ship anchored and still. If the whirr of an electric buggy wasn't just in the background I could have drifted off. There was someone with her. A Crrrrkian. I took another chair from the kitchen and placed it outside and then topped up the kettle ready for an extra cuppa.

Sandra had taken the precaution of inviting the very newly appointed Crrrrkian ambassador. He had an interest in meeting me and Sandra wanted the subject of our conversation to be heard by an important third party.

He introduced himself as Khall, shaking my hand firmly. Then told me that I was held in high regard by Pic and Dom and did I realize how much the Crrrrkian's should do the same. I only shrugged. He didn't understand my response and then after a few seconds laughed and shook my hand for a second time. That was a convenient moment to pour the tea.

"The famous tea. I've heard about this. I was hoping to get one, if the truth be told."

"There's always more. Milk and sugar to taste. I'll leave that up to you. But I'll get another mug in case you need to start afresh."

I paused before leaving the kitchen. Reflecting on old memories of friends visiting with all the demands that produces. Lovely. Days and nights talking nonsense but it meaning everything, priceless. Happily wasting quality time with friends, priceless. I had to explain my smile on my return.

"That's what you have here," Sandra said.

"Only, there's no familiarity, and, I'm not from here. It's nearly home, there's my house, but it's not, home."

"By the time we get, home, you would have lived longer in this place than you did, at home," she stated, dis-compassionately. I wasn't sure if that was supposed to being reassuring or she was telling me to get a life?

"… It's going to take that long? What we hanging around for then? Four earth weeks alright?" I held up my hands as if to surrender and added, "I don't know, you tell me."

"I don't see why not?" Khall agreed.

"We could actually go tomorrow, but, four weeks, so everyone knows to sort out their affairs. So we finalize all talks, leave an ambassador and a team to snag any loose ends, have some fireworks and a big send off," Sandra said, without smiling.

"Simple and sweet," I said smiling then held up my tea, "Cheers." Khall joined in once seeing Sandra clinking my mug with her own.

"What are you going to do when you get there?" Khall asked. The answer took a very long time to submerge but he seemed to like it.

"I'm not totally sure, I'll be playing it by ear, doing what I need to do, one thing I do know is that, I will be doing it all whilst, having a tea?" Khall's laugh took a moment to form itself, a pleasure to listen to, loud and hearty. Sandra just tutted whilst shaking her head stopping momentarily, allowing me to catch a glimpse of a very small hint of a half-smile, but then it went in a flash and she became very Presidential.

"Well, I'm glad that's sorted," she said.

CHAPTER 28

On the morning I could finally say that I was on way home all I wanted to do was stay in bed and stop my head from pounding and sleep off the mighty hangover I had acquired with Sam the previous night after a celebratory send off. Fireworks and all, which didn't help, it still felt like some of the bangers were going off in my skull. I had intended to have a quiet night, get up early and see the planet in the morning light for the last time. Unless I came back, which I might do but bearing in mind the very long travel time let's face it, I might not...

My plans were easily dashed by many a goodbye and even more salutations all involving the local tipple, with at first the crew and other dignitaries and then others also somehow important people. Then lots more. I couldn't tell you how many as things got very blurry after drink number four. At that point Sam found it very easy to persuade me that his moonshine would help get rid of the citrus taste the local brew left behind. Why I thought that would help I don't know? Maybe my brain was one step ahead of me and was making sure I enjoyed myself, or attempted to, before I had the chance to think of an excuse and bail out. Unfortunately, my brain had never experienced this drink before and soon after consuming it my brain went on holiday and left me to my own devices and actions... none of which I could now remember. Maybe that's why my brain went off somewhere else, so it didn't have to witness what was about to happen? I certainly couldn't remember much, how I got home, or to bed was a mystery to me. Two days later Ray would show me a recording of himself carrying both myself and Sam home. When I say carrying I must also add there was a fair amount of dragging and holding down in the back of a taxi. We didn't offend or annoy anyone, but we definitely broke the ambience. Then a shuttle back to the ship and then another buggy ride back home. Where Ray dumped Sam on his porch but at least helped me up the stairs before shoving me in the direction of my bed.

I awoke upon take-off. The humming rumble reminding me of an old vacuum cleaner. Here we go, I thought, we're on our way. Only another fifty odd years of this and I'll be there. At least there's no connections I have make, and my banging head might have gone by then too.

In reality I was up and about after a good breakfast a quick lay down and then dinner. I then took a stroll down to the lake and phoned Nelson asking for a rowboat taxi booking, for immediately. Ten minutes later he turned up smiling and handing me the oars.

"You happy now, Colin? We're going home, we are going home. Just one thing, don't ever ask if we're nearly there yet. We're going to have to refuel, restock, and stretch out legs when we can. Ray seems to think that all going well shouldn't be any more than sixty years, at worst. What could possibly go wrong?" Nelson leant back and stretched sighing. "Once around the lake Colin?"

I didn't take him up on the offer. Going straight to the ship felt much more sensible, and besides I don't think he was being serious. It wouldn't have been too polite to his guests for starters. Everyone was gathered in the galley. I went straight for the coffee accompanied with shouts of encouragement from Sam and Ray and laughter from most of the others. I must have been more drunk than I thought. What did they witness?

"I was asked not to show this until we were all gathered," said Ray. His eyes span in their sockets and he projected on the table a scene in which a very drunk Colin asks the new ambassadors' wife for the next dance. She accepts. Once on the dance floor I get down on my knees to equalize the height difference and then proceed to knock over others around with my trailing limbs which eventually leads to me tripping over myself and dragging my partner down with me, more on me where of course we end up very nearly kissing. The ambassador certainly earnt his money that night... I made profuse apologies of course and tip toed off the dance floor hoping that being extra quiet would also somehow make me invisible. Then Ray paused an image and zoomed in closely to droopy drunk face halfway through saying something that contorted it into something a gurning champion would be proud of.

I don't think I've ever gone so red. Noticing how embarrassed I was helped to block out the raucous laughter trumpeting like canon around me. Bernie was the first to ask for tissues. No one had time to respond as he then ran off to the toilet howling all the way. This only prolonged the moment during which time I was able to make a fresh coffee.

"Did I miss something?" Bernie said innocently as he could upon his return.

I had no choice but to suck it up and guessed that they would be dragging out that story for years to come. Over the whole journey to planet Earth it turned out there was further mention of it about once a year, fifty-six times in total.

It was a long journey home... We stopped half a dozen times along the way. Restocking and refuelling when necessary as Nelson had mentioned, always eager to step on land at the same time. Sometimes stopping in order to do just that, stand on land, experience any wind, and all sunsets, and some planets had more than one. To hear the crunch or squelch under foot. On some planets we met new beings and engaged with them as we did the Crrrrkian's. Once they heard our story and knew of our journey they promised to help mainly with donations of food and water. This news only encouraged more planets to help us.

"How many ships does it take for it to be a convoy?" I asked one day when I noticed seven trailing behind, although they could have been masking more. I wish I'd never asked as Ray proceeded to sing the song from the film 'Convoy' for the rest of the day. He then persuaded everyone to have an impromptu film night. No prizes for guessing the main feature... I ended up singing the song the next day. Ear bombed to kingdom come from the previous day, couldn't help myself. Occasionally Ray would whistle the tune and the ten minutes later I'd be off on it. Another ten minutes would pass and then I'd shout an insult in his direction and stop singing.

Keeping ourselves and each other entertained, having fun along the way became the norm. By the time we reached Earth we had ran out of ways to insult each other, in that way only friends can, Ray's insults were generally best because he could do accents and impersonations. He was also the hardest to insult because he was mostly computer.

He was also however, an amazing chef and I set out to learn as much as I could from him. We would watch old cookery shows, that he projected on my kitchen wall and we'd cook the meal as we went. If I didn't understand something or needed extra information he would simply show something else or drag up some literature and project that simultaneously. Once every two weeks or so I'd have a go at doing a dish en-masse and invite the crew around to get stuck in. Ray always cooked something up for film night which we maintained for the whole journey.

Just cooking things after a few years became less daunting so I decided to add some spice by also learning, for the duration of the cooking session, the language of the people who would normally cook it. Even though they were all mostly now defunct. I could ask for a beer and directions to the football stadium in thirty languages by the time I had perfected sushi.

216

Some things I didn't do was join any committees or groups that had interest of any sort. I was often asked but always declined. In truth I only wanted my quiet life back. The one in which I had the choice of doing something or not after not having the choice because of life and the trappings of it. The mortgage, the overdraft, the fridge that needed filling, and the electricity to keep it running. The life I had now could be filled with so much more but, the one thing I learnt a thousand years ago is that you have to make it enjoyable, as you go, and if you get trapped by work and business you'll forget to do that. So, I didn't commit to anything that involved that possibility... some organizations felt duty bound to ask me for my input considering the part I played. I understood they would but still declined. I did a couple of spots on a few chat shows to try and let everyone know that at heart I was a shy, quiet sort of bloke. I was left with the impression that I wasn't believed and that I was just trying to look modest. So, in-light of that I decided that I should demonstrate the quiet life I was desiring by having one and declined all further press invitations... I always keep the kitchen door open slightly and told all my friends not to bother knocking. Half of them never knocked anyway, I'm just trying to say that I didn't close down socially. Friends get forgotten when we become too busy, the second victim of modern life. I wasn't going to fall into that trap... They could all still get lost after a long day so I could reach a moment of quietness, but I'd look forward to seeing them next time. I suppose we all seek a part of the day we can call private? I can't be that much different from the next bloke? The question is, how far to go on the Hermit scale?

I asked myself this question a lot over the next fifty-six years as part of me wanted to get to Earth, find the exact spot where I used to live and plonk my house down on right there. I could close the curtains and It'll be like nothing had happened. Apart from the lack of neighbourly noise and bearable temperatures. Then I realized that if I made a satellite with some form of sunblind that I could open and shut on command things might not be so bad? Give myself some shade whenever I wanted it. I would also need something to cool the place down if my small tea plantation idea was to ever work? Ray had his reservations about the plan. Too much work for one person, he said. I disagreed even though I hadn't the faintest idea of what I was talking about and forgot that I didn't want to be busy busy busy. I then told Ray that he was right and asked if he could help build a tea picking auto-bot. I'd try to make it all myself, I told him, but the satellite was going to take more time than I thought. He looked at me quizzically not sure if I was joking or not and then said he could help with both. The sunblind satellite could be quite small, just send it far enough out in a stationary orbit until you have the required amount of shade. The tea bots could also be small, the size of a bumble bee, just lots of them. Once we got going it only took a couple of years to build what we thought we needed… Whether it was going to work or not who knew? It was finished twenty years before we'd get to use it. It did however suggest that a greater part of me was going to settle. No more travelling. I could open up a small café and serve cream tea and be a stopover point for my travelling friends? Uh oh, more work? Perhaps not, so much for the quiet life? I still had decades to consider everything.

Then, in the slowest way possible, twenty or more years whizzed by. On the day the Earth was going to be visible for the first time I was invited to the Bridge to watch. I declined knowing that they would be using screens with massive magnification lenses and I wanted to see it as it happened, so I chose the forward observation suite to let it appear live. Everyone joined me.

We slowed to a mere fifty thousand miles per hour. Much faster than anything NASA made but not so fast as to spoil the crescendo of excitement coursing around my system. I forgot to breathe for a short moment when I first caught sight. Home, I'm back home. She doesn't look as colourful as I remember, I thought to myself. We all had a look of loss about us. More memories of very different days. When things around you had a lushness about them, from the colours of flowers to the smell in the wind and the warmth of the rain. The colours now reminded me of over dry straw, volcanic sand, or the swirl in a milky coffee. It looked dirty, ill and old, like a smoker's teeth. No discernible outlines of continents, no landmarks, no Islands, no countries. If BBC radio 4 was still broadcasting they'd have a program called 'desert planet discs' I'm sure…. I should have built a jukebox.

We then spent two weeks taking all manner of survey and scan without anyone being allowed to go to the surface. I therefore contemplated building that juke box, when Ray told me an amplifier and a set of decent speakers would do. Plug it directly into my phone or attach a wireless connection, easy. Smokey knew where to find everything I needed and turned up within a couple of days with a box full of goodies.

On the third day of the self-imposed curfew, or the massively long health and safety check, as someone put it. I persuaded President Sandra to allow me to pop down to the surface in the Flying Fish. She didn't hesitate to say yes.

"Do what you want, it's your barbecue," she said.

"Really, do you want to come down?"

"No, I'm far too busy to be messing around. I don't want to have to send out a rescue party or anything, so please, don't be stupid, and is two hours enough?"

"More than. And I won't get out the ship."

"Why are you so eager? What are you going to do when you get there?"

She couldn't see my expression over the phone, but the lack of response was enough for her to guess.

"Oh dear, you're going down there just to have a cup of tea, aren't you?"

I giggled before hanging up. I then sent the same message to the crew. "Flying Fish, be there in ten minutes. Going down to the surface." Ten minutes later we were all gathered in the dock at the foot of our ship. I handed Smokey a scrap of paper with a set of numbers on it.

"Can you take us here, please?"

Within a few minutes we were coming to rest on a flat plain, savannah like, a few grassy shrubs here and there trying to get by. A massive tumble weed the size of a double decker bus slowly lumbered over the surface hoping to hit the jackpot, water. None of that here my friend. Apart from the hot stuff presently brewing away in the tea pot. Tea isn't normally allowed in the bridge, but hey, the occasion calls for it. I brought enough cups for everyone, but some didn't want any. That's okay, it wouldn't go to waste. I'm sure Nelson could polish off another one.

"I think I've found my spot," I said, staring blankly ahead at the view through the screen whilst blowing on the surface of my tea.

"How do you work that out?" asked Smokey.

I smiled and took a sip. Nelson kindly answered for me.

"He's home. This is where your house used to stand right? We're probably at roof level, or there abouts, we could all be huddled around your old chimney," he suggested, and I hoped correctly. He could make out my smile over the rim of my mug

"Not much of a view is it?" Nelson continued, sarcastically, and then sipped his own tea.

THE END

Printed in Poland
by Amazon Fulfillment
Poland Sp. z o.o., Wrocław

60594075R00125